# Mr. PANTS

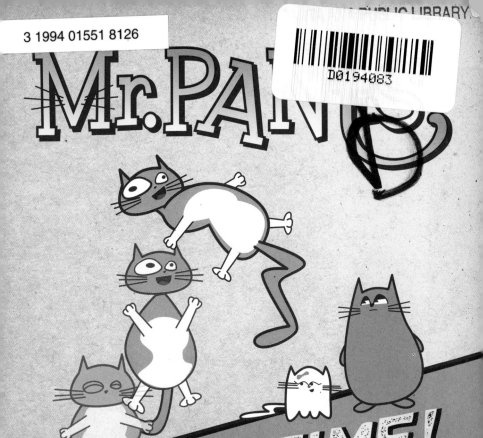

# IT'S GO TIME!

**WORDS BY
SCOTT McCORMICK**

**PICTURES BY
R. H. LAZZELL**

PUFFIN BOOKS
An Imprint of Penguin Group (USA)

## TO SOEN AND SADIE, THE COOLEST CATS I KNOW
## "ALL . . ."

**—S.M.**

## FOR MY PARENTS, CAROLE AND BOB

**—R.H.L.**

PUFFIN BOOKS
Published by the Penguin Group
Penguin Group (USA) LLC
375 Hudson Street
New York, New York 10014

USA * Canada * UK * Ireland * Australia * New Zealand * India * South Africa * China

penguin.com
A Penguin Random House Company

First published in the United States of America by Dial Books for Young Readers, an imprint of Penguin Young Readers Group, 2014
Published by Puffin Books, an imprint of Penguin Young Readers Group, 2015

Text copyright © 2014 by Scott McCormick
Pictures copyright © 2014 by R. H. Lazzell

THE LIBRARY OF CONGRESS HAS CATALOGED THE DIAL BOOKS EDITION AS FOLLOWS:
McCormick, Scott, date.
Mr. Pants : it's go time! / words by Scott McCormick ; pictures by R. H. Lazzell.
pages cm
Summary: On the last day of summer vacation, all Mr. Pants wants to do is play laser tag,
but Mom and his sisters, Foot Foot and Grommy, have other ideas.
ISBN 978-0-8037-4007-5 (hardcover)
[1. Brothers and sisters—Fiction. 2. Cats—Fiction. 3. Behavior—Fiction.]
I. Lazzell, R. H., illustrator. II. Title.
PZ7.M47841437Mqi 2014  [E]—dc23  2013001969

Puffin Books ISBN  978-0-14-751710-4

Manufactured in China

1  3  5  7  9  10  8  6  4  2

# CONTENTS

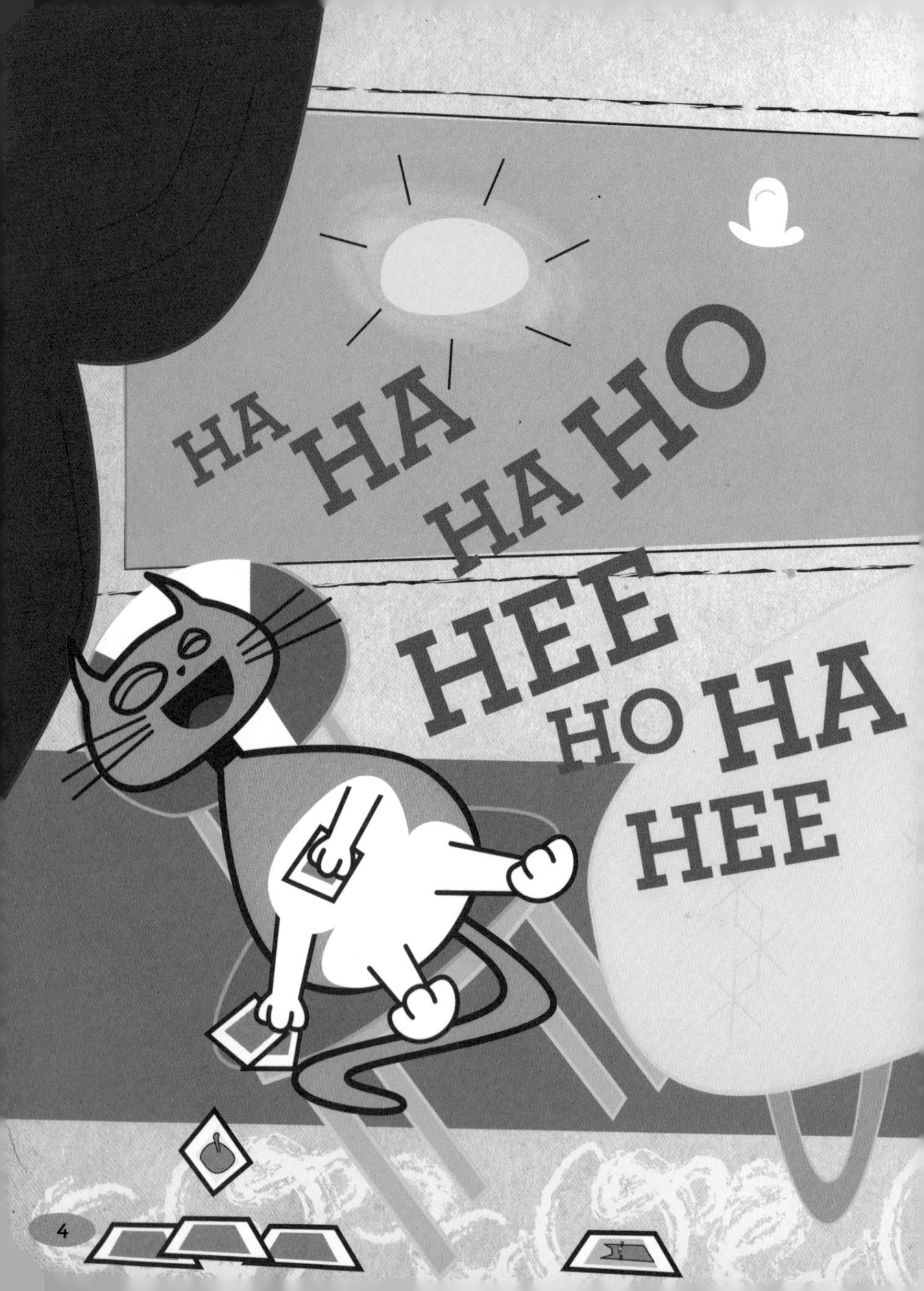
HA
HA
HA
HO
HEE
HO
HA
HEE

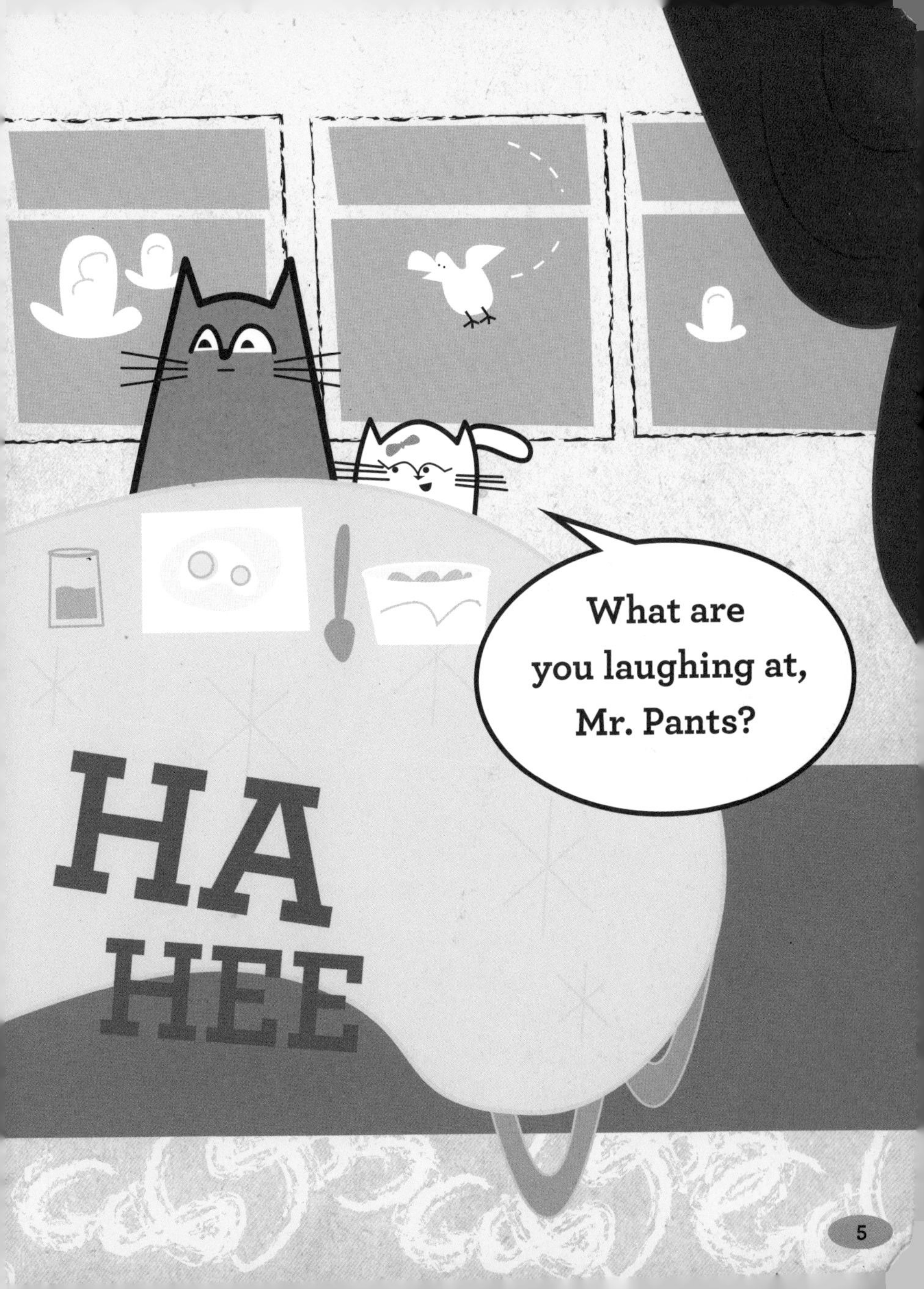
What are you laughing at, Mr. Pants?
HA
HEE

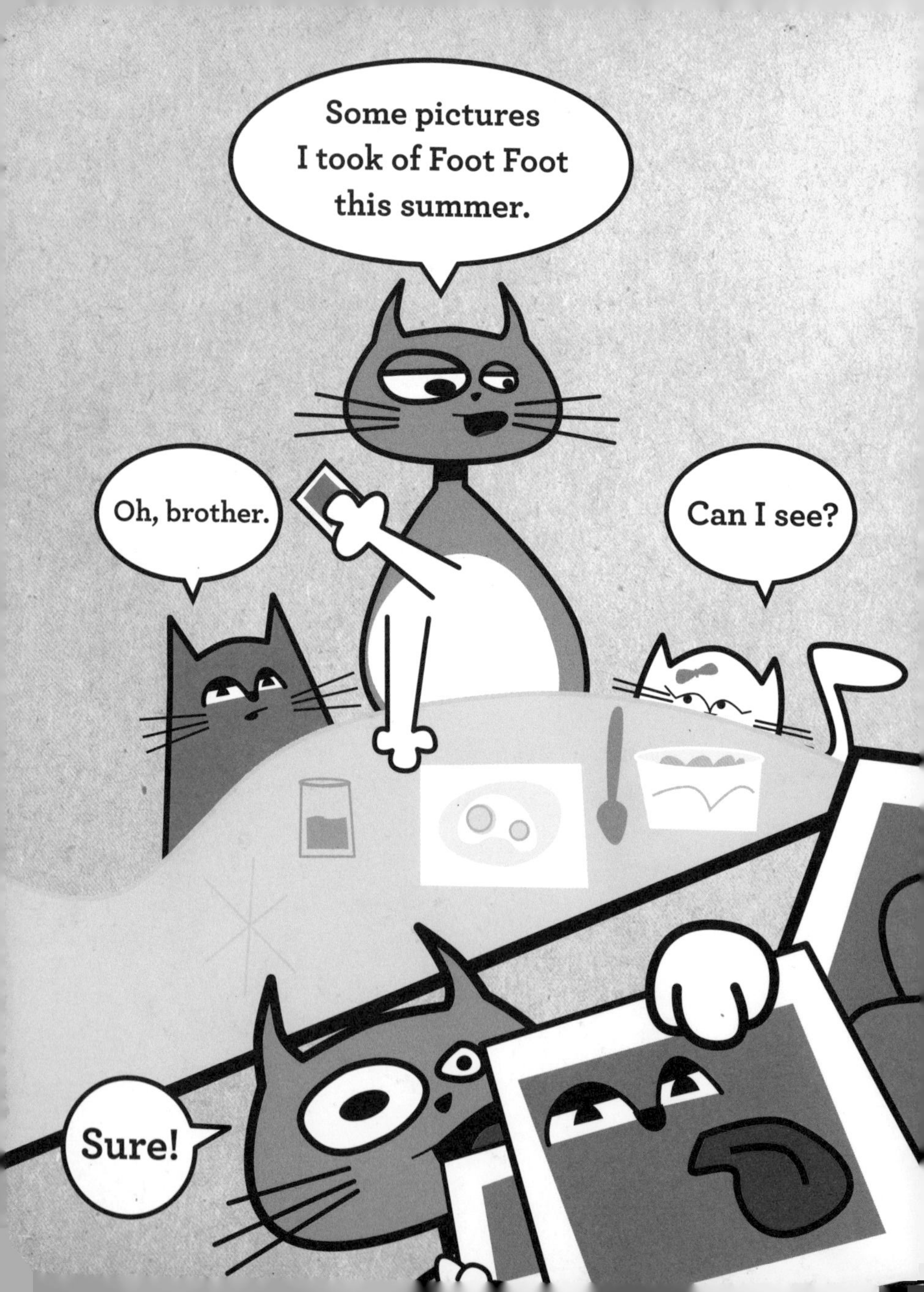
Some pictures I took of Foot Foot this summer.
Oh, brother.
Can I see?
Sure!

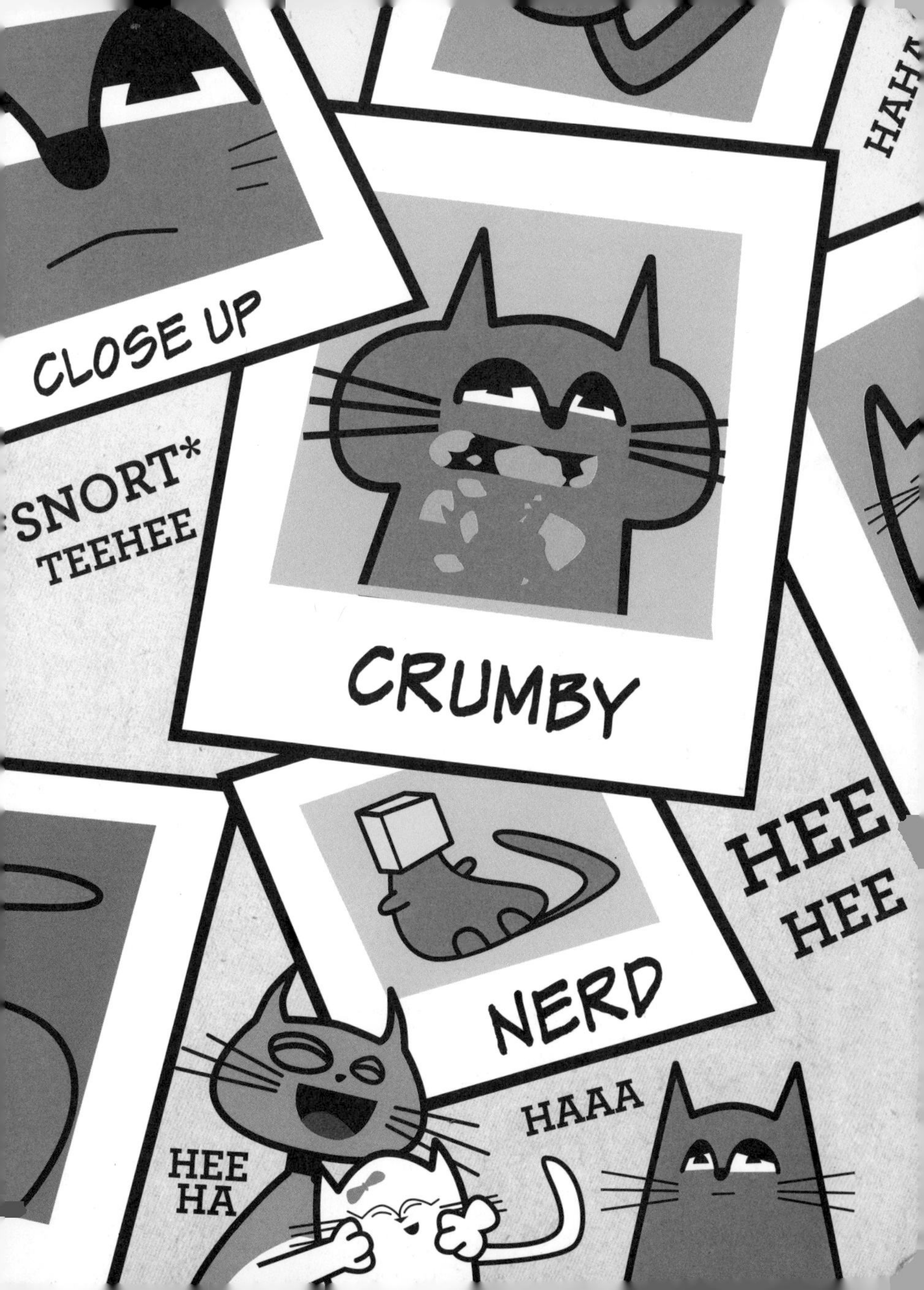
CLOSE UP
*SNORT*
TEEHEE
CRUMBY
HEE
HEE
NERD
HAAA
HEE
HA

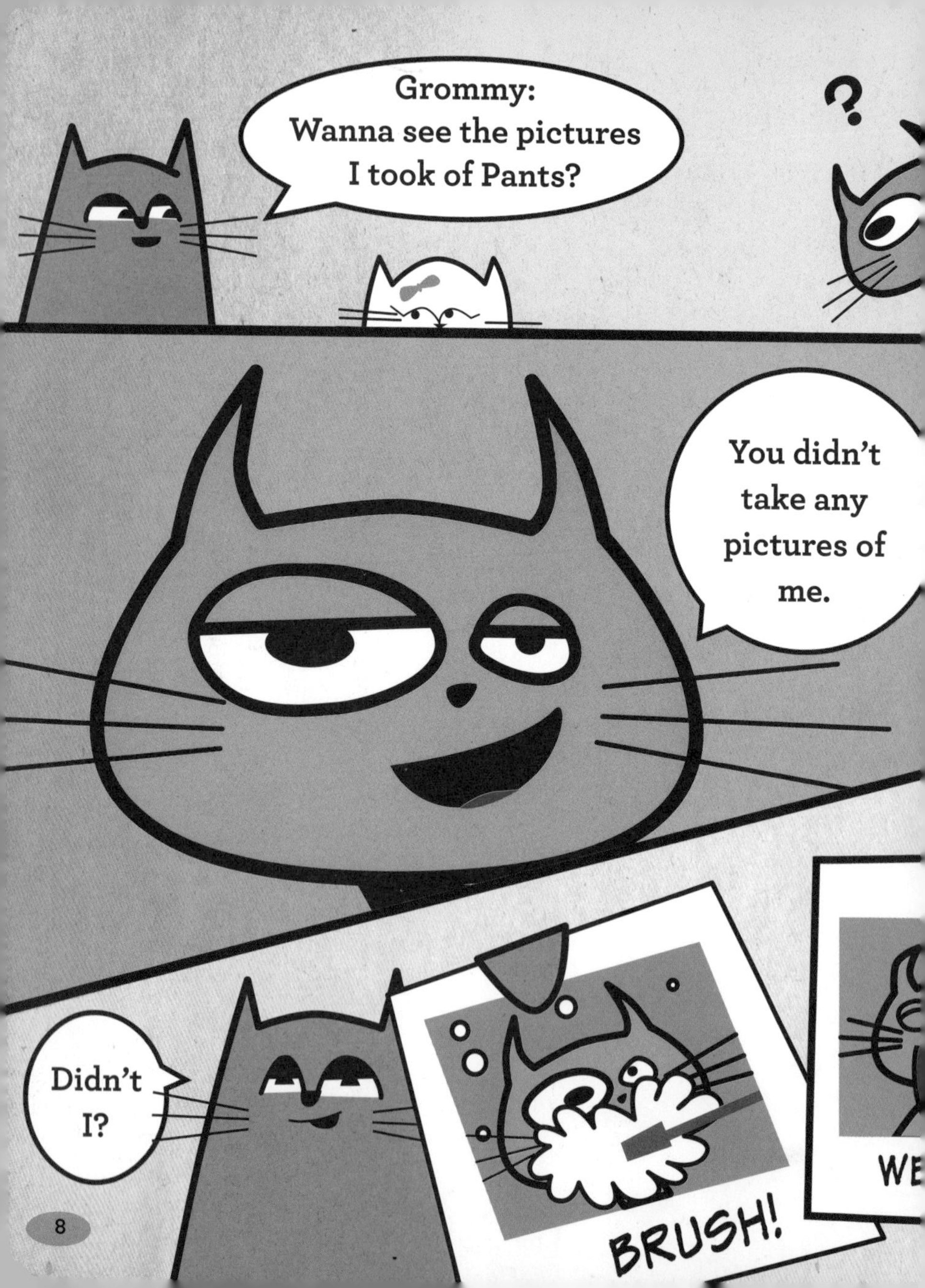
Grommy:
Wanna see the pictures
I took of Pants?
?
You didn't
take any
pictures of
me.
Didn't
I?
BRUSH!

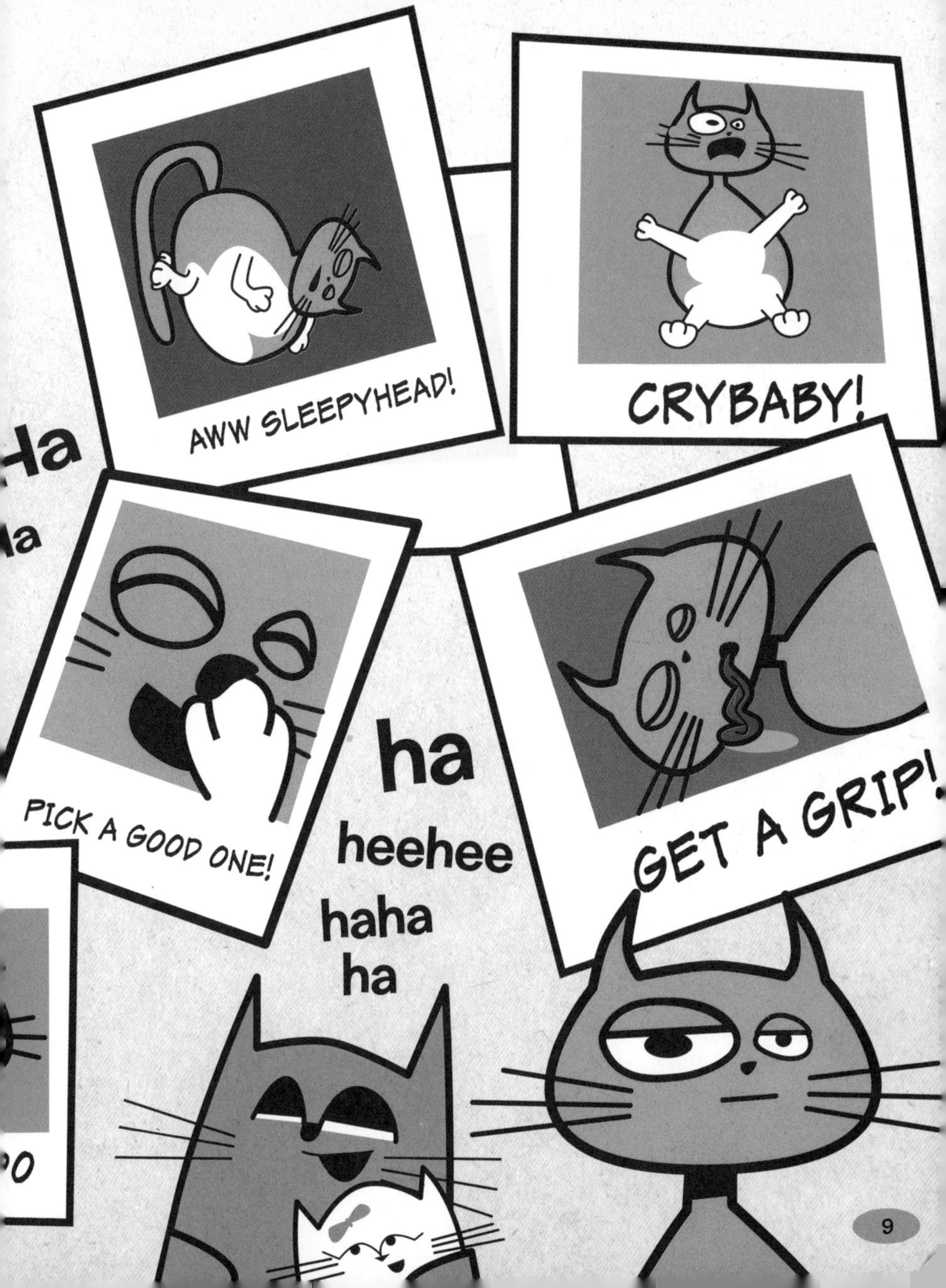
AWW SLEEPYHEAD!
CRYBABY!
Ha
a
PICK A GOOD ONE!
GET A GRIP!
ha
heehee
haha
ha
O

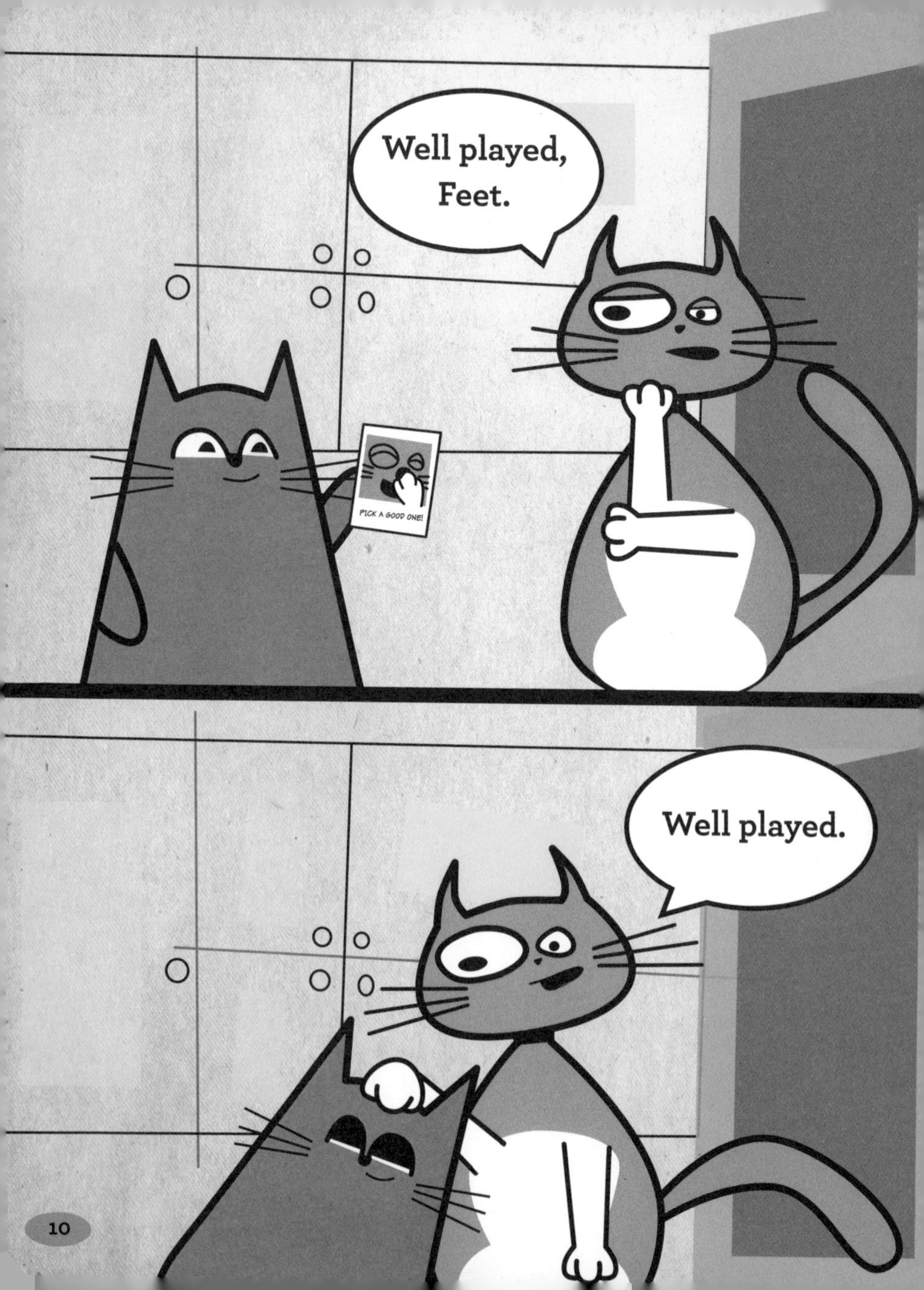
Well played,
Feet.
PICK A GOOD ONE!
Well played.

# Chapter One: THE DEAL

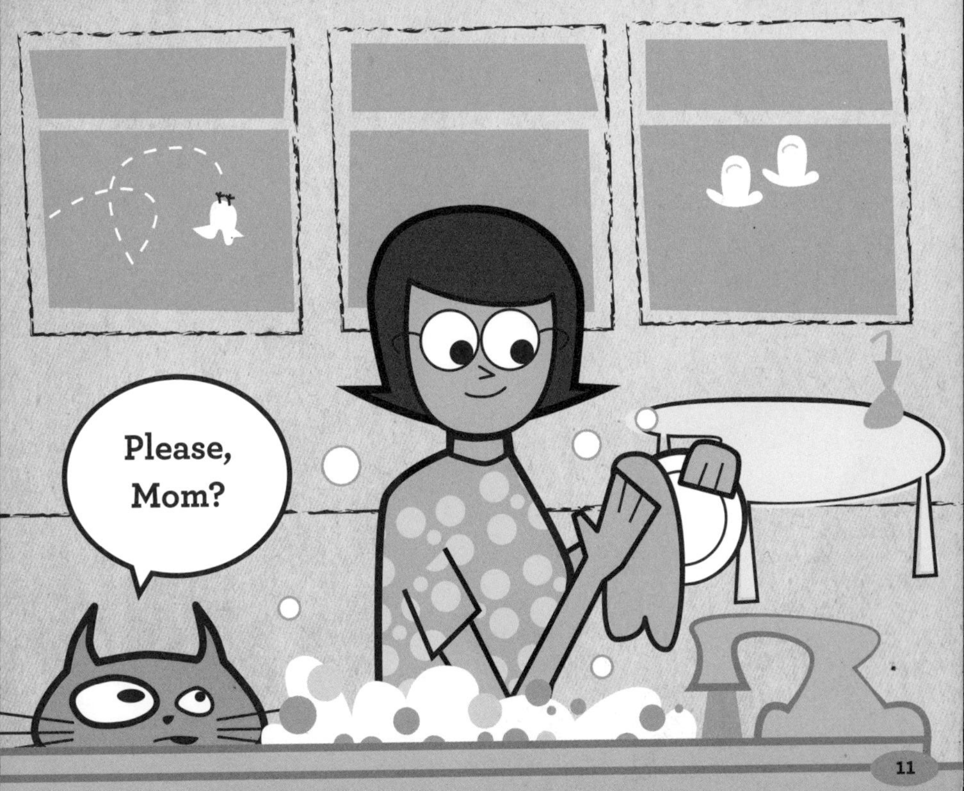
Please, Mom?

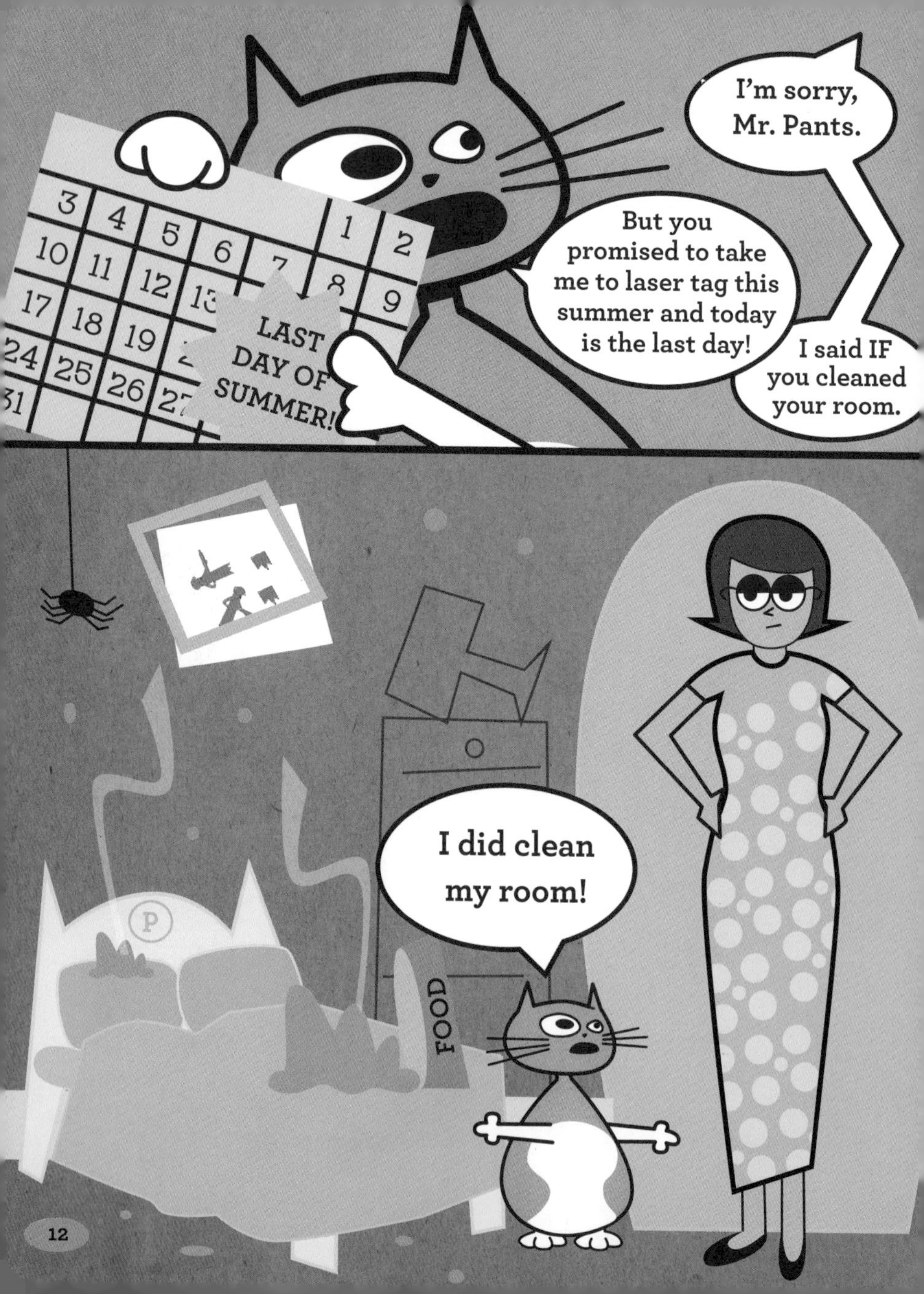

LAST DAY OF SUMMER!
I'm sorry, Mr. Pants.
But you promised to take me to laser tag this summer and today is the last day!
I said IF you cleaned your room.
I did clean my room!
FOOD

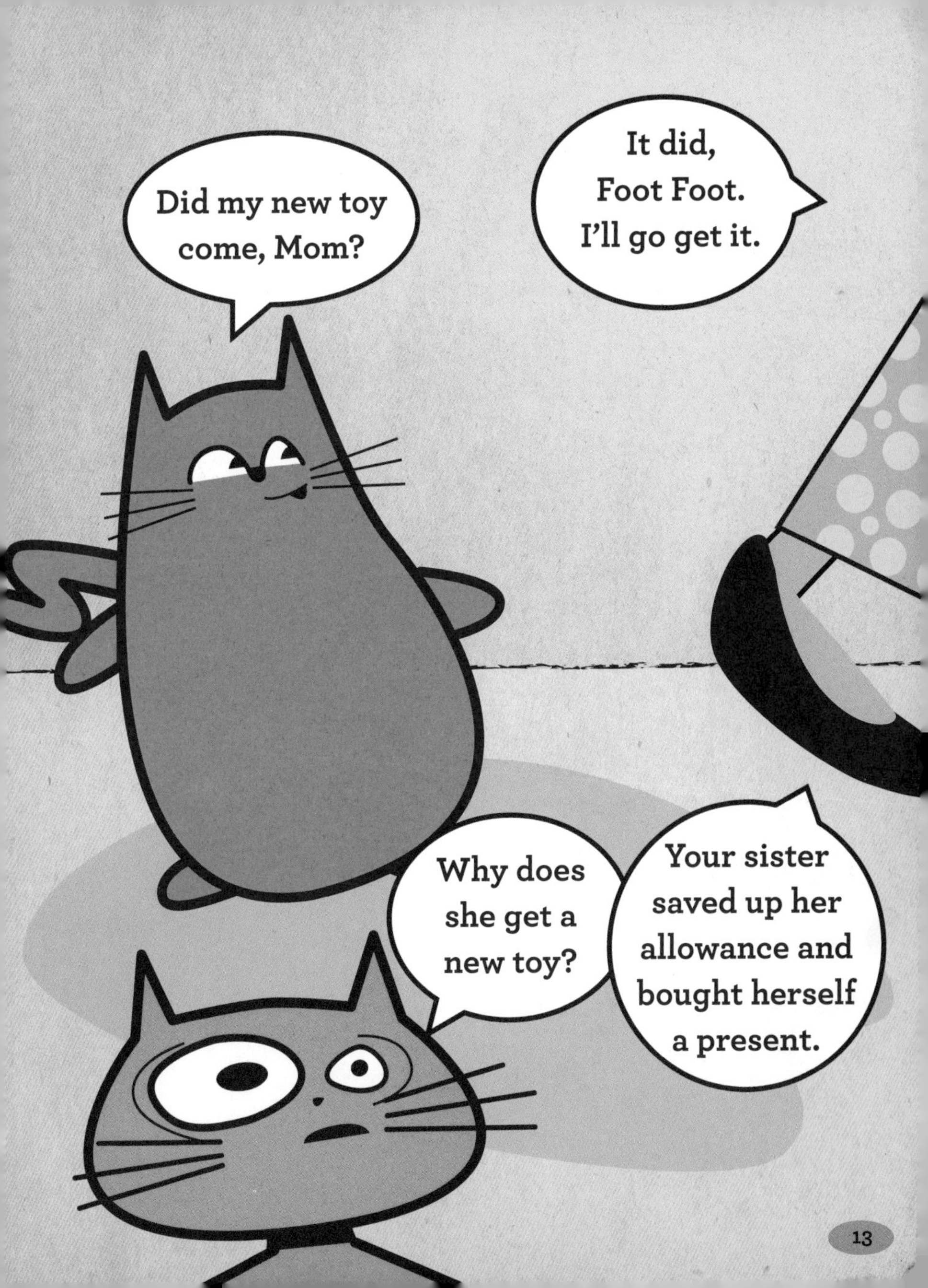
Did my new toy come, Mom?
It did, Foot Foot. I'll go get it.
Why does she get a new toy?
Your sister saved up her allowance and bought herself a present.

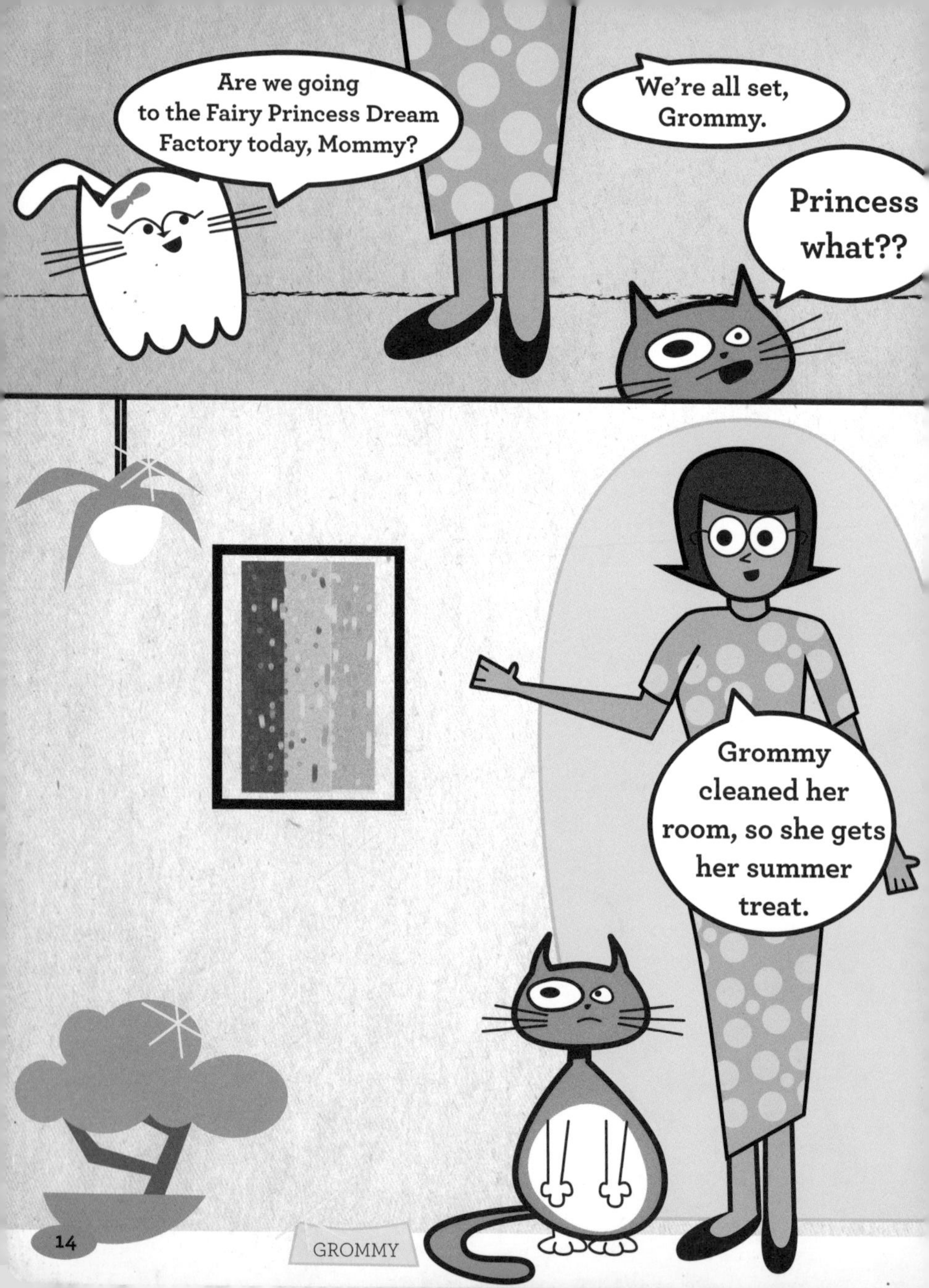
Are we going to the Fairy Princess Dream Factory today, Mommy?
We're all set, Grommy.
Princess what??
Grommy cleaned her room, so she gets her summer treat.

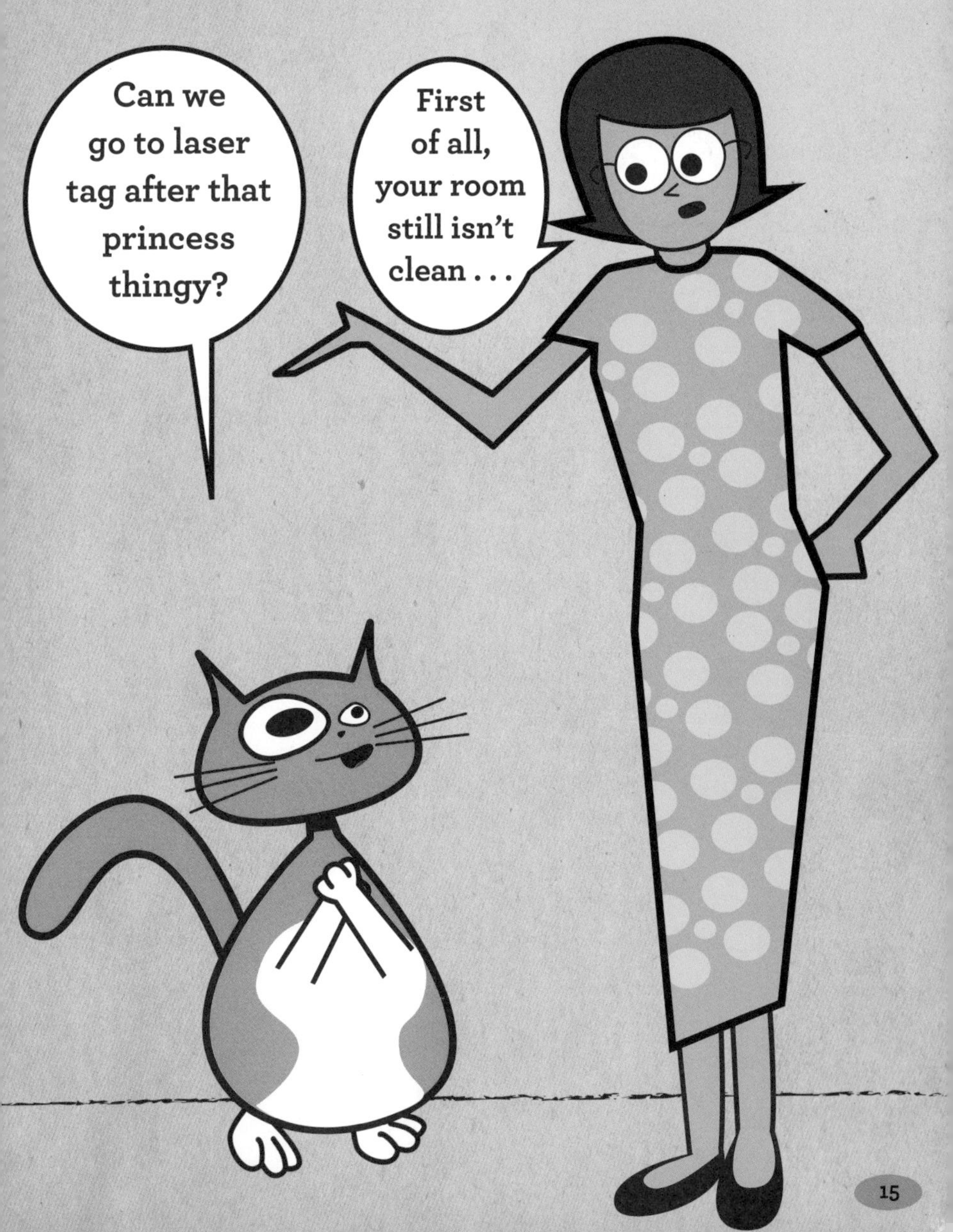
Can we go to laser tag after that princess thingy?
First of all, your room still isn't clean . . .

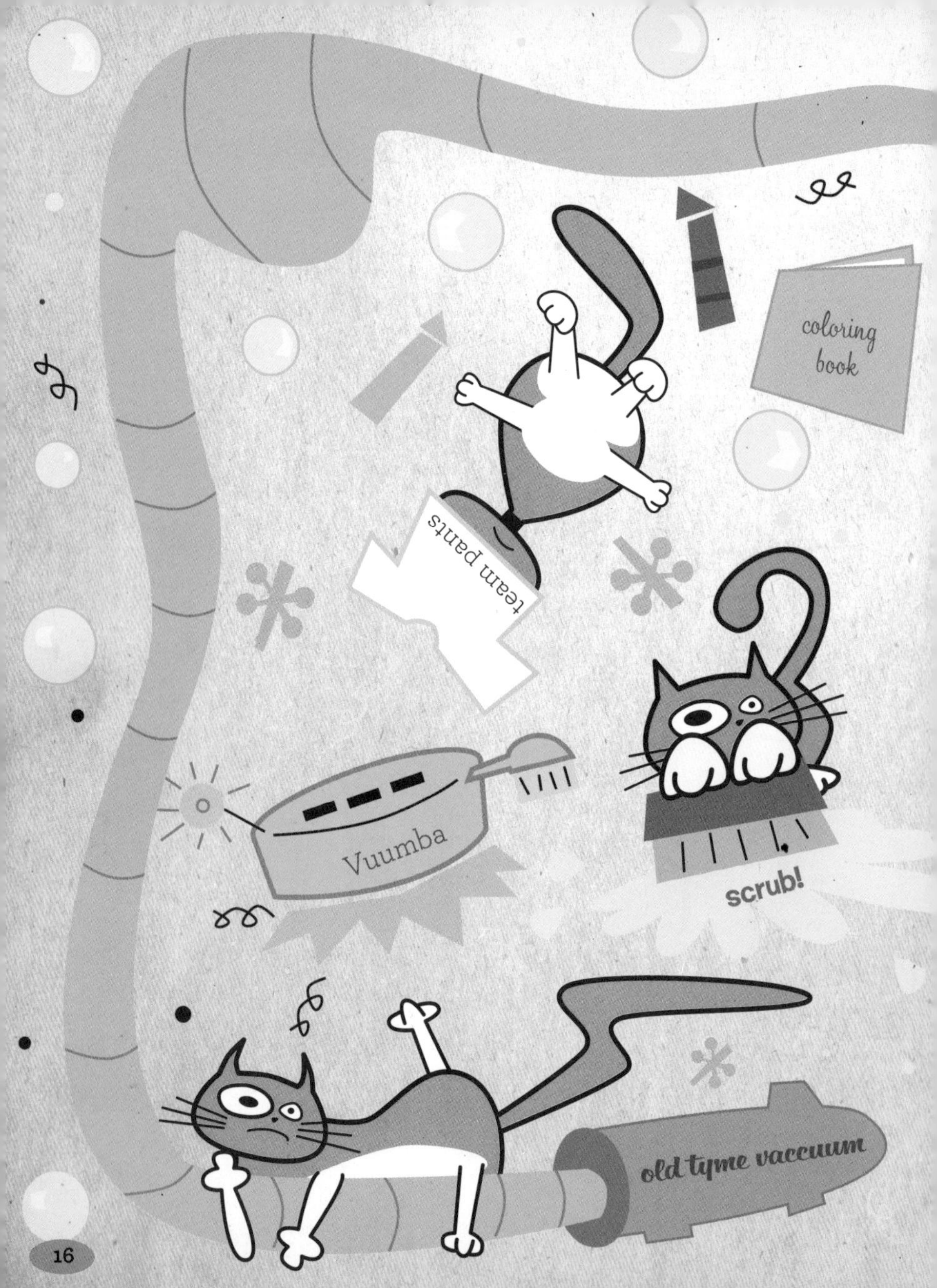
coloring book
team pants
Vuumba
scrub!
old tyme vaccuum

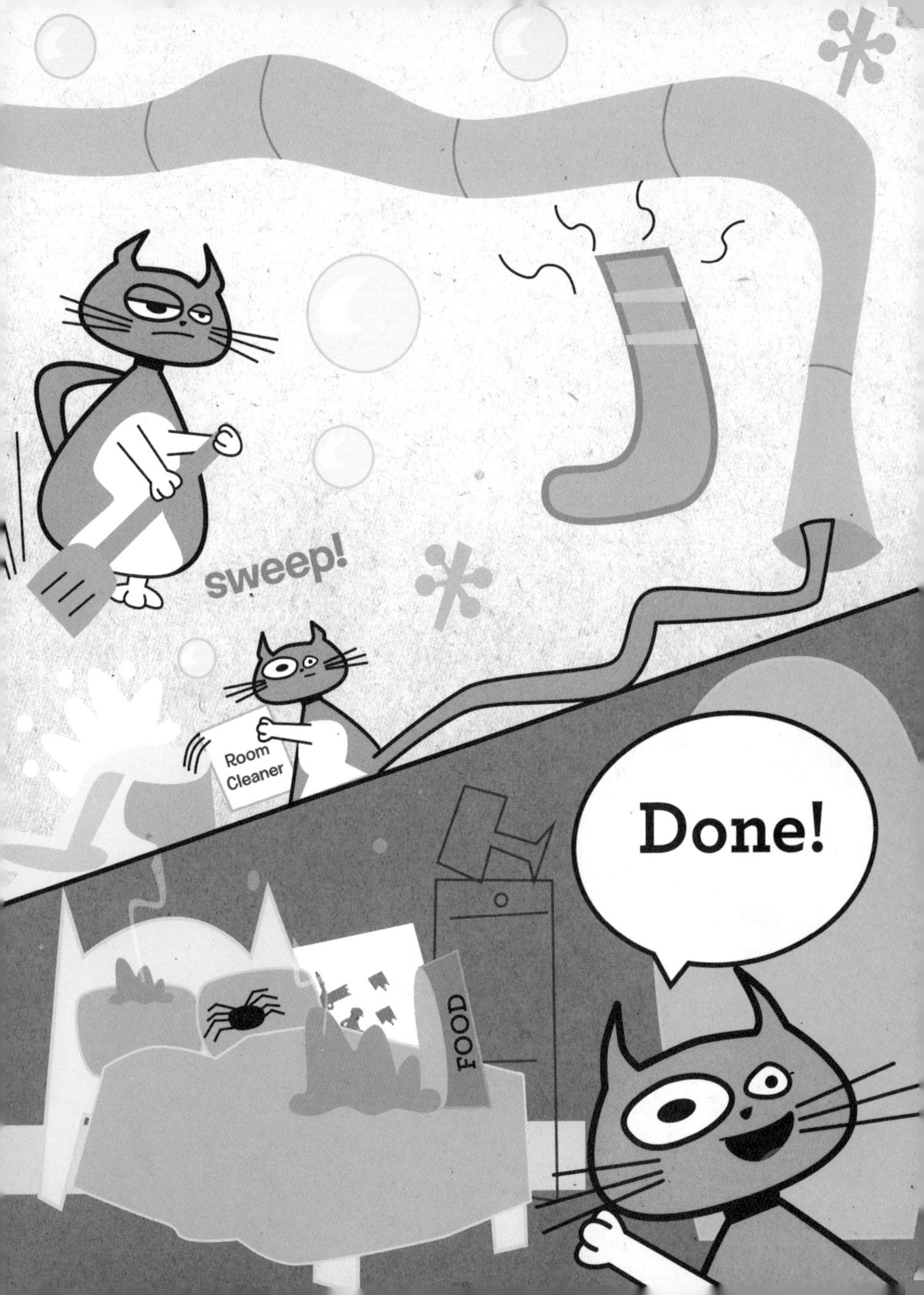
sweep!
Room Cleaner
Done!
FOOD

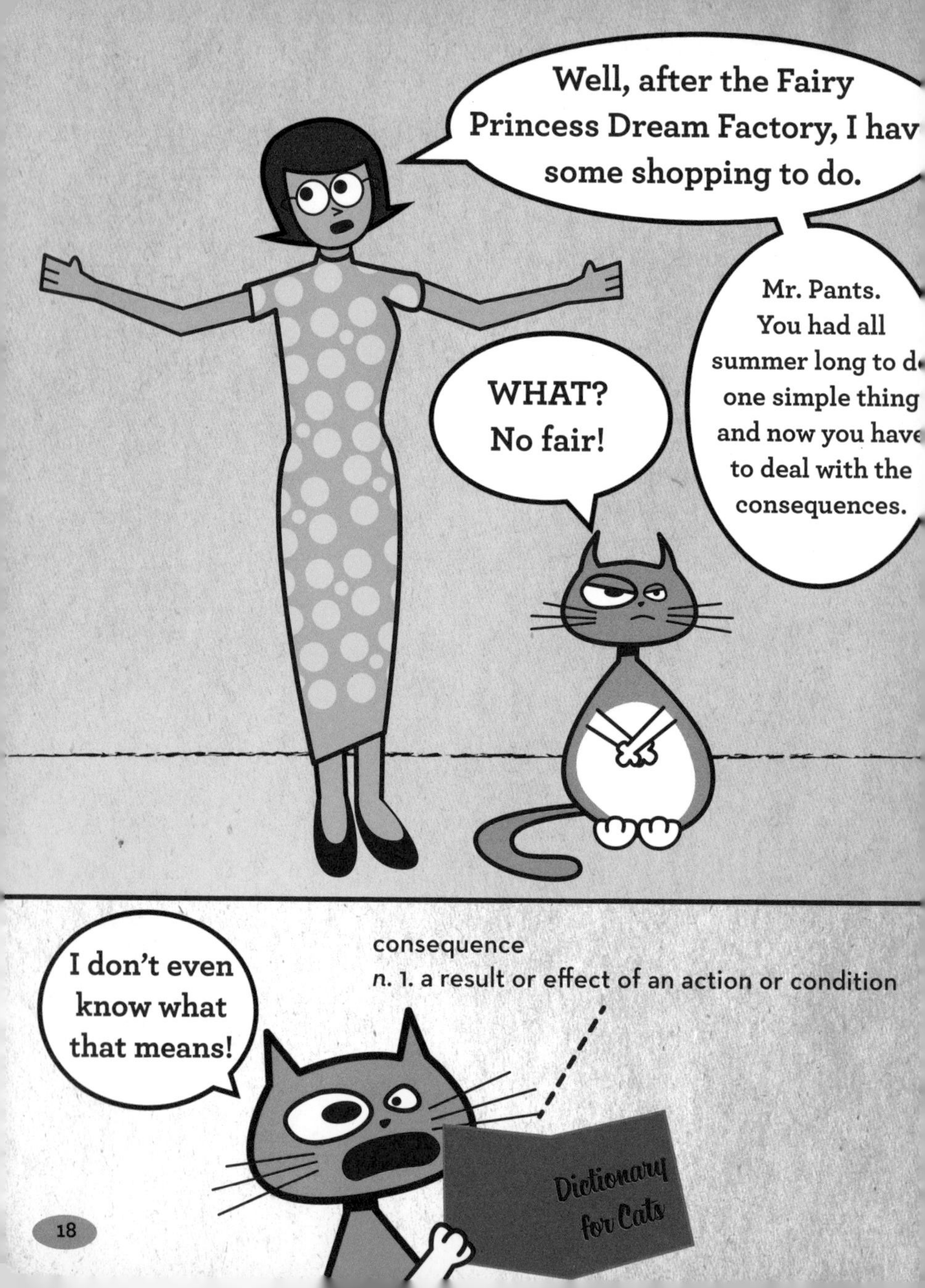
Well, after the Fairy Princess Dream Factory, I hav
some shopping to do.
Mr. Pants. You had all summer long to d
one simple thing and now you have to deal with the consequences.
WHAT? No fair!
I don't even know what that means!
consequence
n. 1. a result or effect of an action or condition
Dictionary for Cats

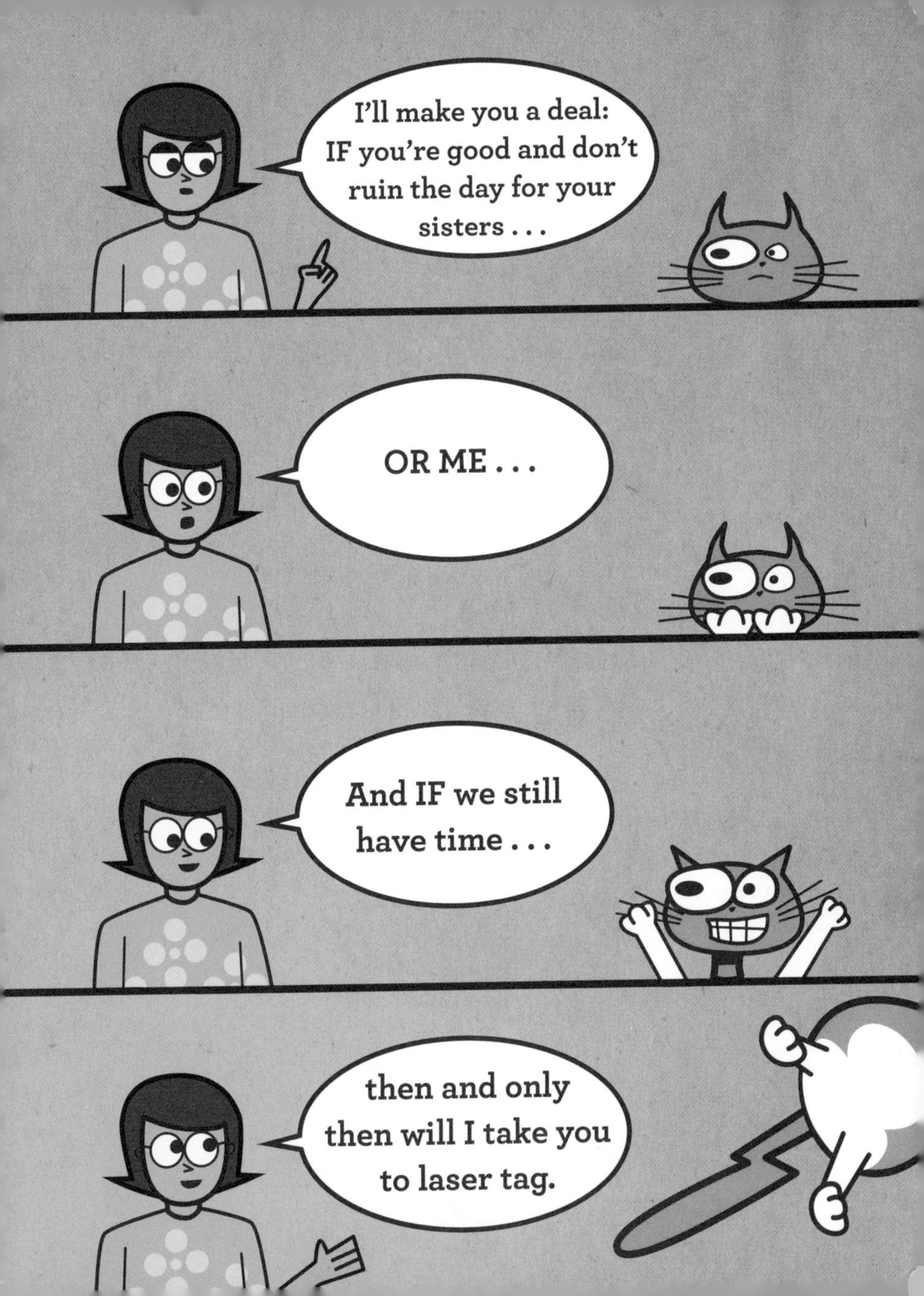
I'll make you a deal: IF you're good and don't ruin the day for your sisters . . .
OR ME . . .
And IF we still have time . . .
then and only then will I take you to laser tag.

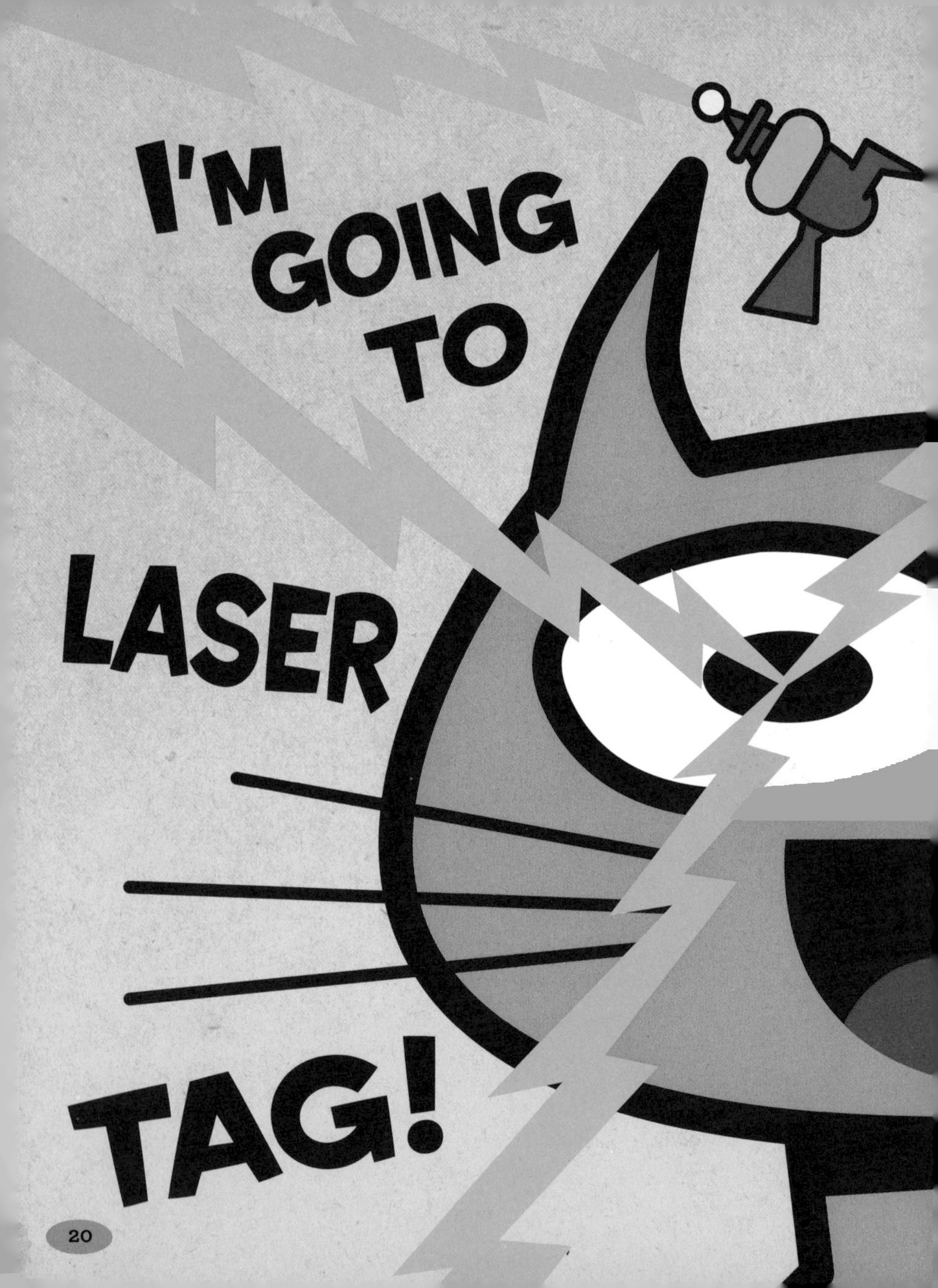
I'M GOING TO LASER TAG!

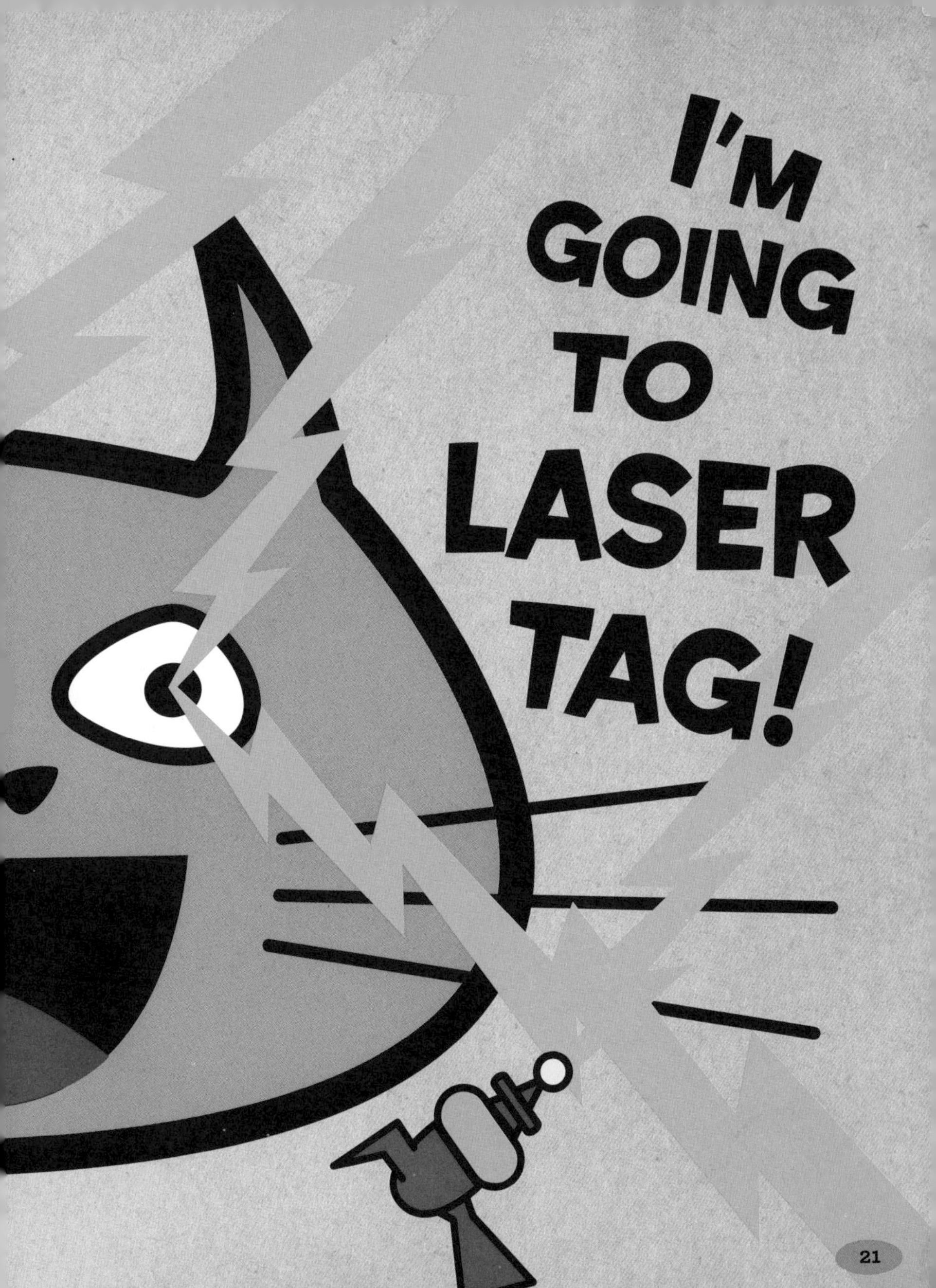
I'M GOING TO LASER TAG!

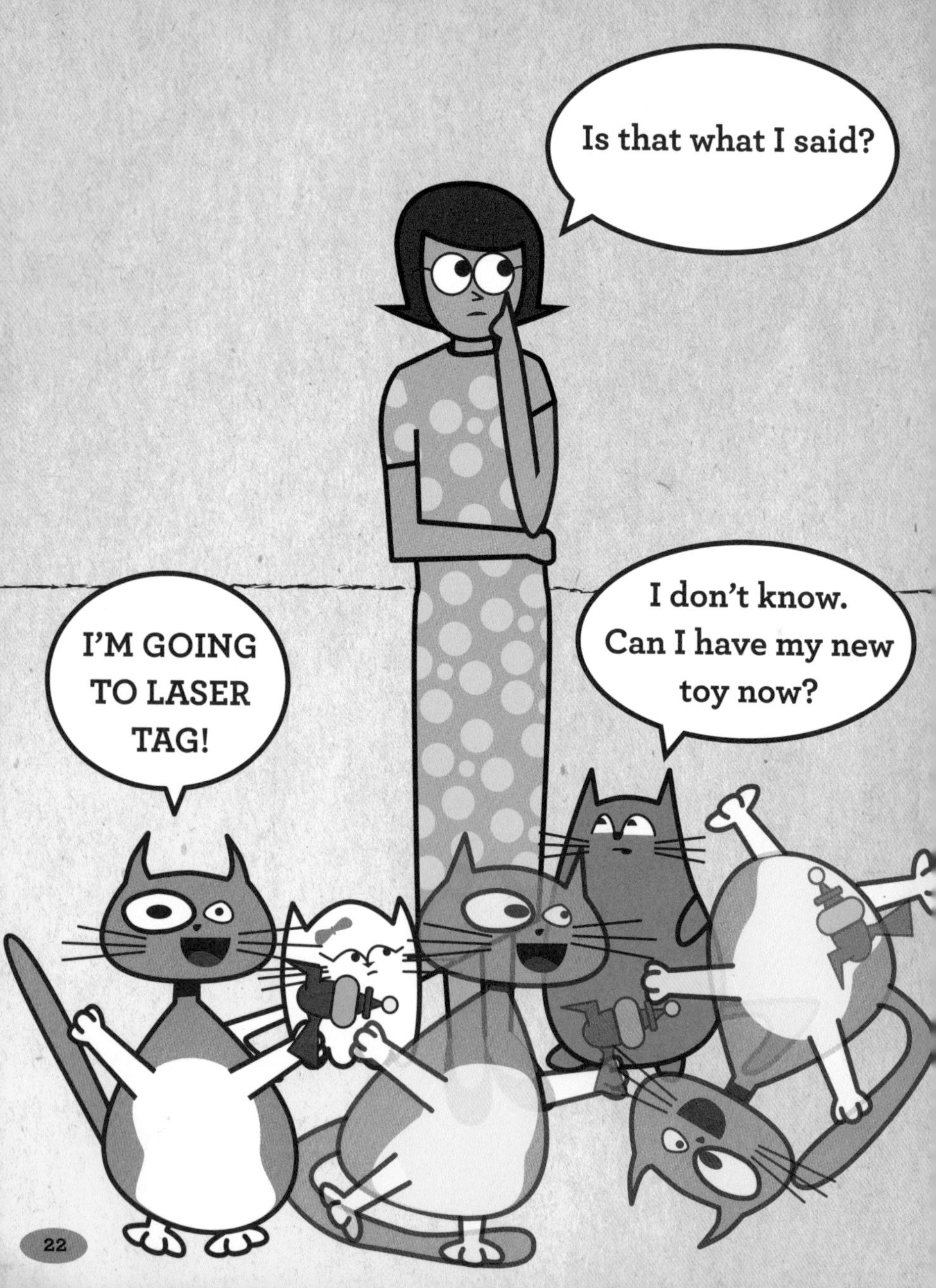
Is that what I said?
I'M GOING TO LASER TAG!
I don't know. Can I have my new toy now?

# Chapter Two:
# BOXY

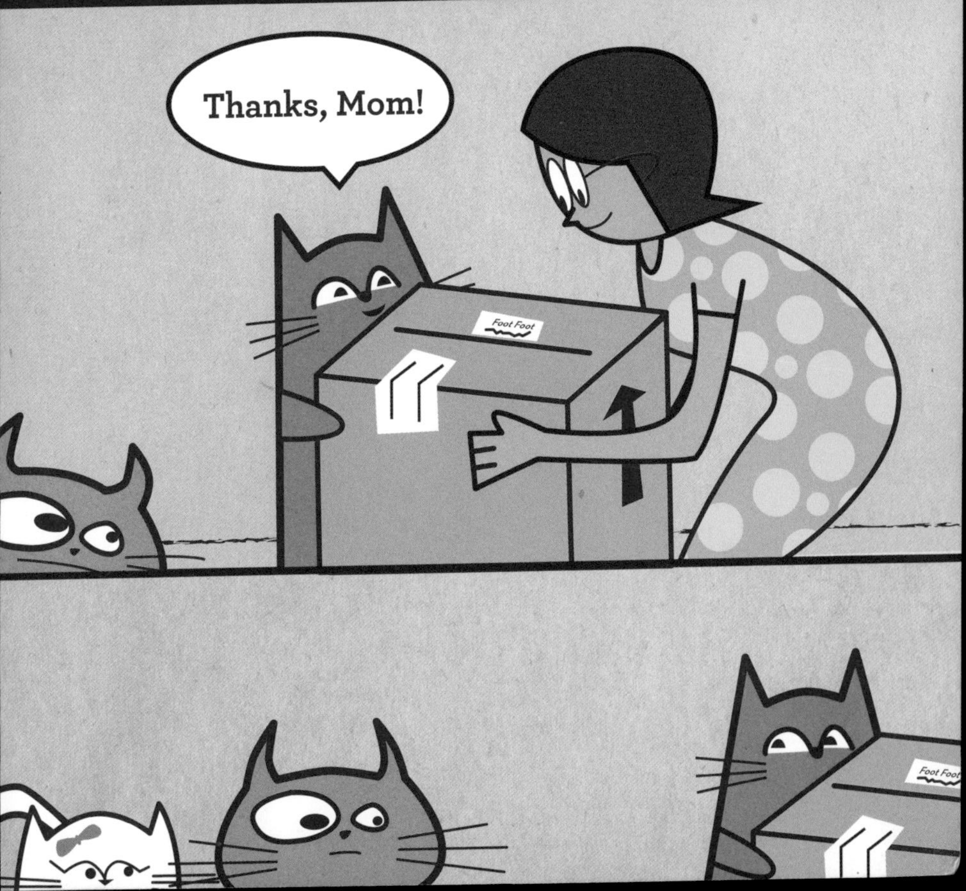
Thanks, Mom!
Foot Foot
Foot Foot

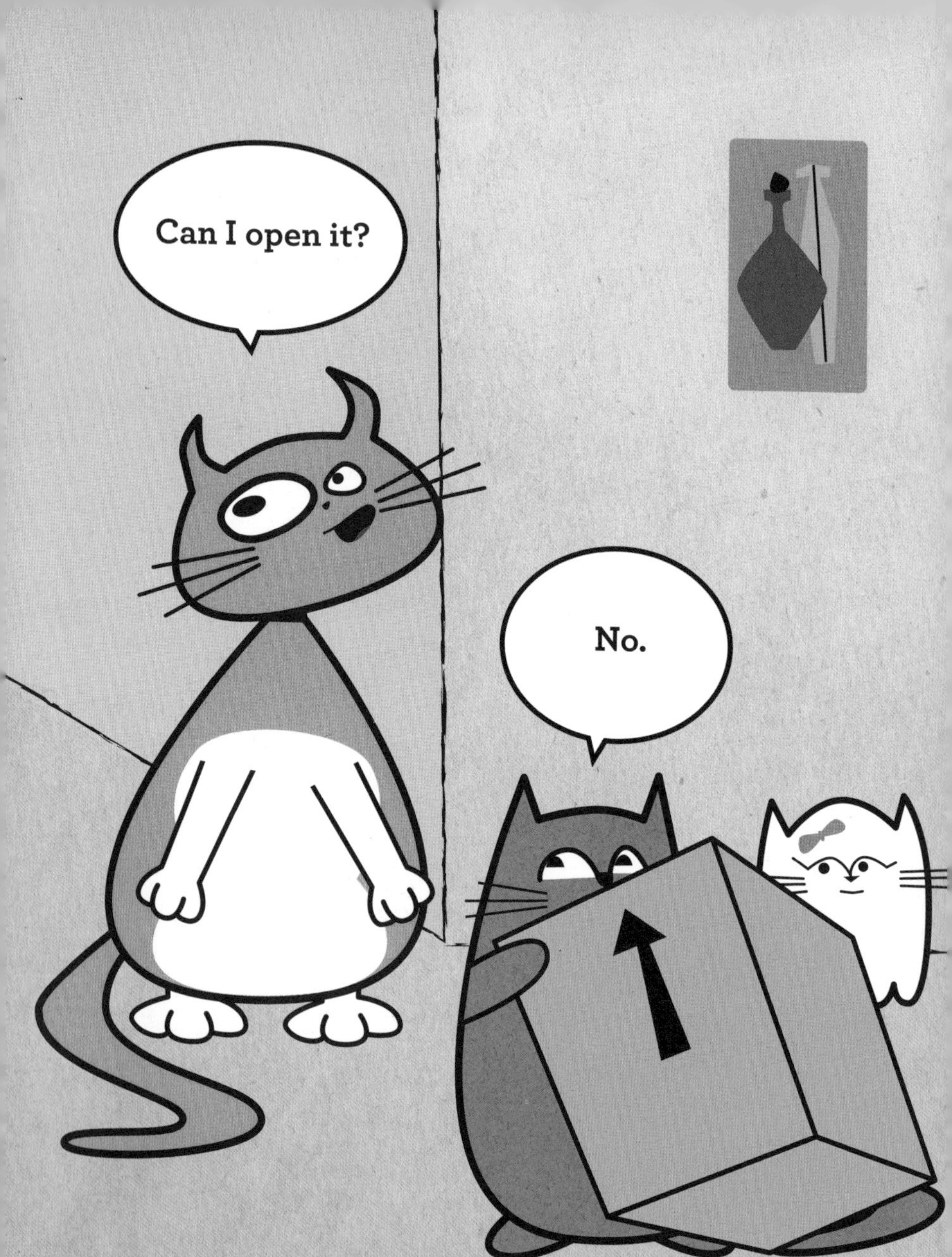
Can I open it?
No.

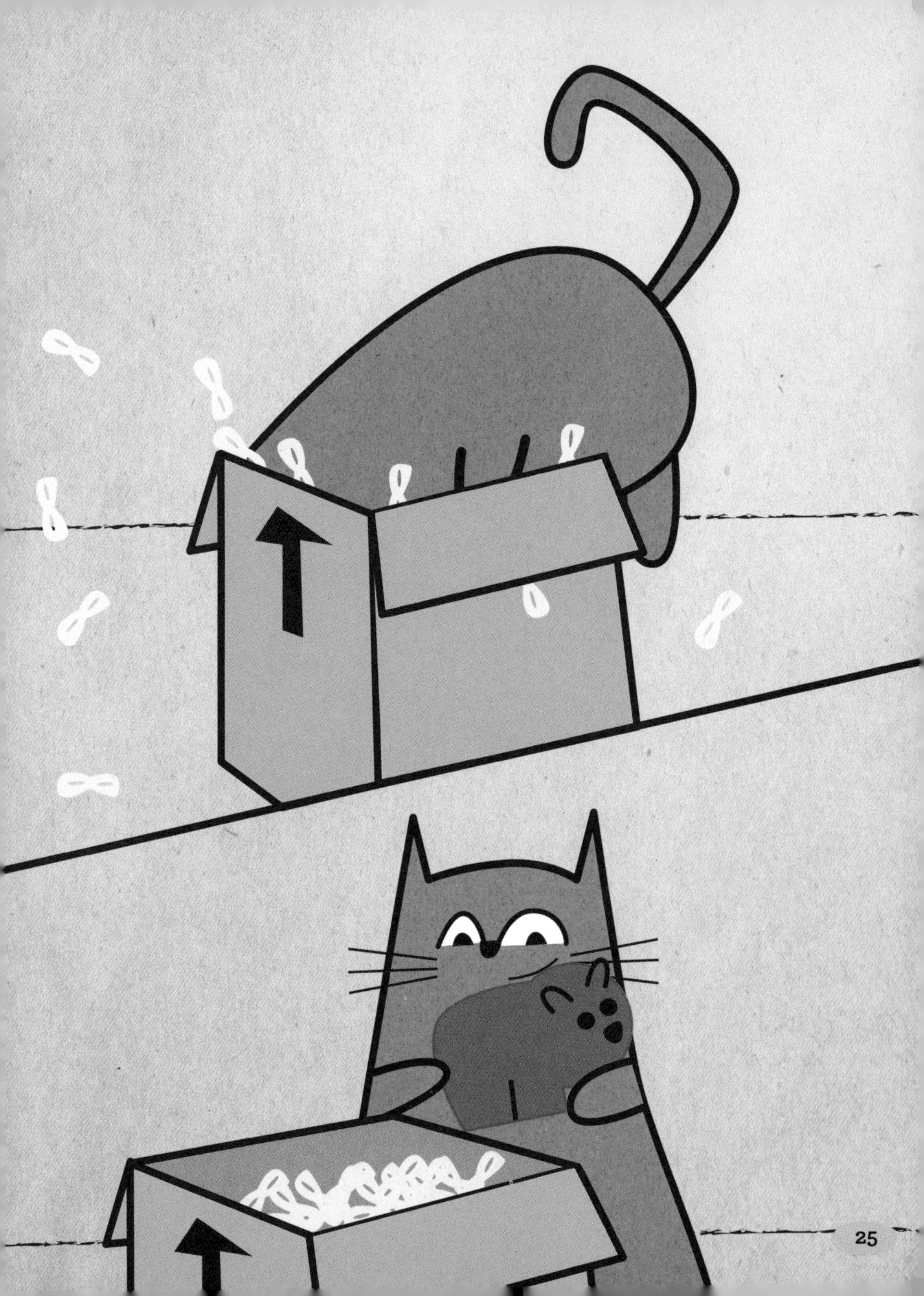

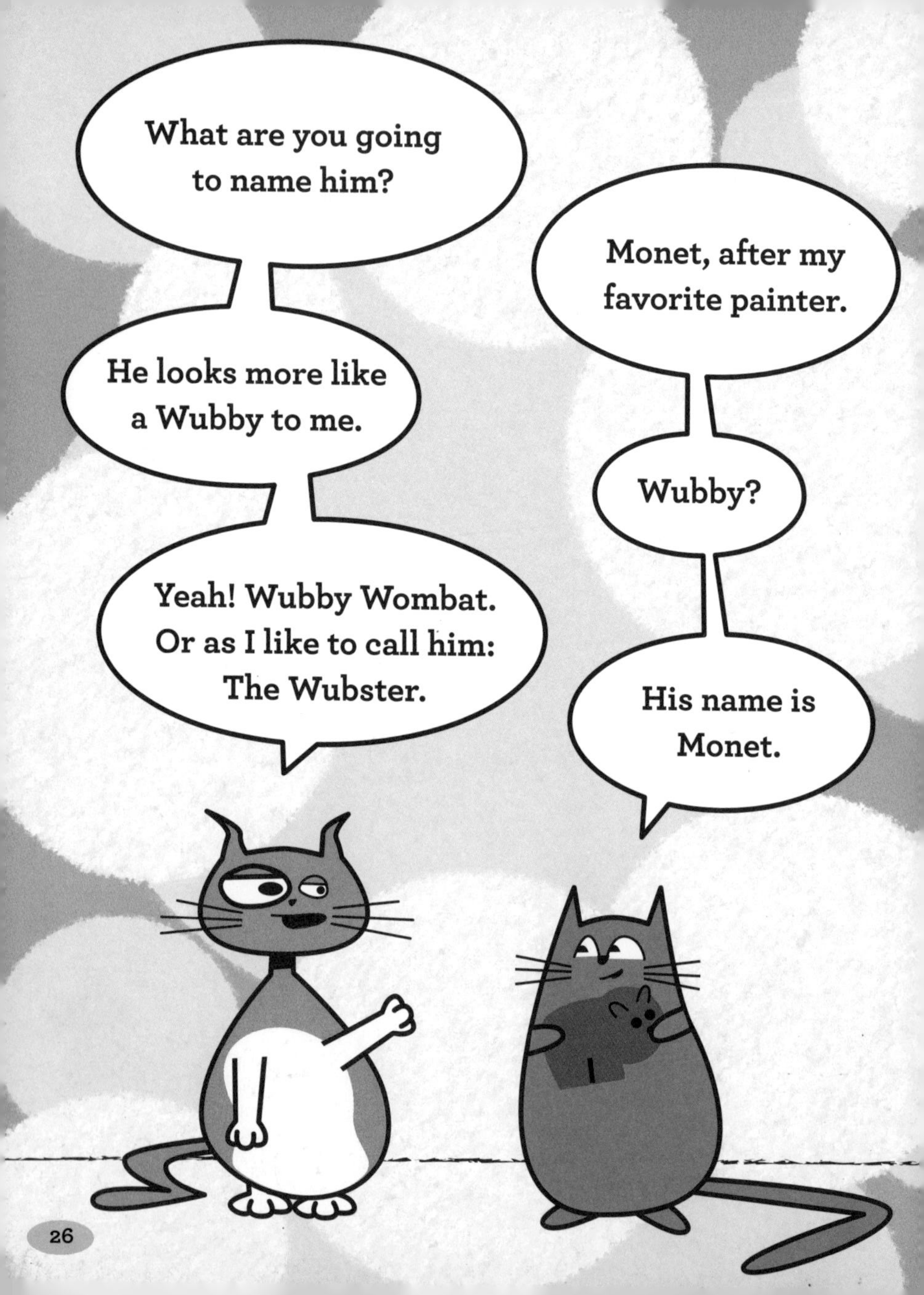
What are you going to name him?
Monet, after my favorite painter.
He looks more like a Wubby to me.
Wubby?
Yeah! Wubby Wombat. Or as I like to call him: The Wubster.
His name is Monet.

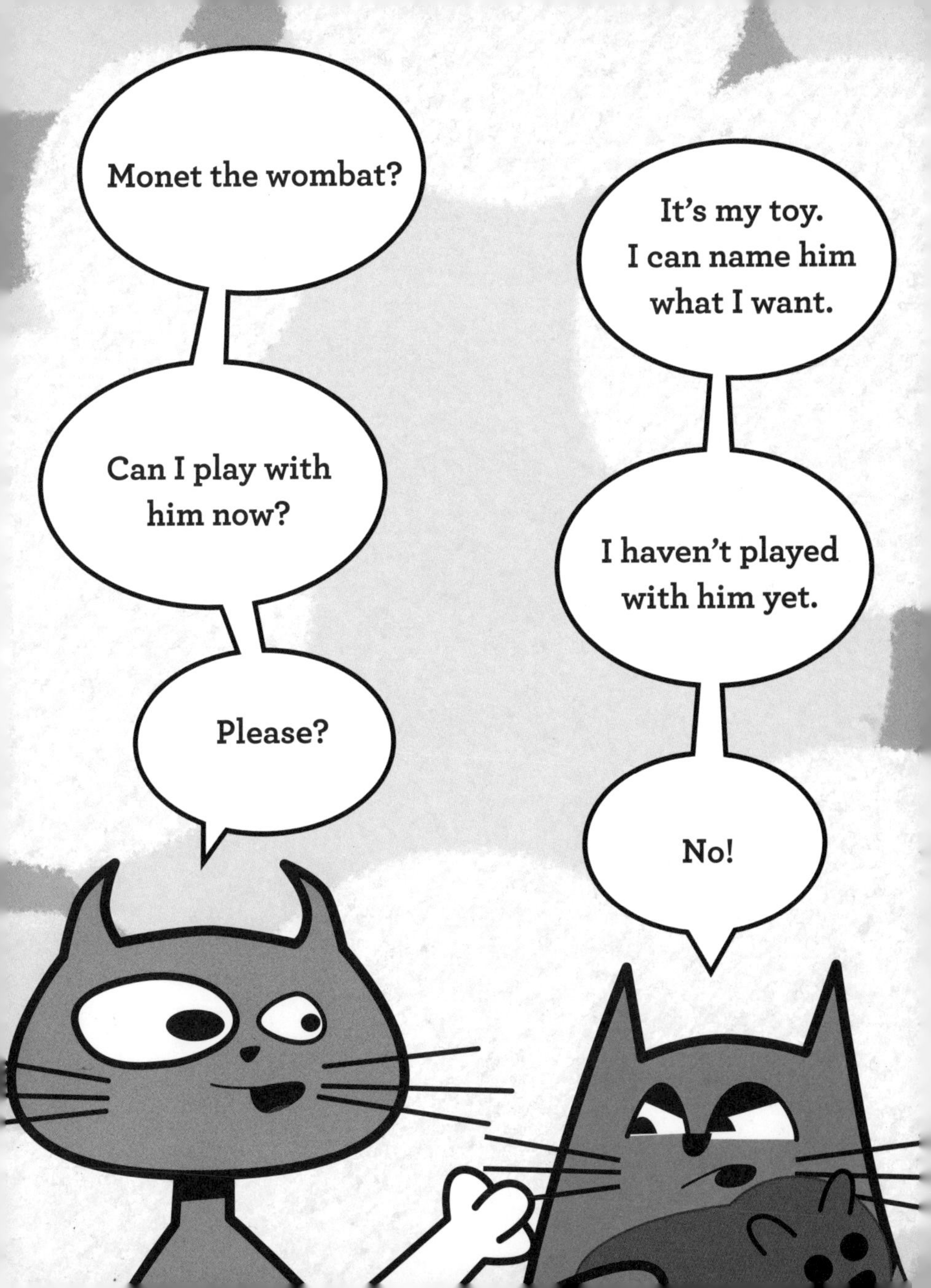
Monet the wombat?
Can I play with him now?
Please?
It's my toy. I can name him what I want.
I haven't played with him yet.
No!

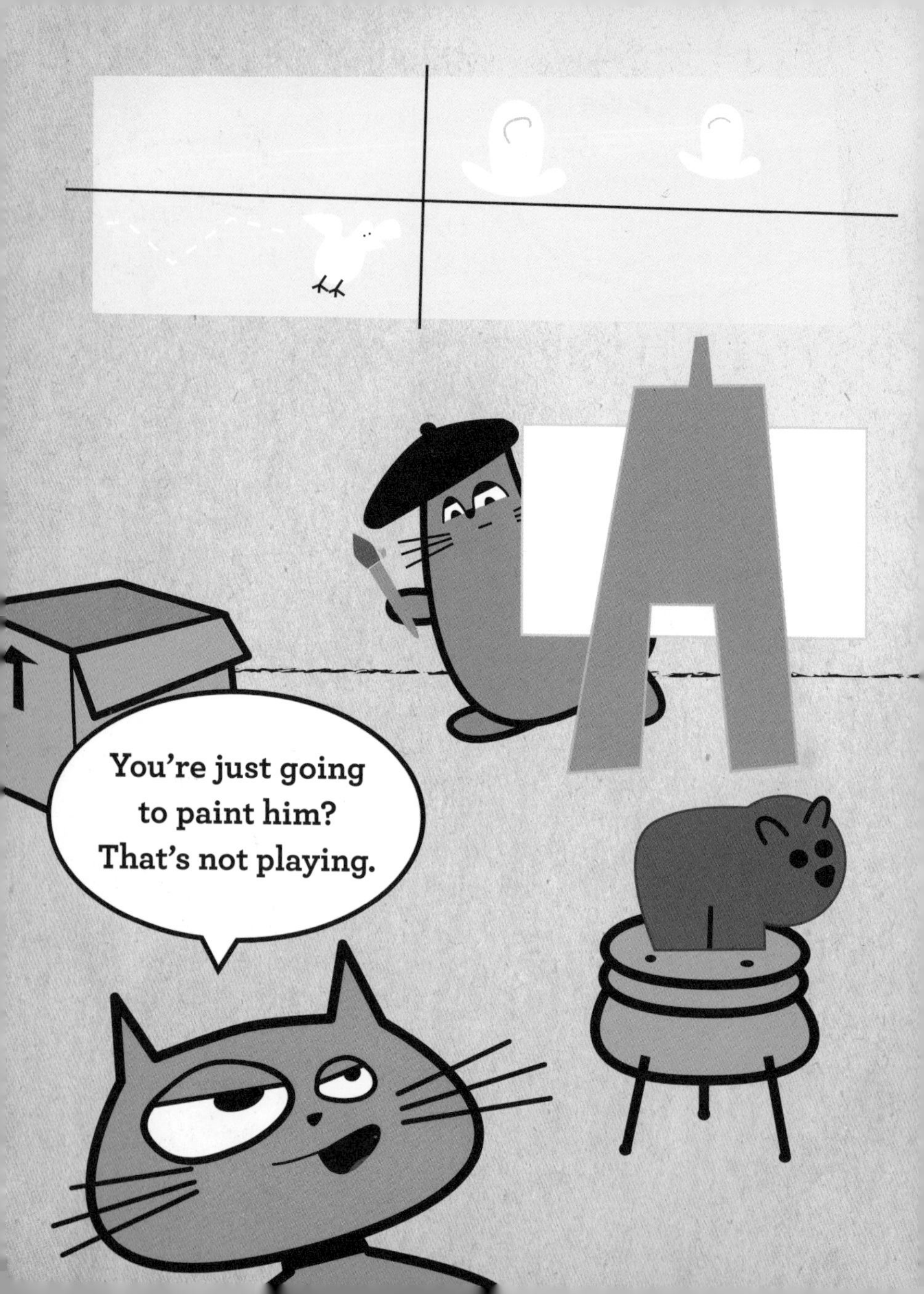
You're just going to paint him? That's not playing.

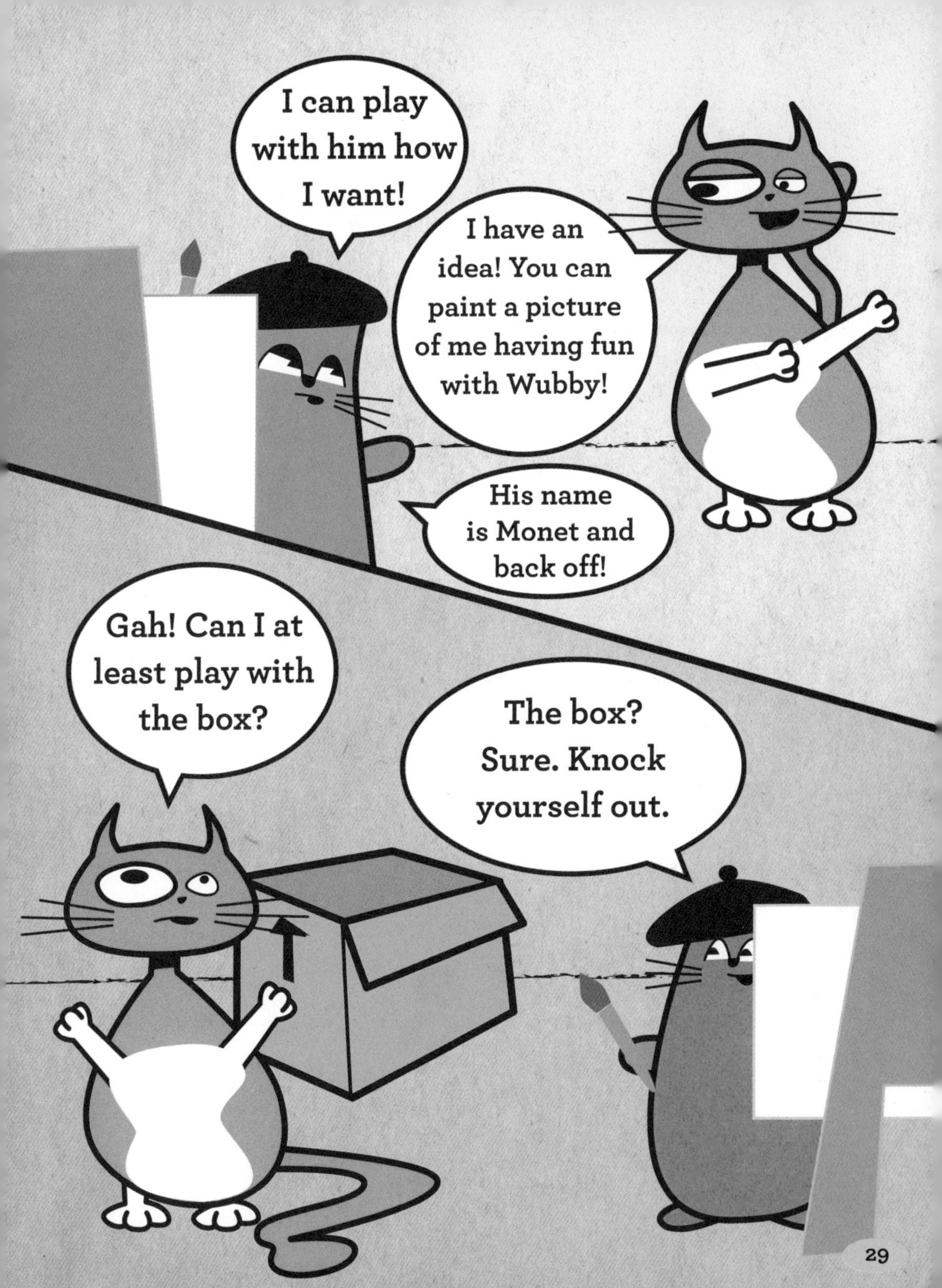
I can play with him how I want!
I have an idea! You can paint a picture of me having fun with Wubby!
His name is Monet and back off!
Gah! Can I at least play with the box?
The box? Sure. Knock yourself out.

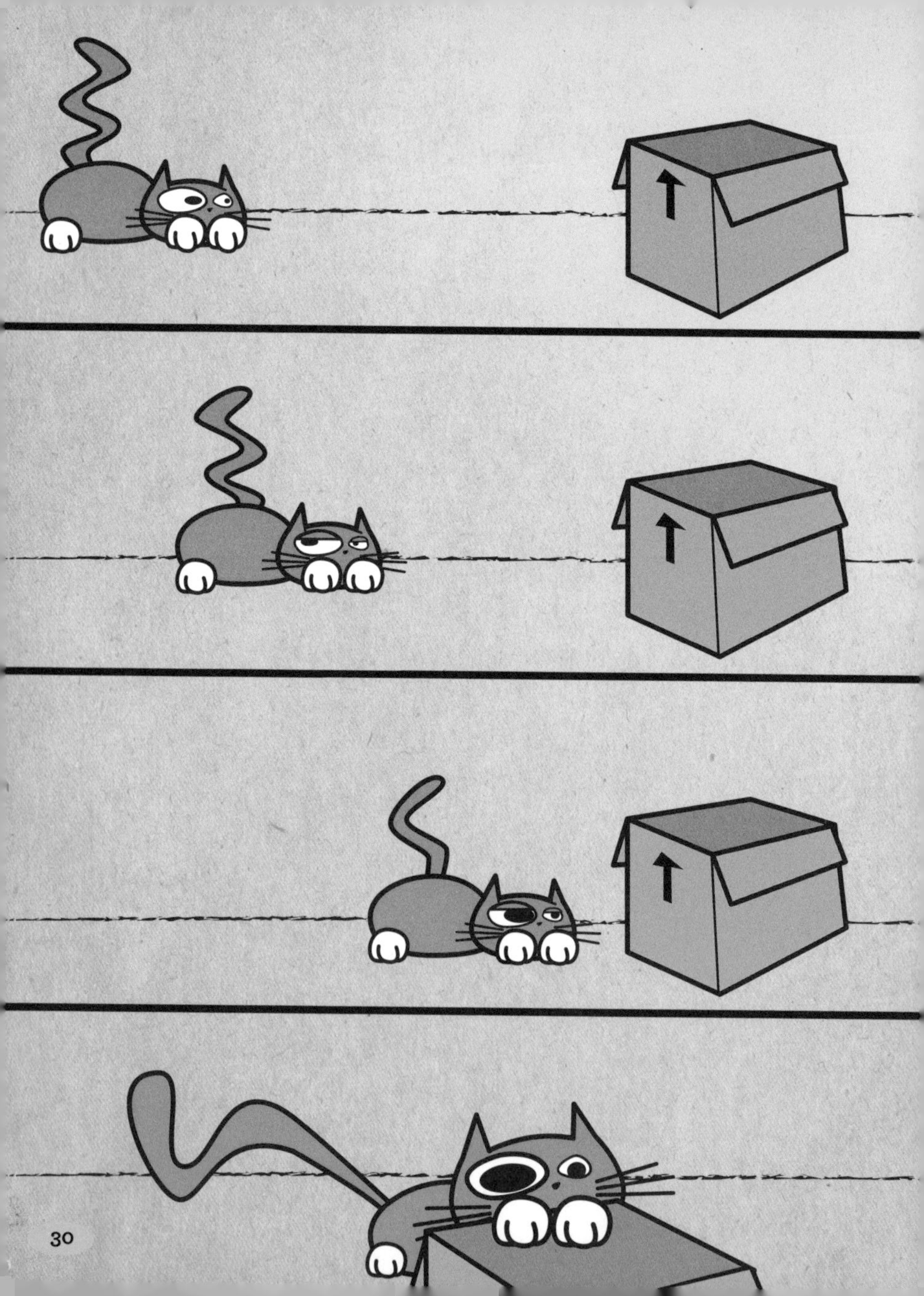

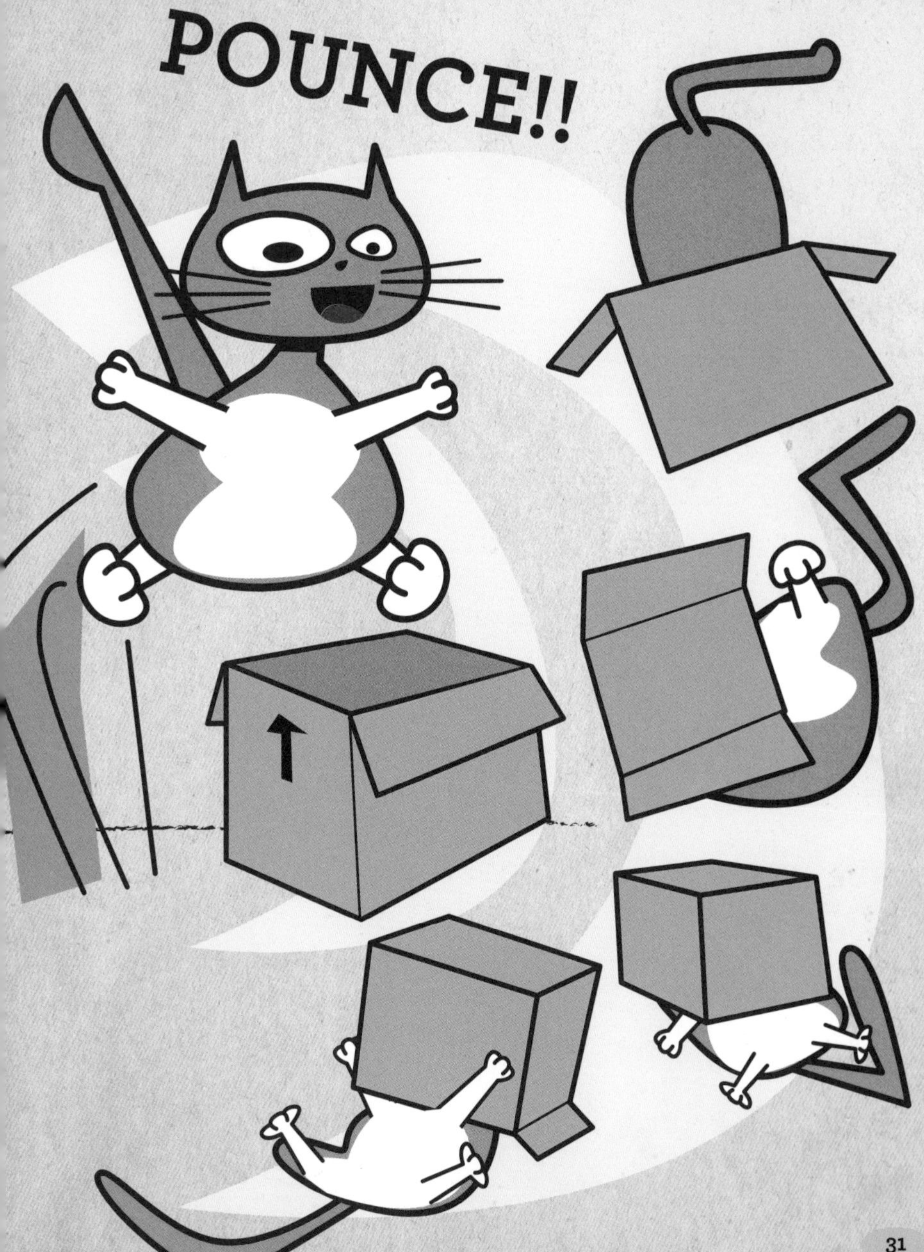
POUNCE!!

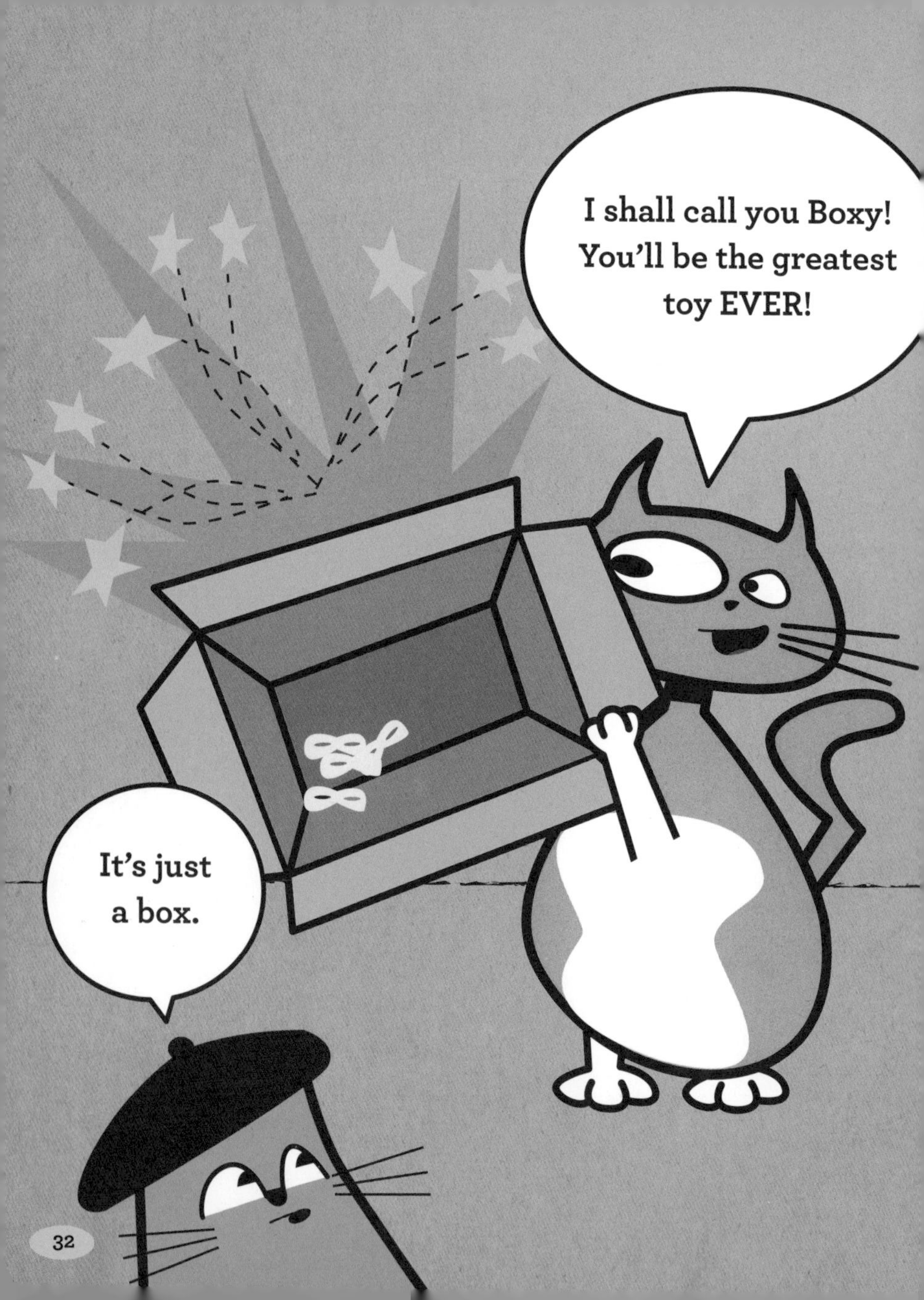
I shall call you Boxy! You'll be the greatest toy EVER!
It's just a box.

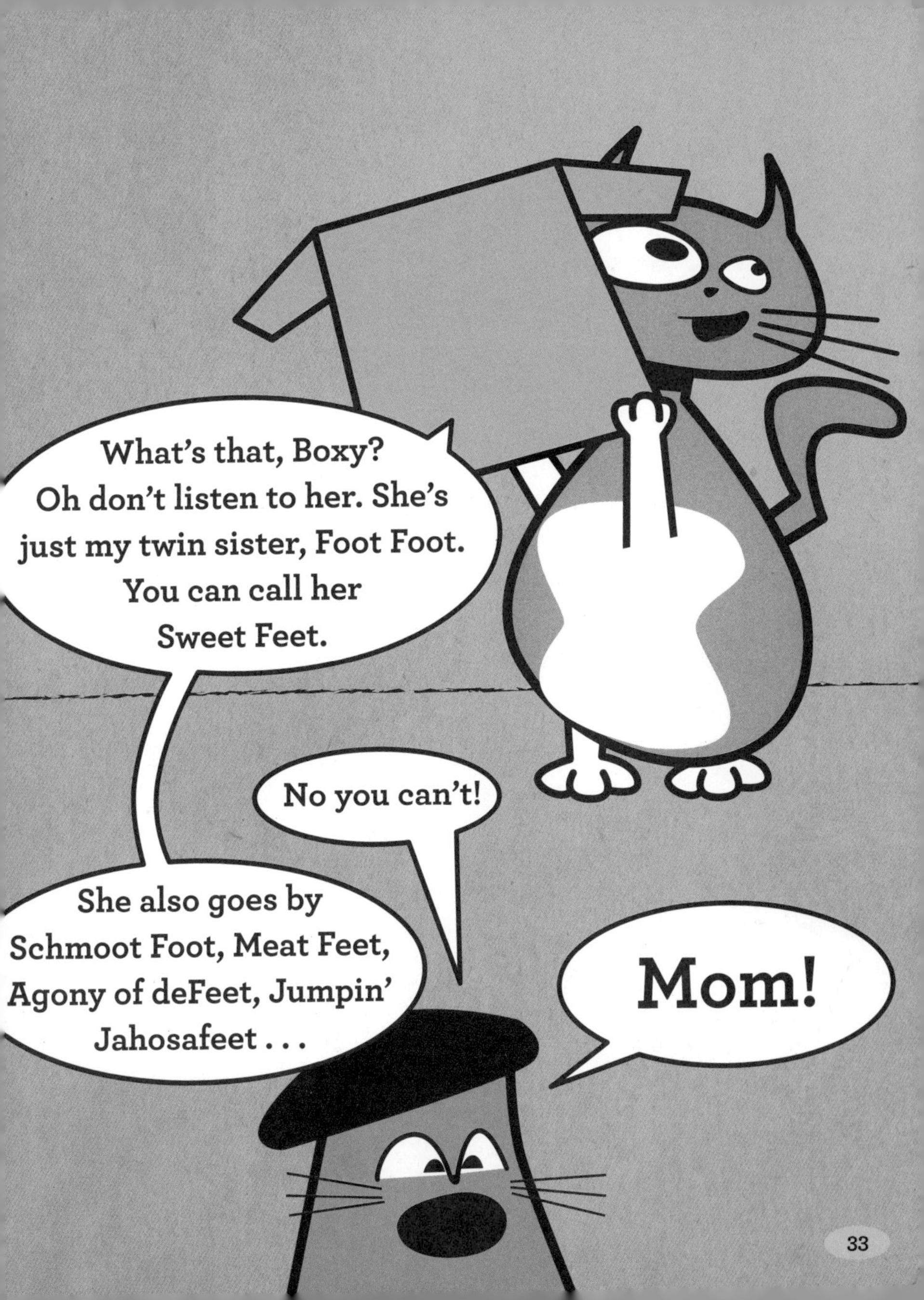
What's that, Boxy? Oh don't listen to her. She's just my twin sister, Foot Foot. You can call her Sweet Feet.
No you can't!
She also goes by Schmoot Foot, Meat Feet, Agony of deFeet, Jumpin' Jahosafeet . . .
Mom!

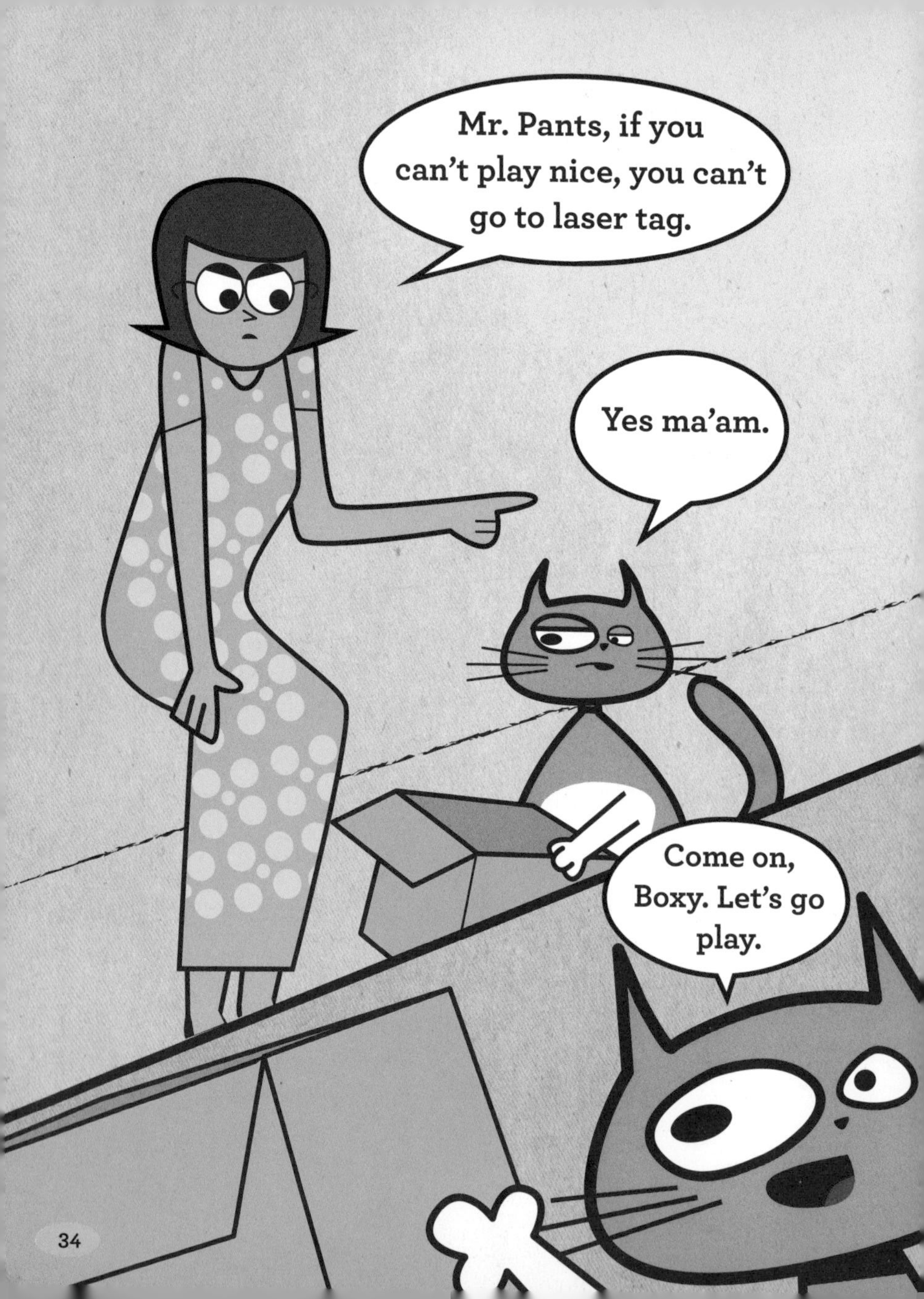
Mr. Pants, if you can't play nice, you can't go to laser tag.
Yes ma'am.
Come on, Boxy. Let's go play.

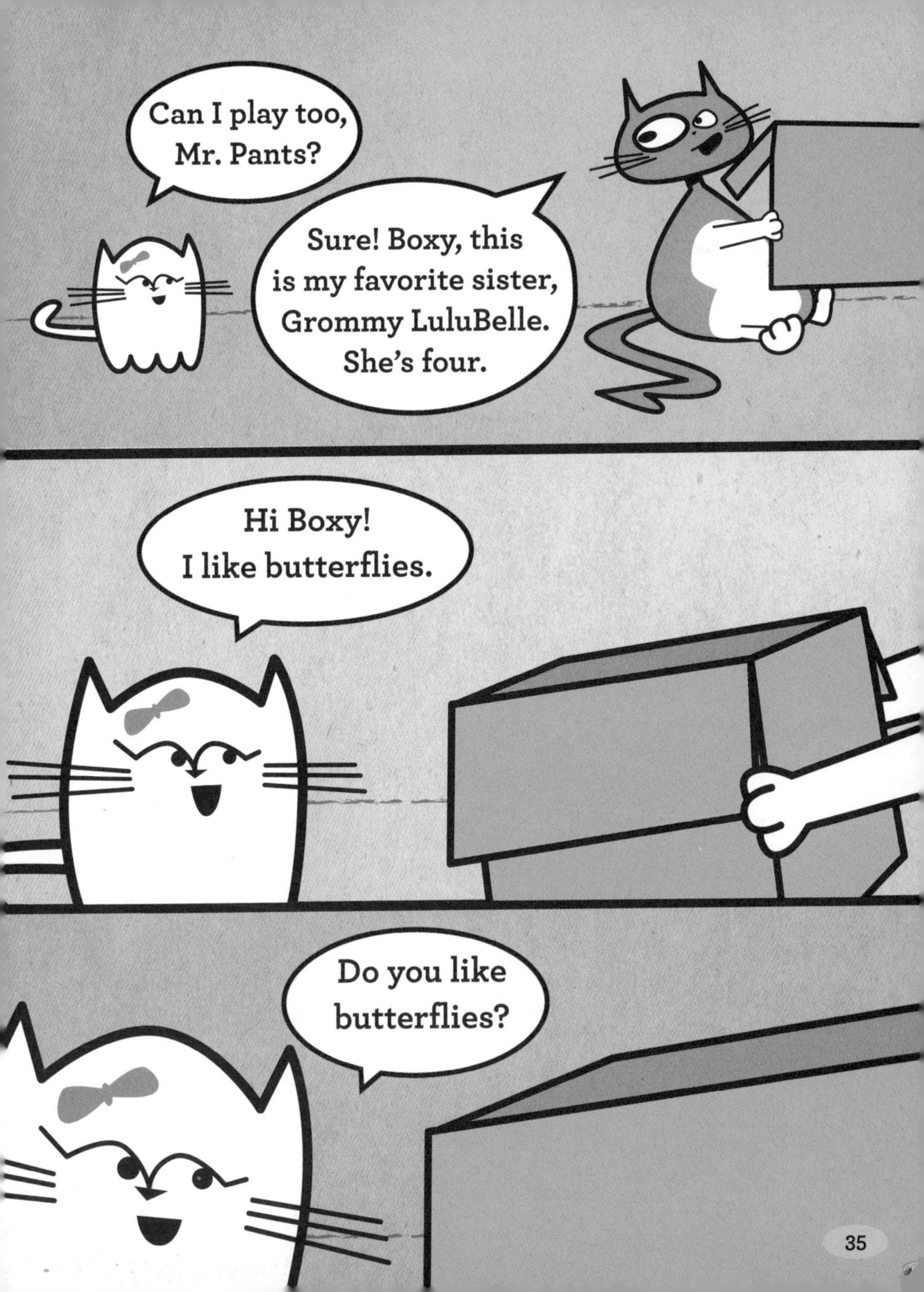

Can I play too, Mr. Pants?
Sure! Boxy, this is my favorite sister, Grommy LuluBelle. She's four.
Hi Boxy! I like butterflies.
Do you like butterflies?

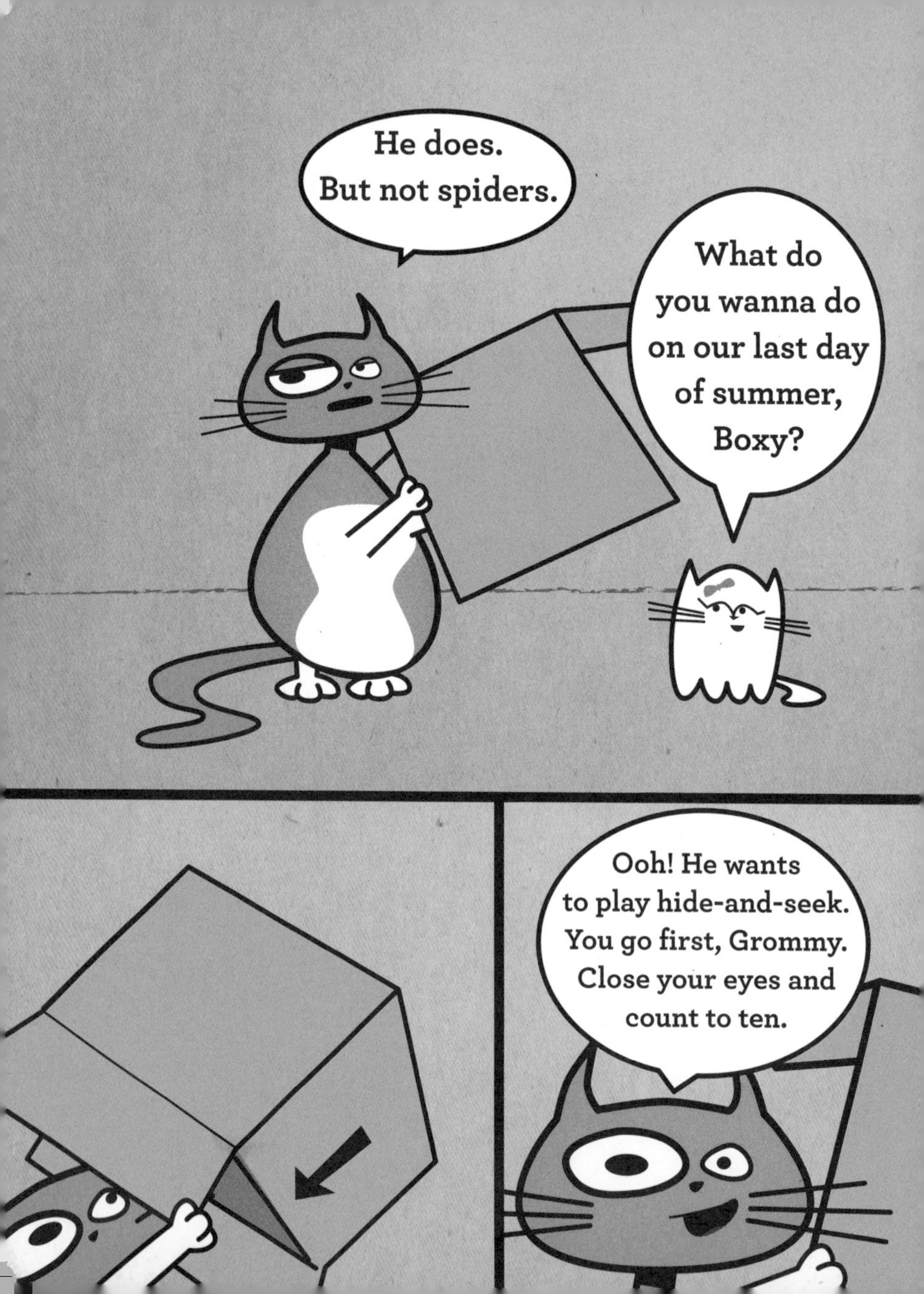
He does. But not spiders.
What do you wanna do on our last day of summer, Boxy?
Ooh! He wants to play hide-and-seek. You go first, Grommy. Close your eyes and count to ten.

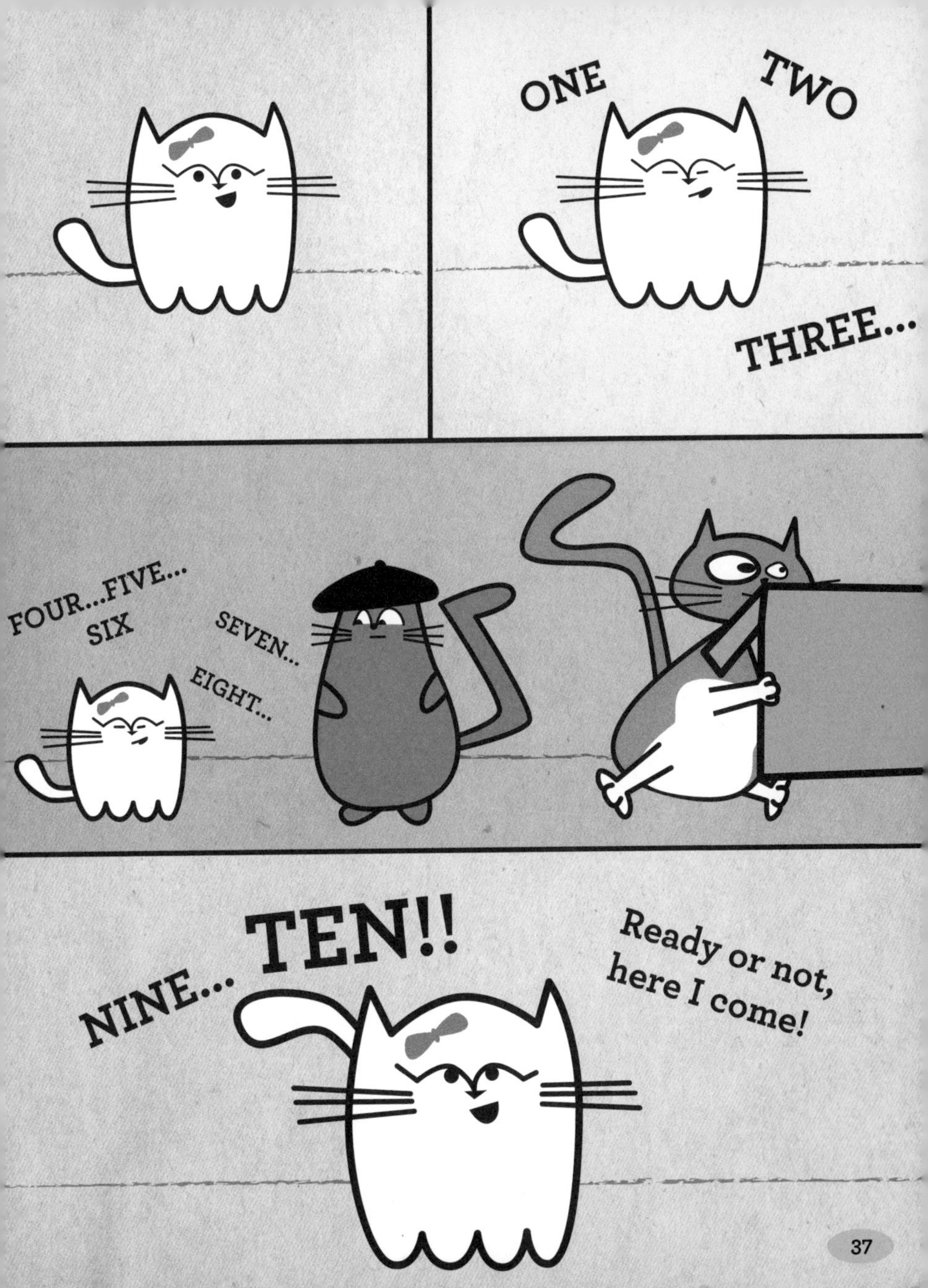

ONE
TWO
THREE...
FOUR...FIVE...
SIX
SEVEN...
EIGHT...
NINE...
TEN!!
Ready or not, here I come!

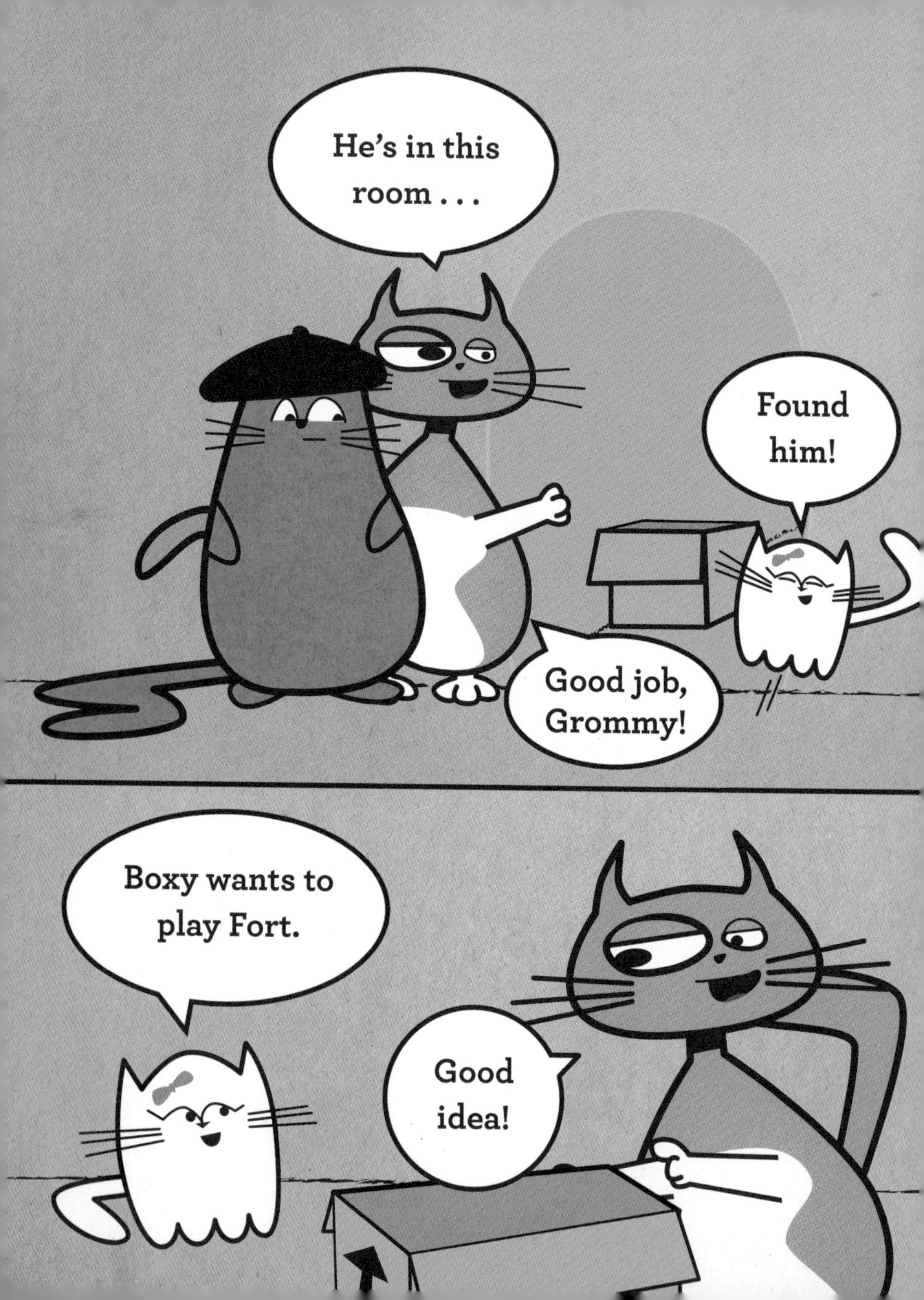
He's in this room . . .
Found him!
Good job, Grommy!
Boxy wants to play Fort.
Good idea!

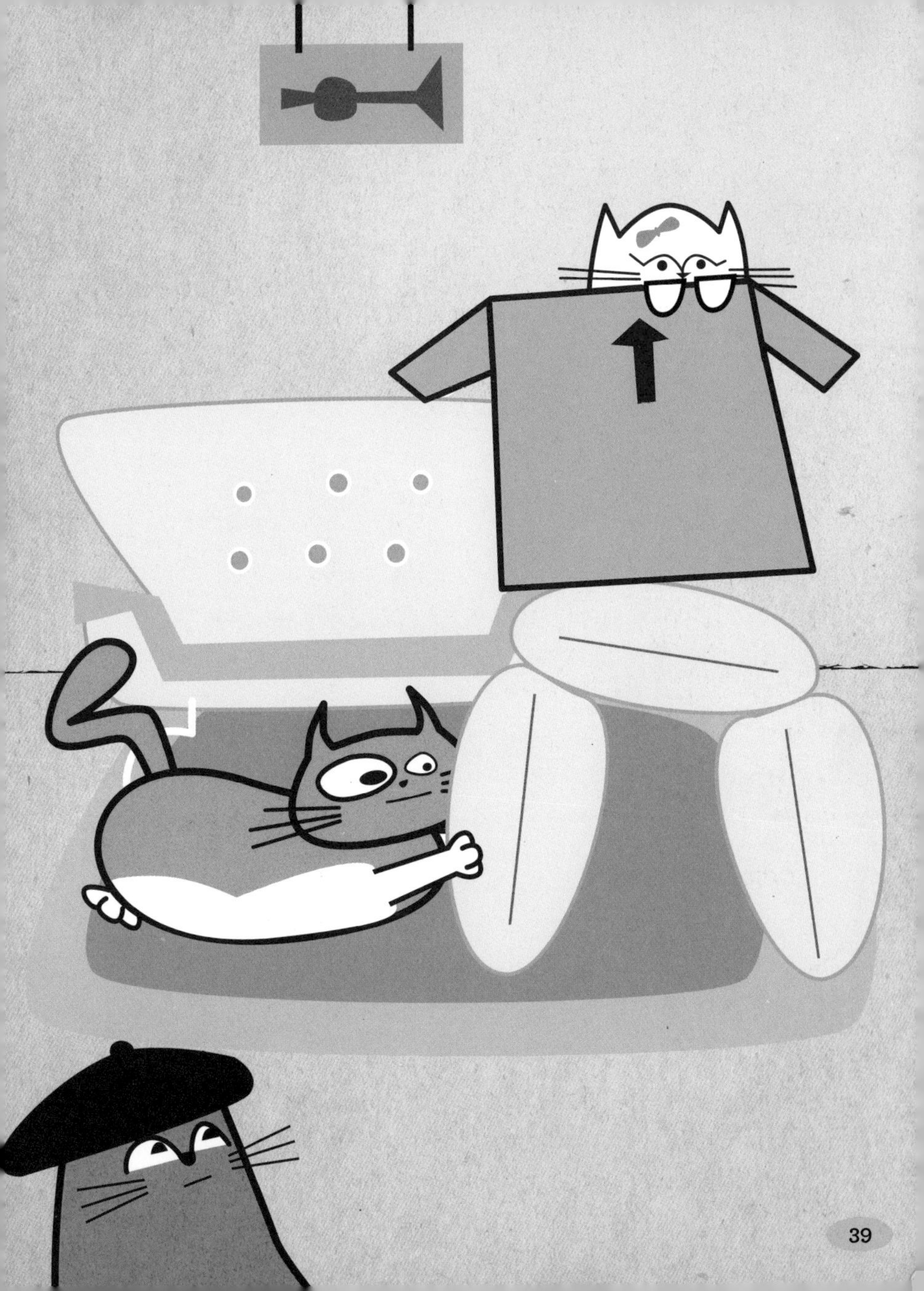

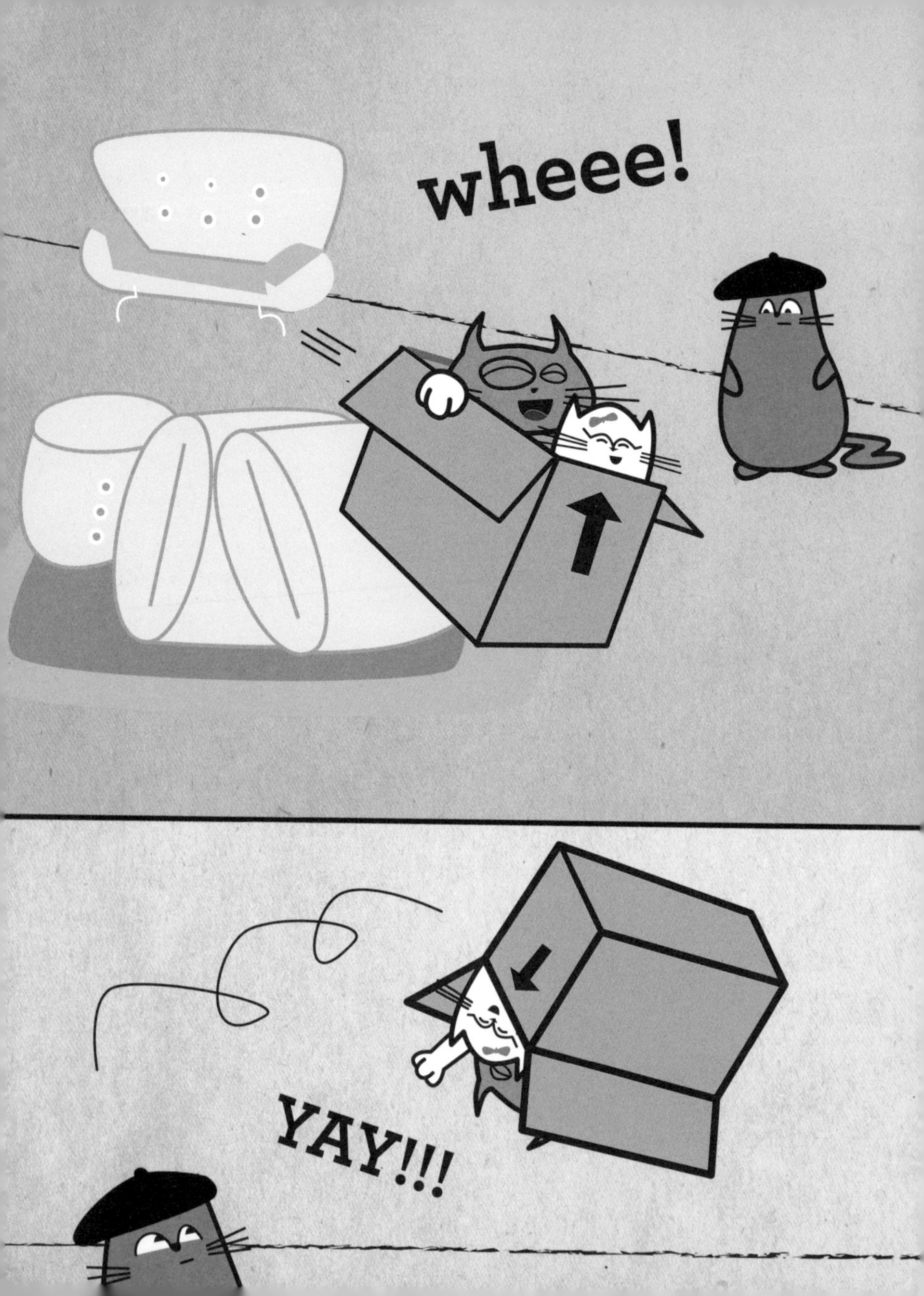
wheee!
YAY!!!

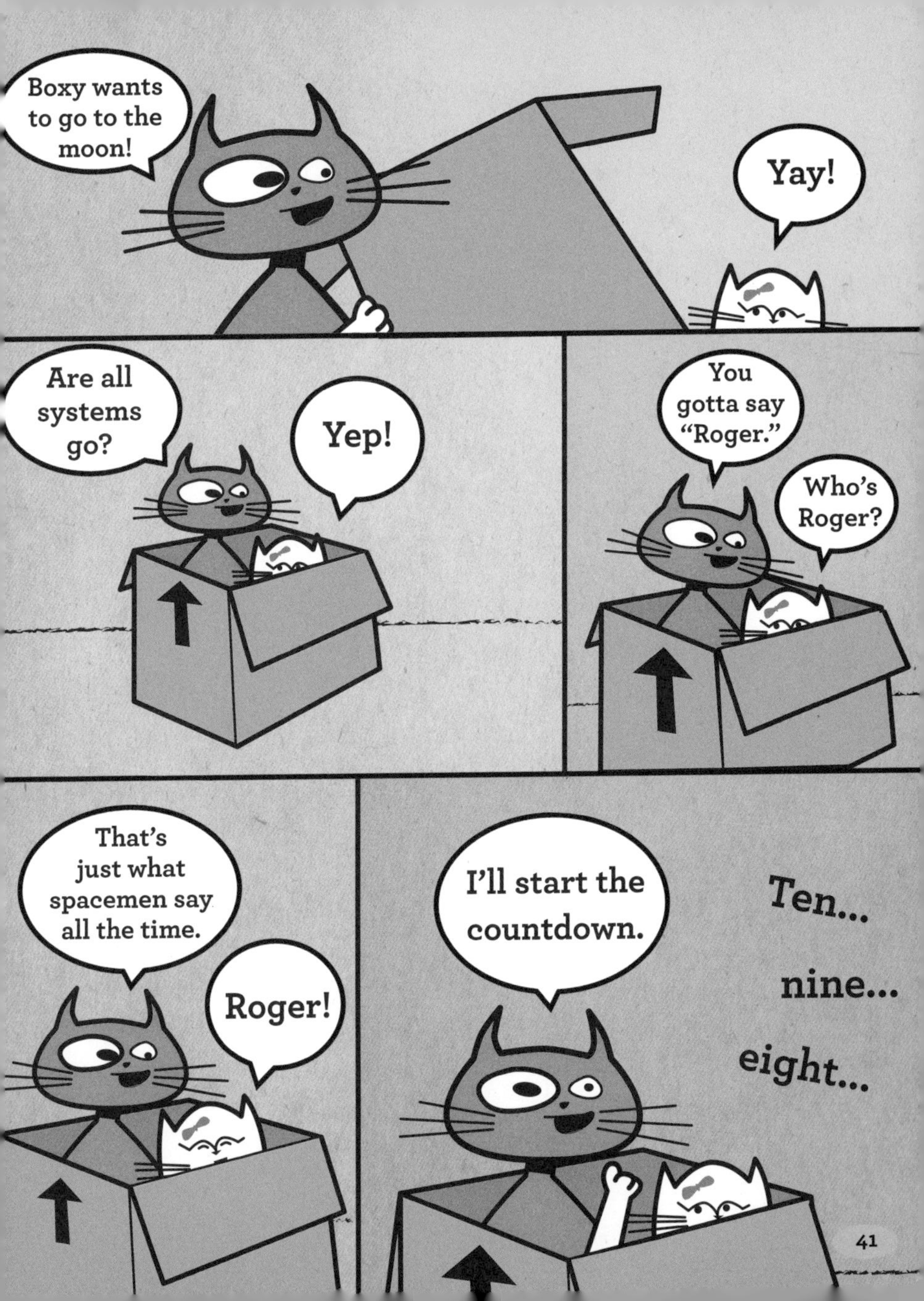
Boxy wants to go to the moon!
Yay!
Are all systems go?
Yep!
You gotta say "Roger."
Who's Roger?
That's just what spacemen say all the time.
Roger!
I'll start the countdown.
Ten...
nine...
eight...

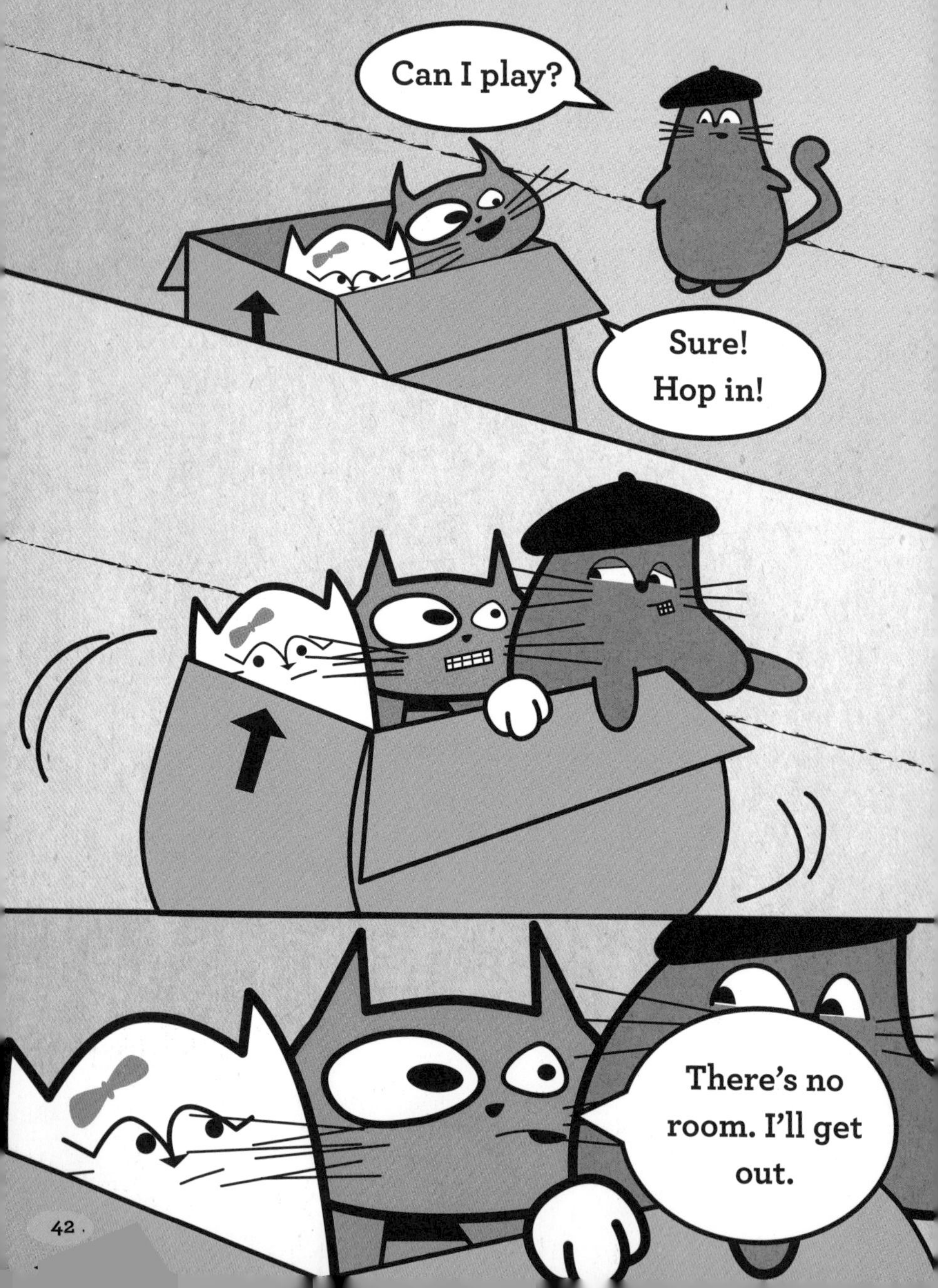
Can I play?
Sure!
Hop in!
There's no room. I'll get out.

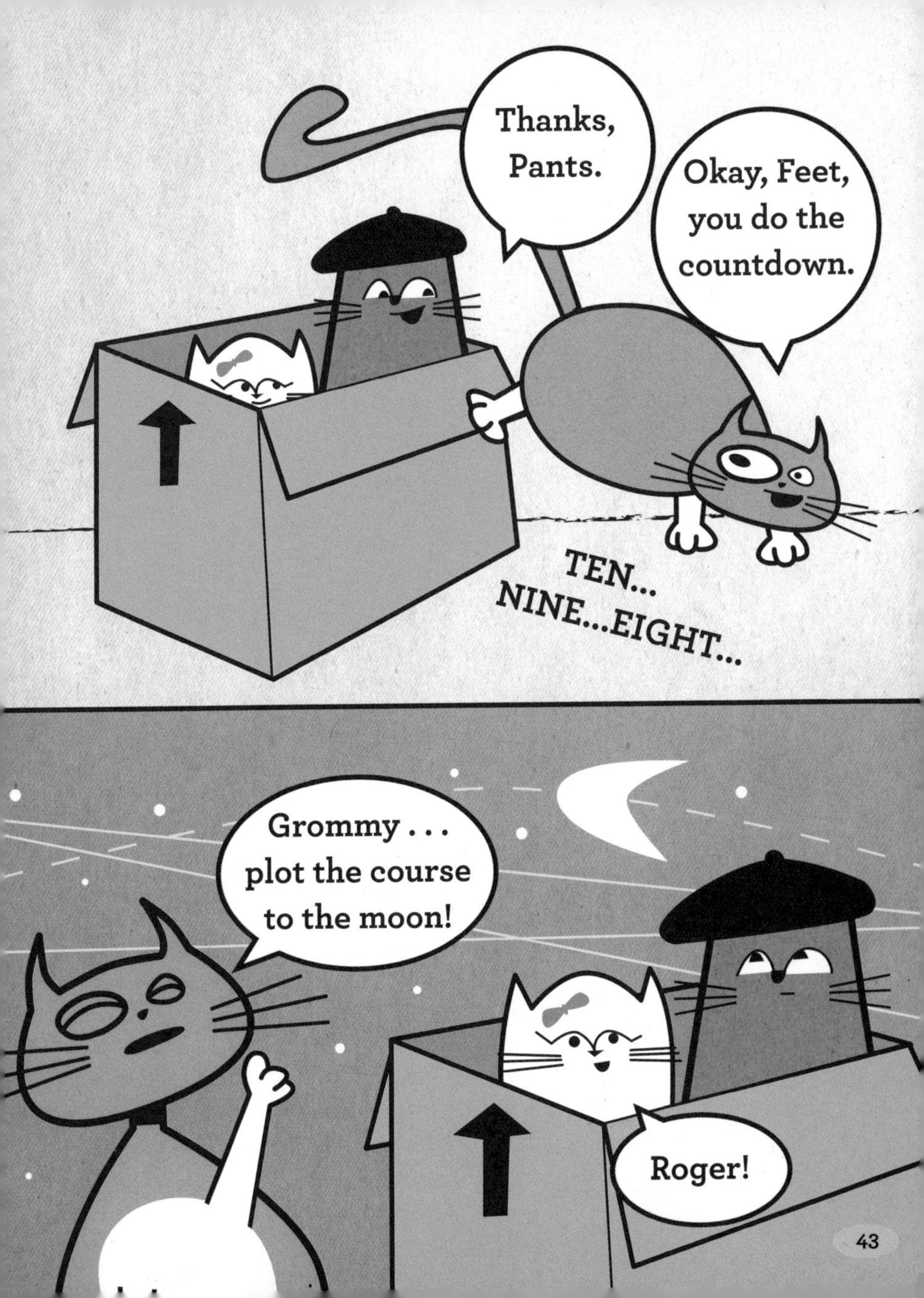
Thanks, Pants.
Okay, Feet, you do the countdown.
TEN... NINE...EIGHT...
Grommy . . . plot the course to the moon!
Roger!

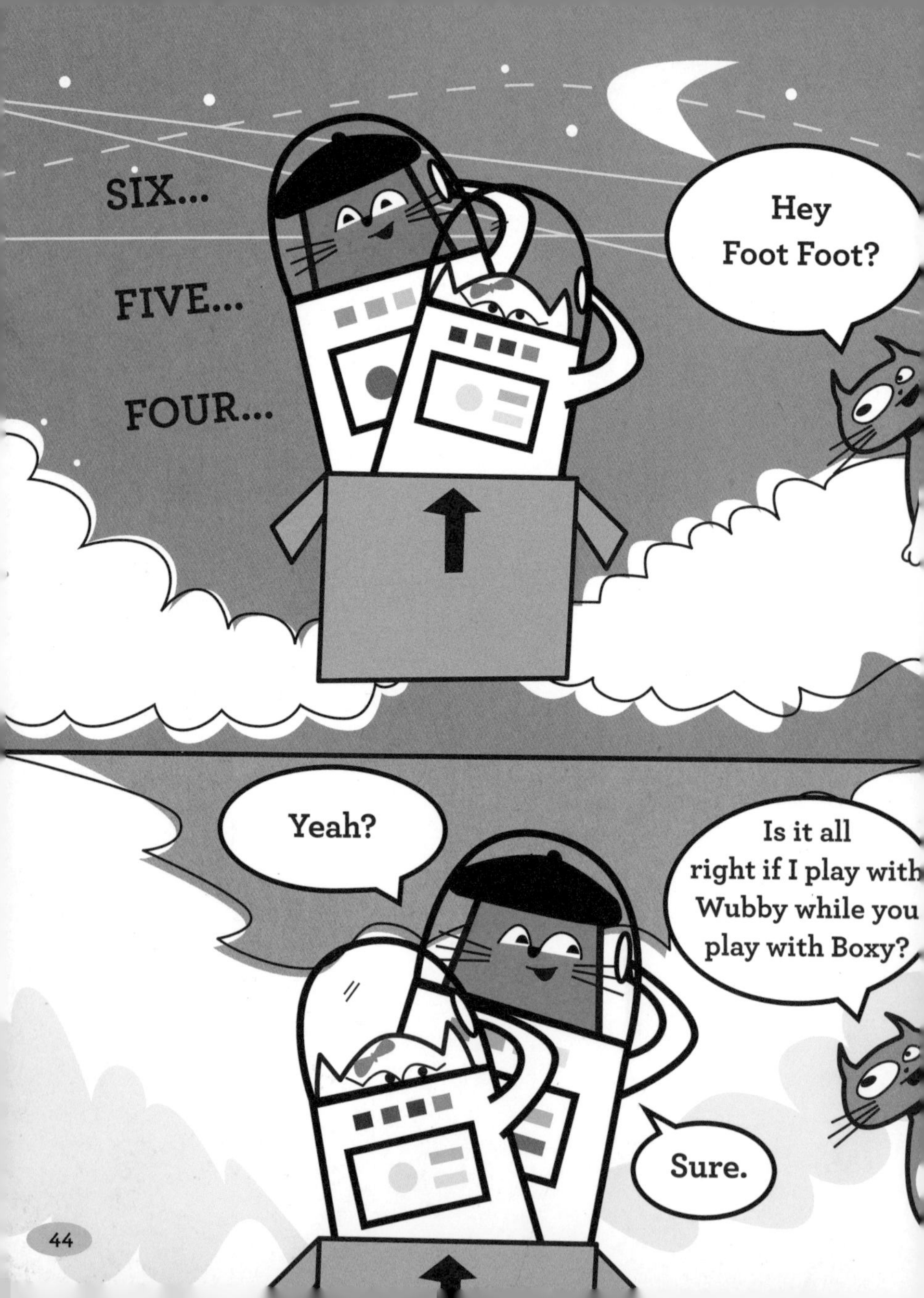

SIX...
FIVE...
FOUR...
Hey Foot Foot?
Yeah?
Is it all right if I play with Wubby while you play with Boxy?
Sure.

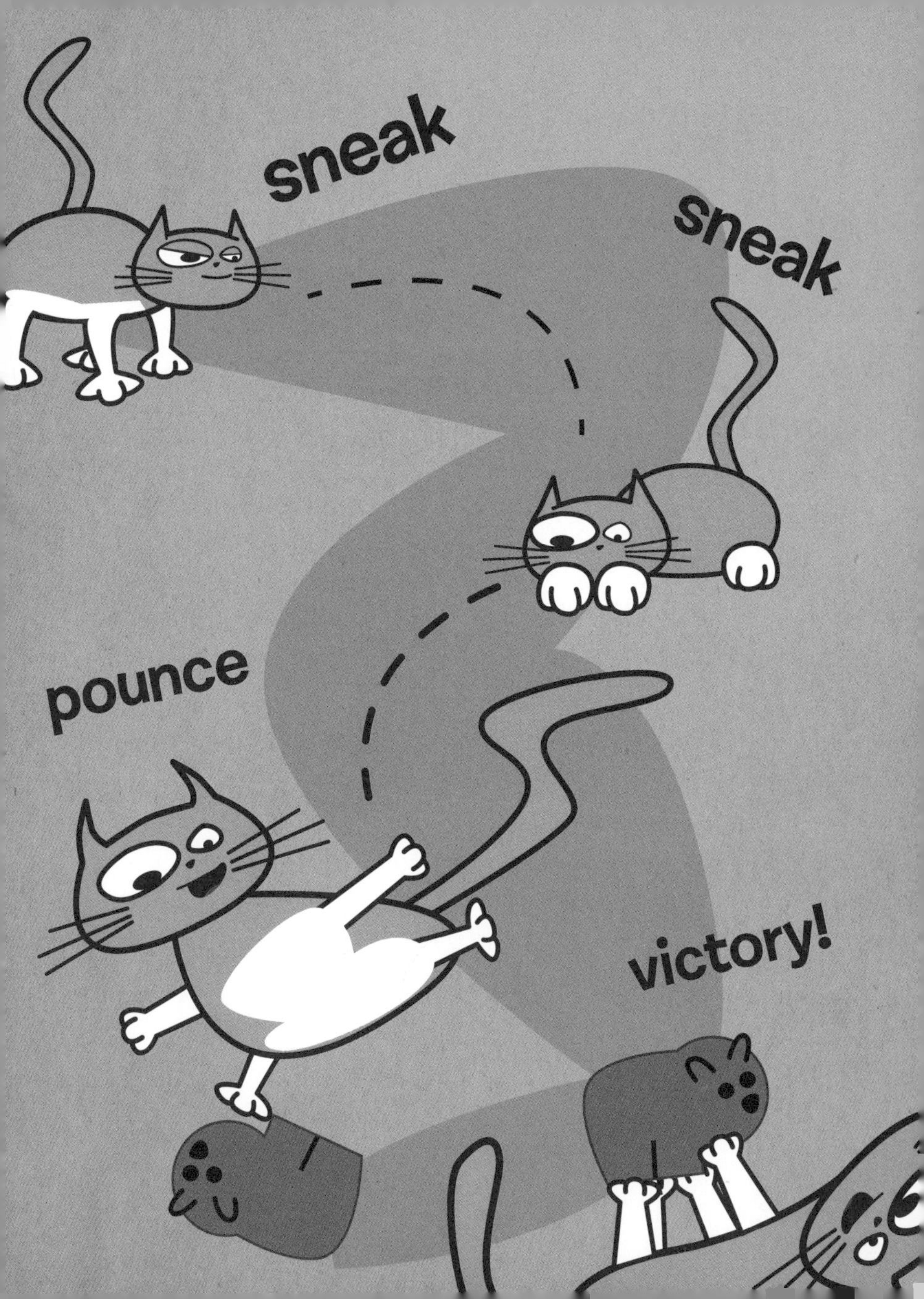
sneak
sneak
pounce
victory!

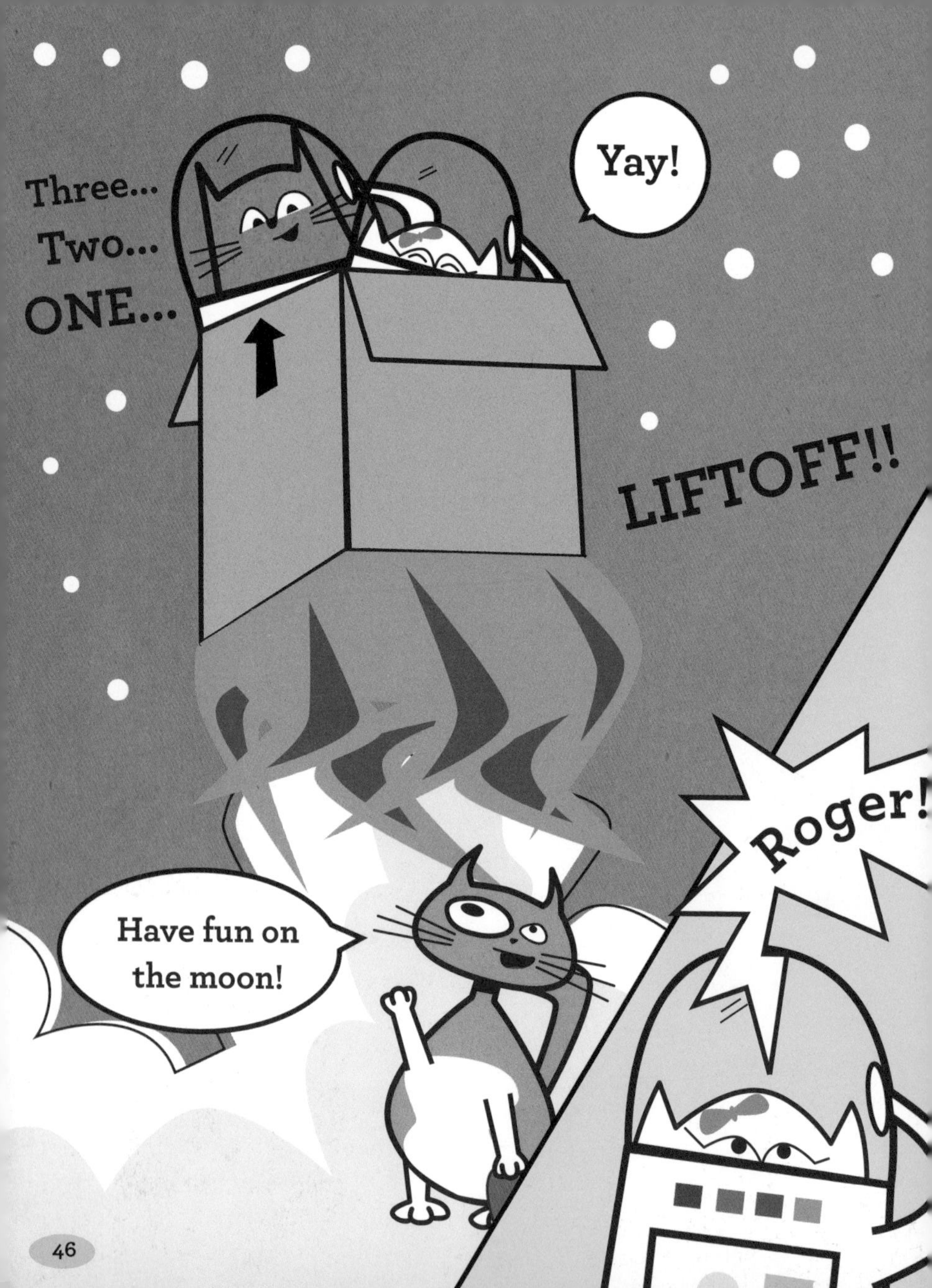
Three...
Two...
ONE...
Yay!
LIFTOFF!!
Roger!
Have fun on the moon!

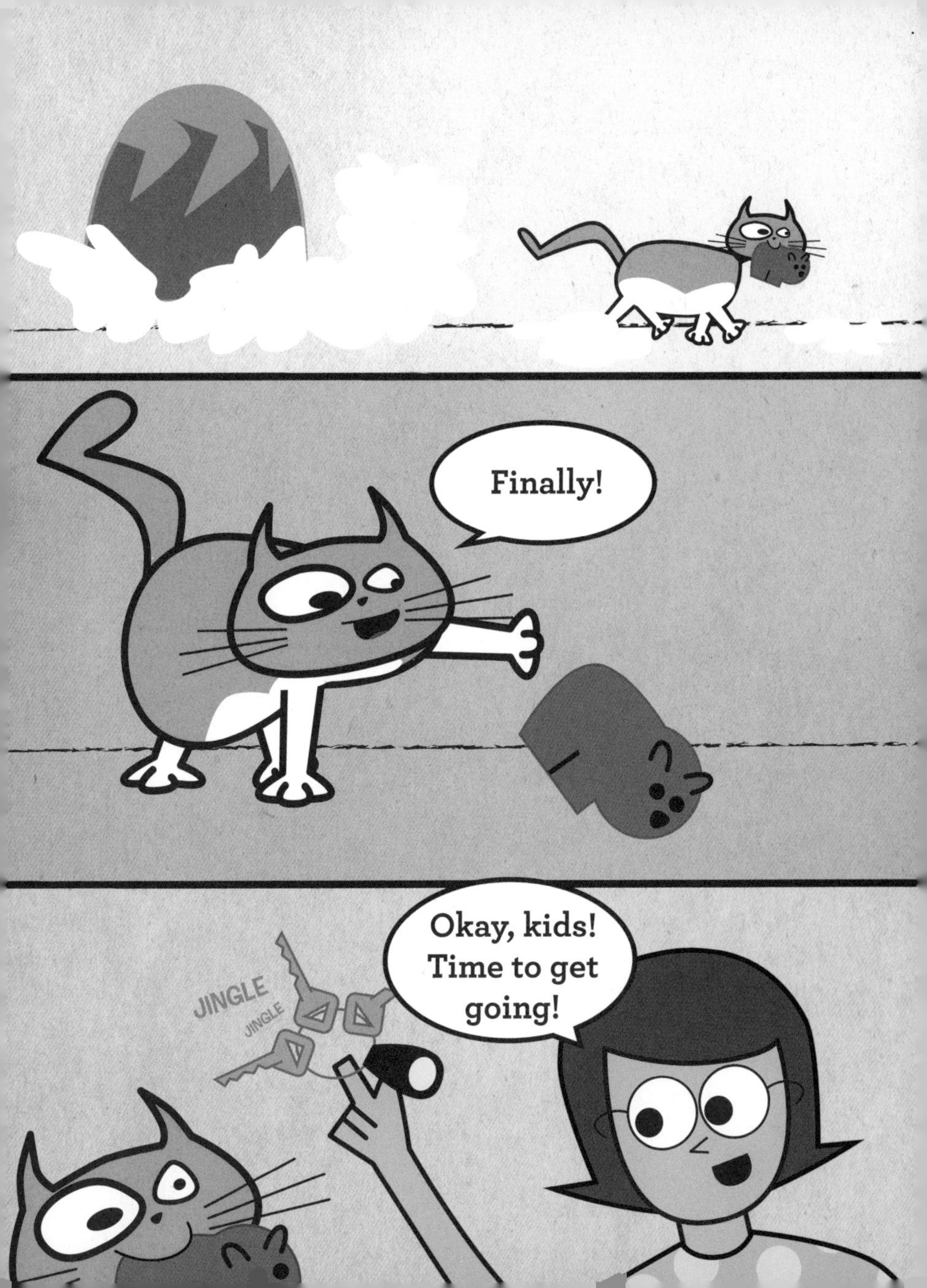

Finally!
Okay, kids! Time to get going!
JINGLE
JINGLE

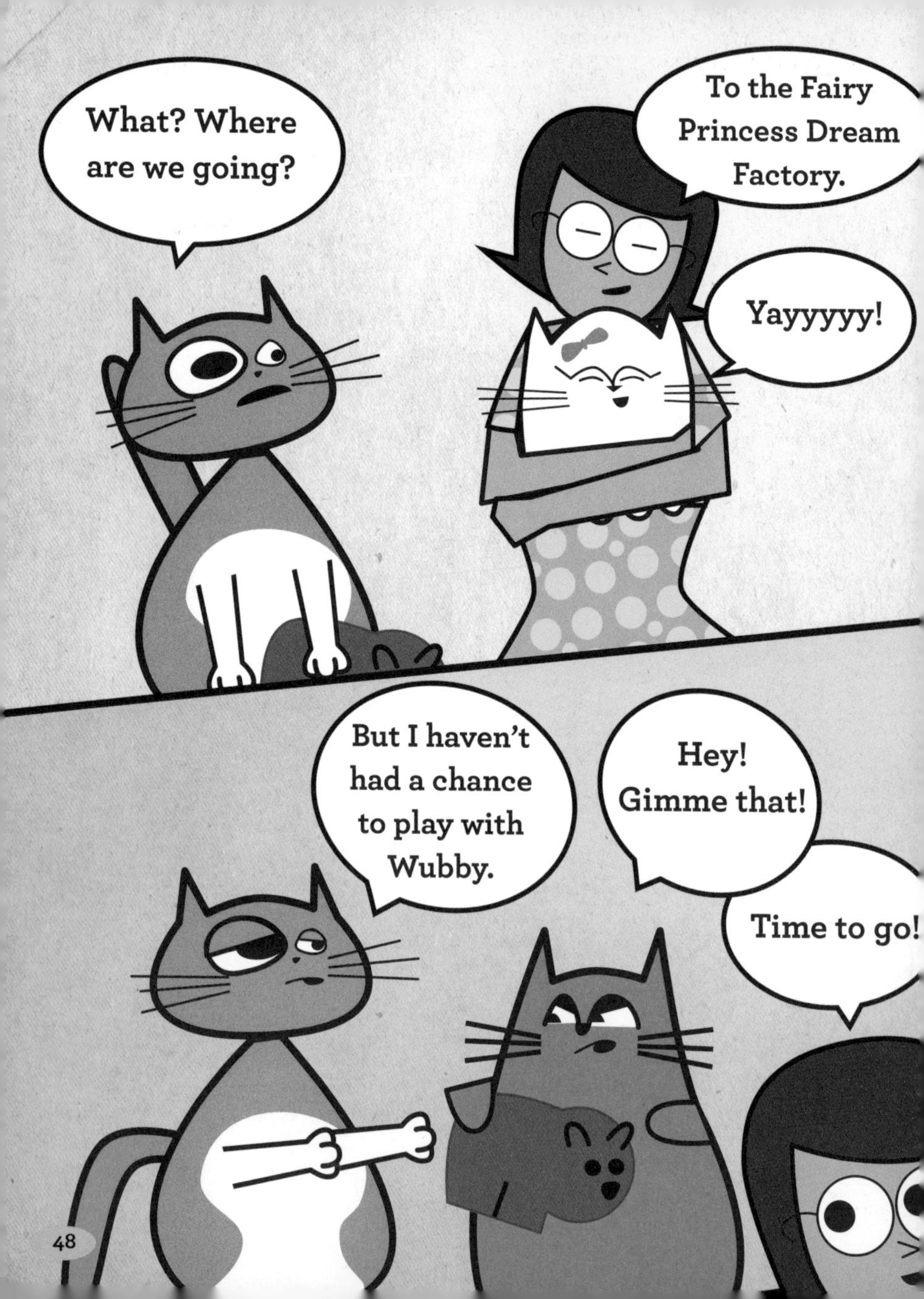
What? Where are we going?
To the Fairy Princess Dream Factory.
Yayyyyy!
But I haven't had a chance to play with Wubby.
Hey! Gimme that!
Time to go!

# Chapter Three:
# PRINCESS PANTS

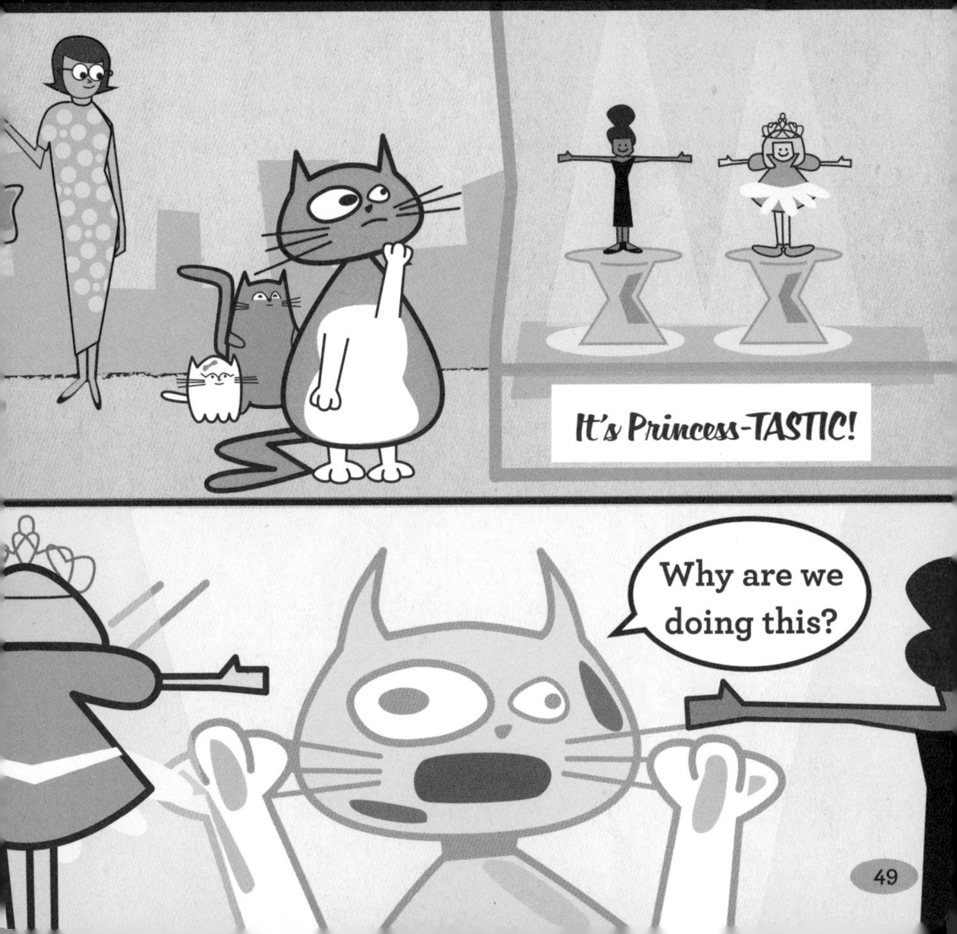
It's Princess-TASTIC!
Why are we doing this?

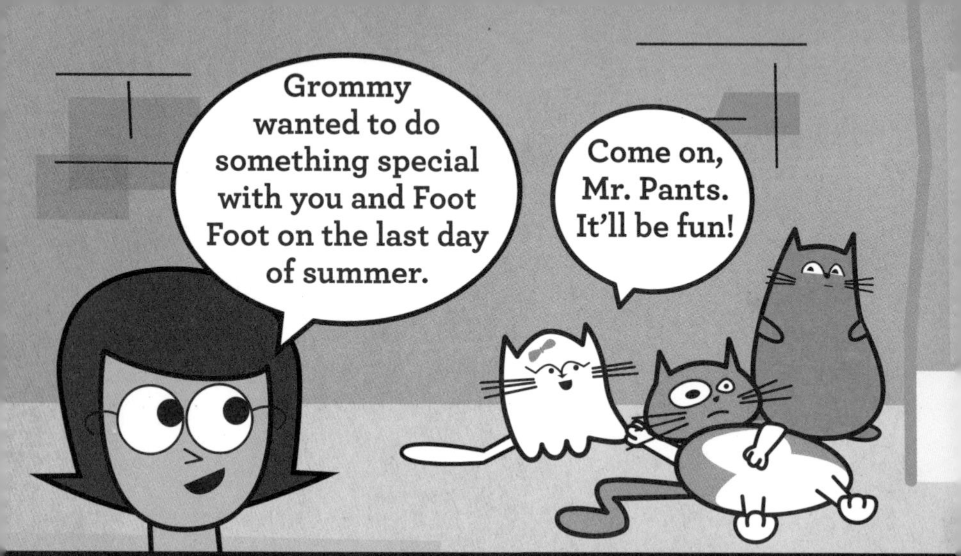
Grommy wanted to do something special with you and Foot Foot on the last day of summer.
Come on, Mr. Pants. It'll be fun!

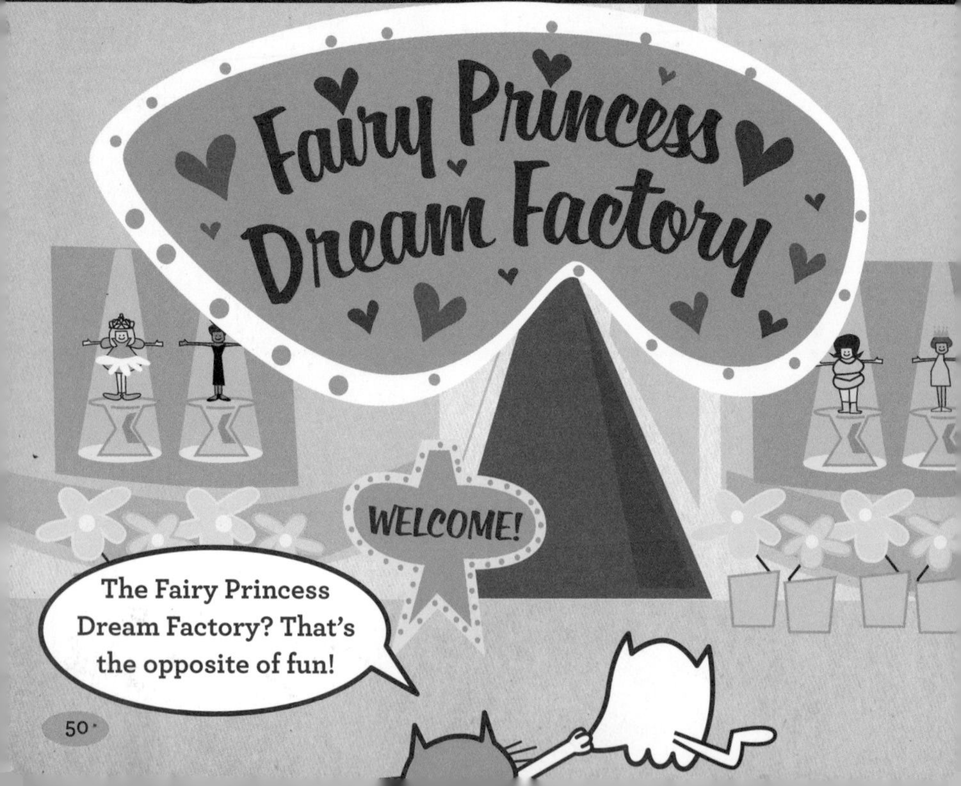
Fairy Princess Dream Factory
WELCOME!
The Fairy Princess Dream Factory? That's the opposite of fun!

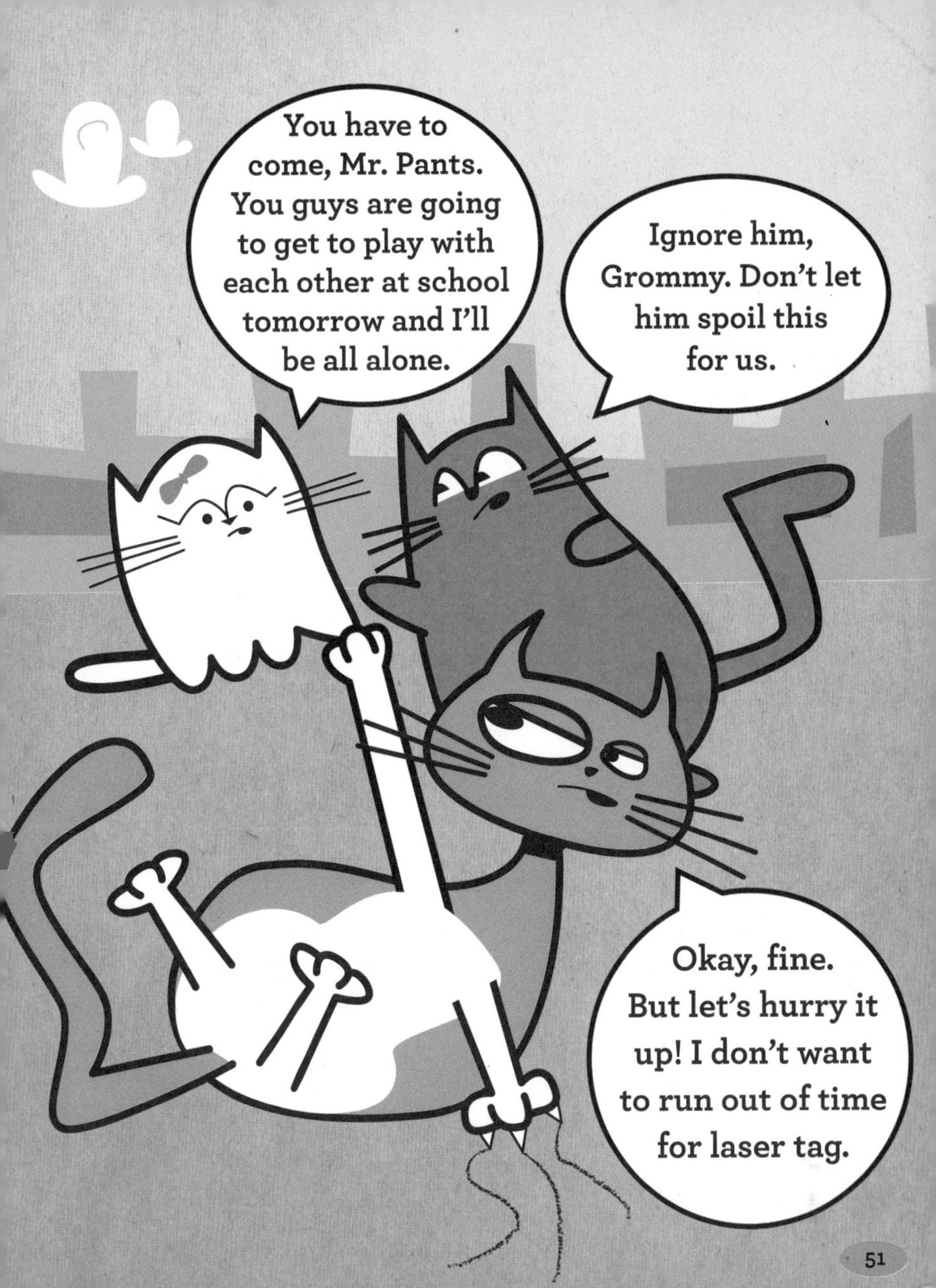
You have to come, Mr. Pants. You guys are going to get to play with each other at school tomorrow and I'll be all alone.
Ignore him, Grommy. Don't let him spoil this for us.
Okay, fine. But let's hurry it up! I don't want to run out of time for laser tag.

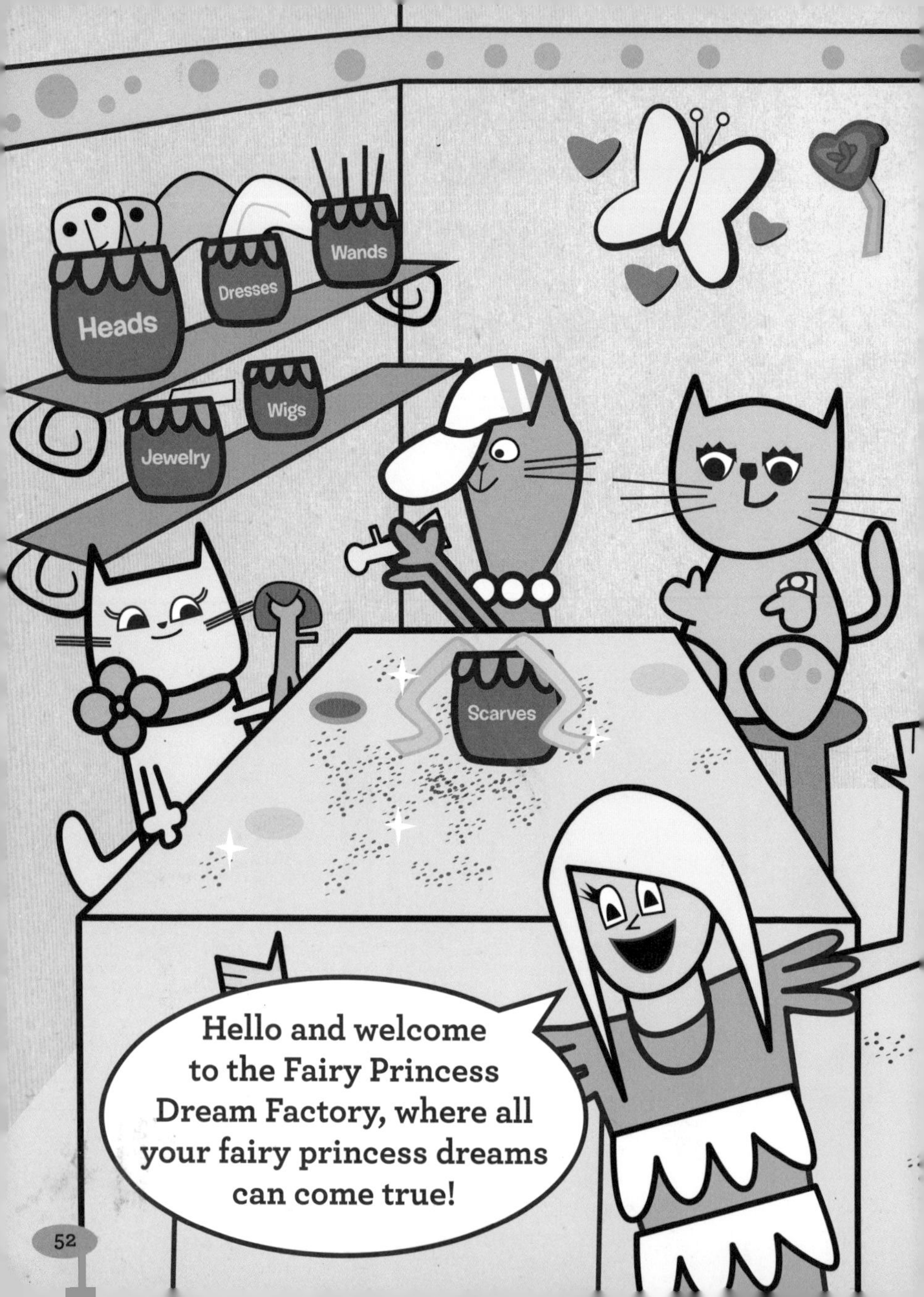
Heads
Dresses
Wands
Wigs
Jewelry
Scarves
Hello and welcome to the Fairy Princess Dream Factory, where all your fairy princess dreams can come true!

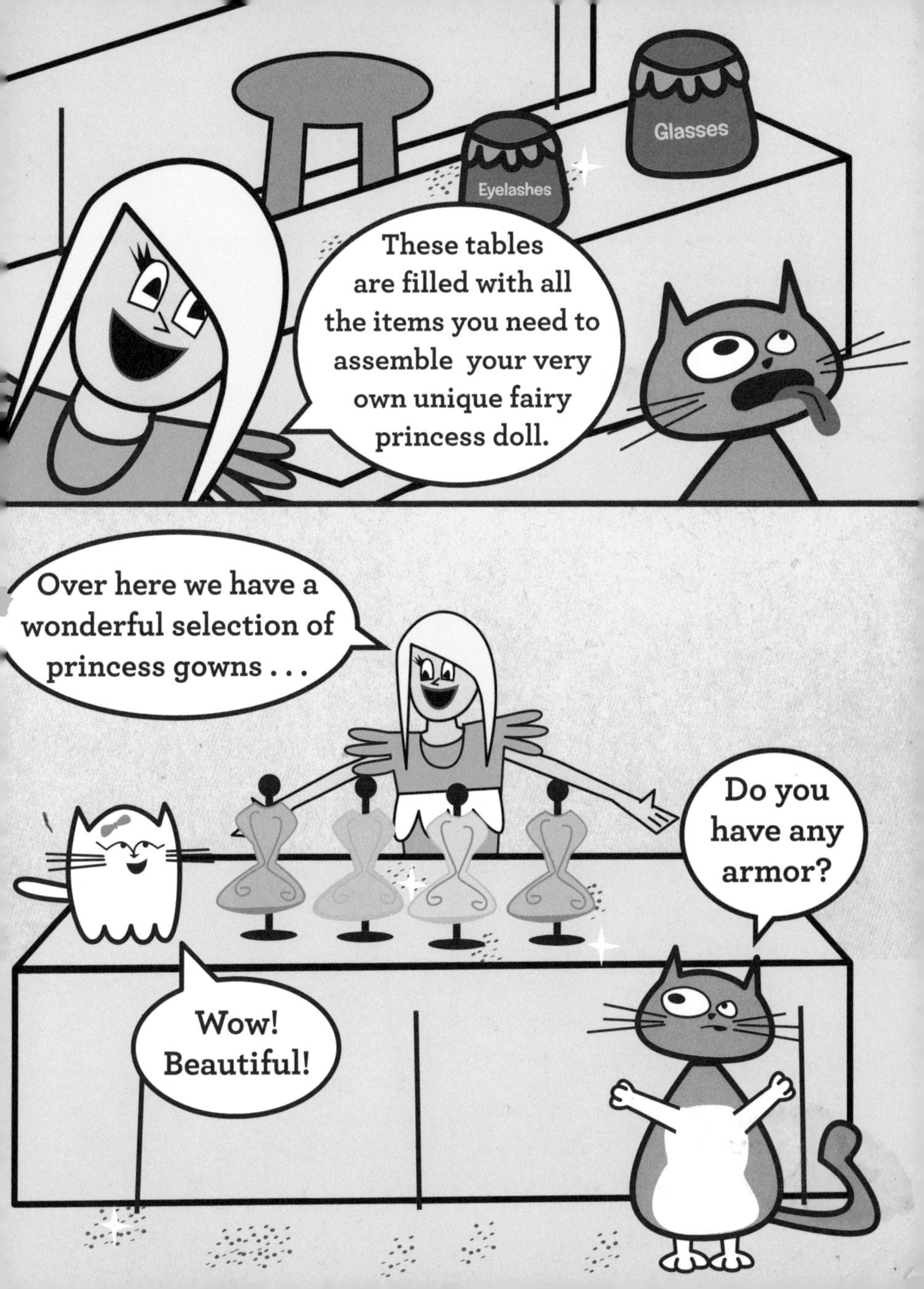
Glasses
Eyelashes
These tables are filled with all the items you need to assemble your very own unique fairy princess doll.
Over here we have a wonderful selection of princess gowns . . .
Do you have any armor?
Wow! Beautiful!

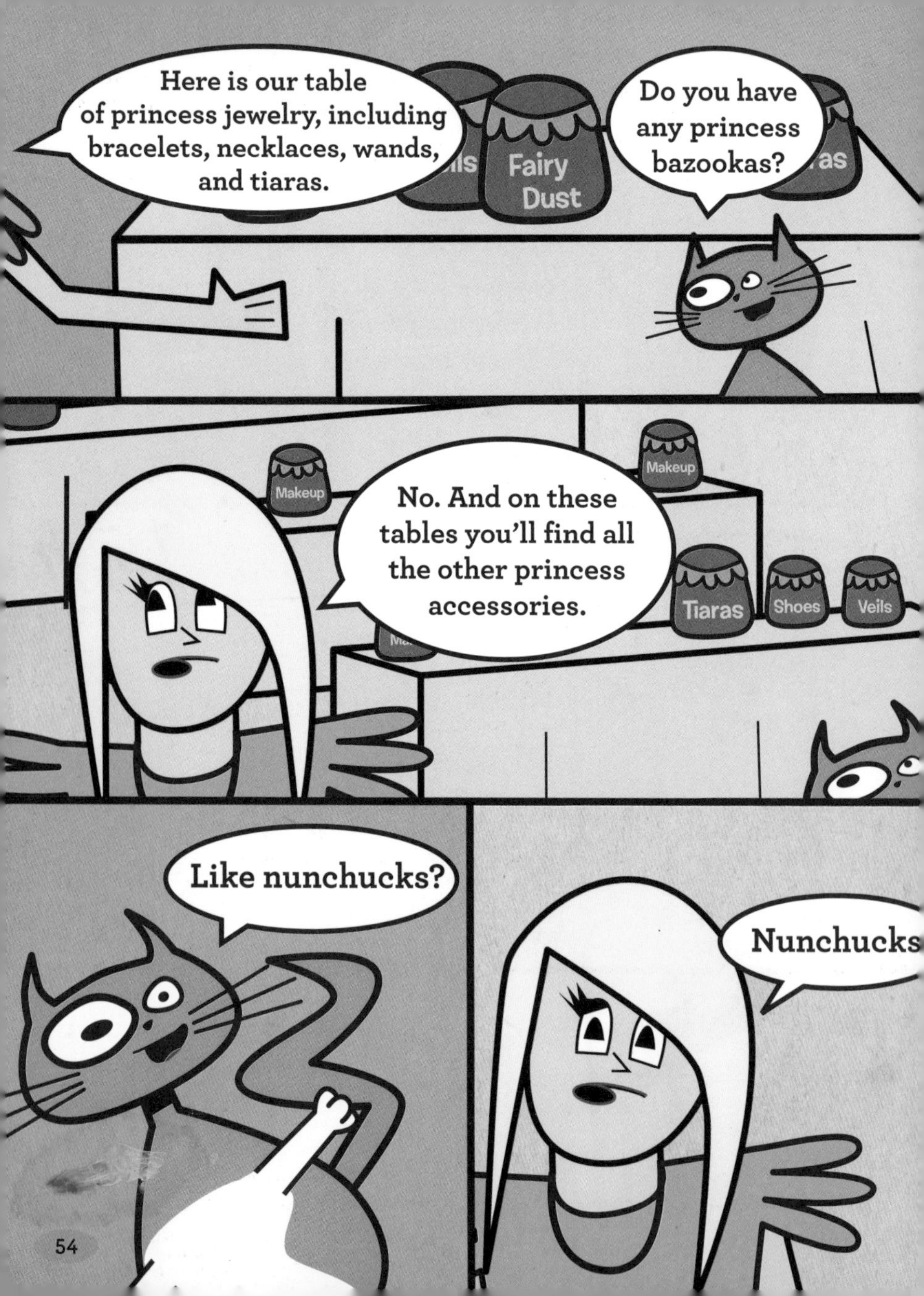
Here is our table of princess jewelry, including bracelets, necklaces, wands, and tiaras.
Fairy Dust
Do you have any princess bazookas?
Makeup
Makeup
No. And on these tables you'll find all the other princess accessories.
Tiaras
Shoes
Veils
Like nunchucks?
Nunchucks

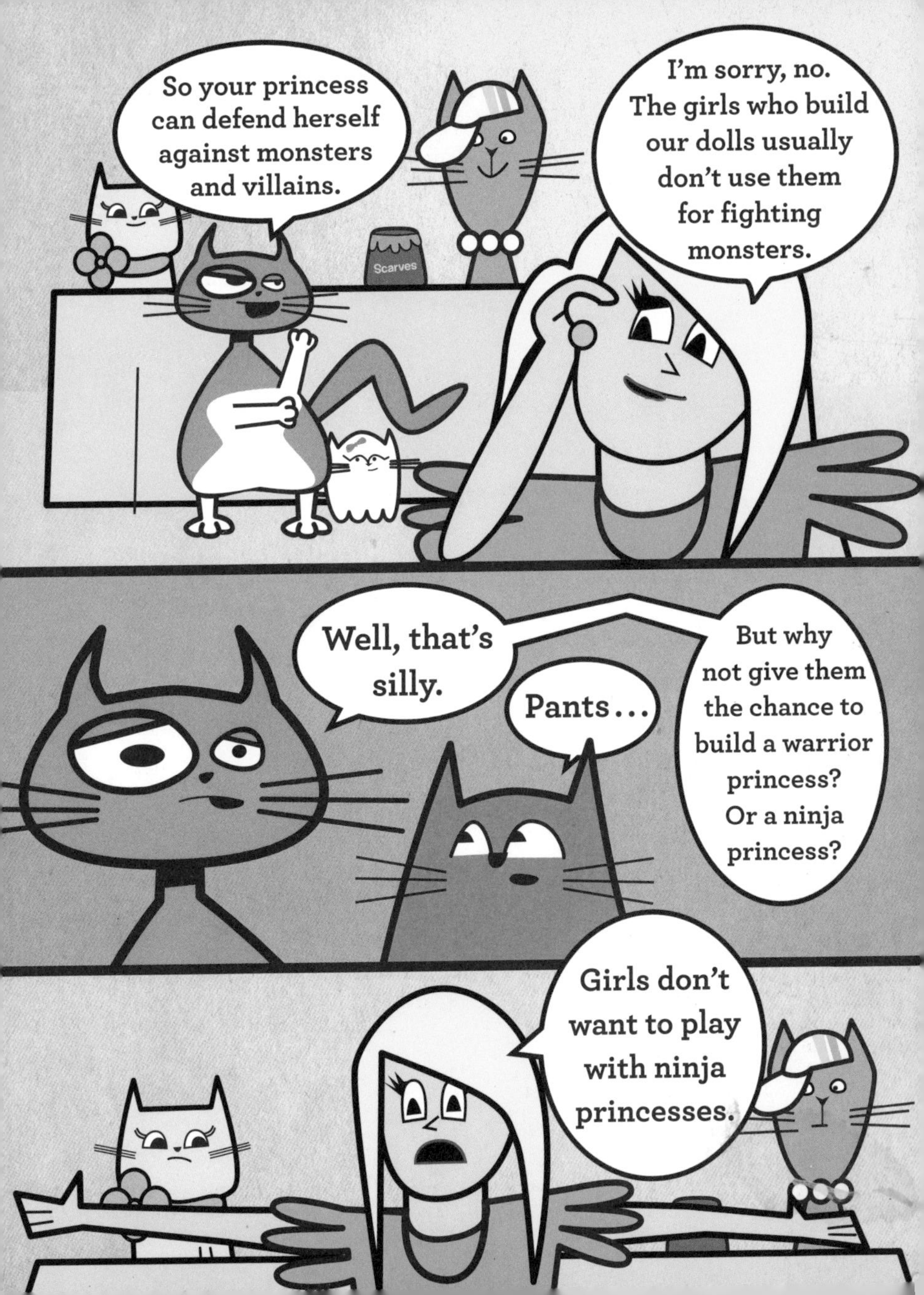
So your princess can defend herself against monsters and villains.
Scarves
I'm sorry, no. The girls who build our dolls usually don't use them for fighting monsters.
Well, that's silly.
Pants...
But why not give them the chance to build a warrior princess? Or a ninja princess?
Girls don't want to play with ninja princesses.

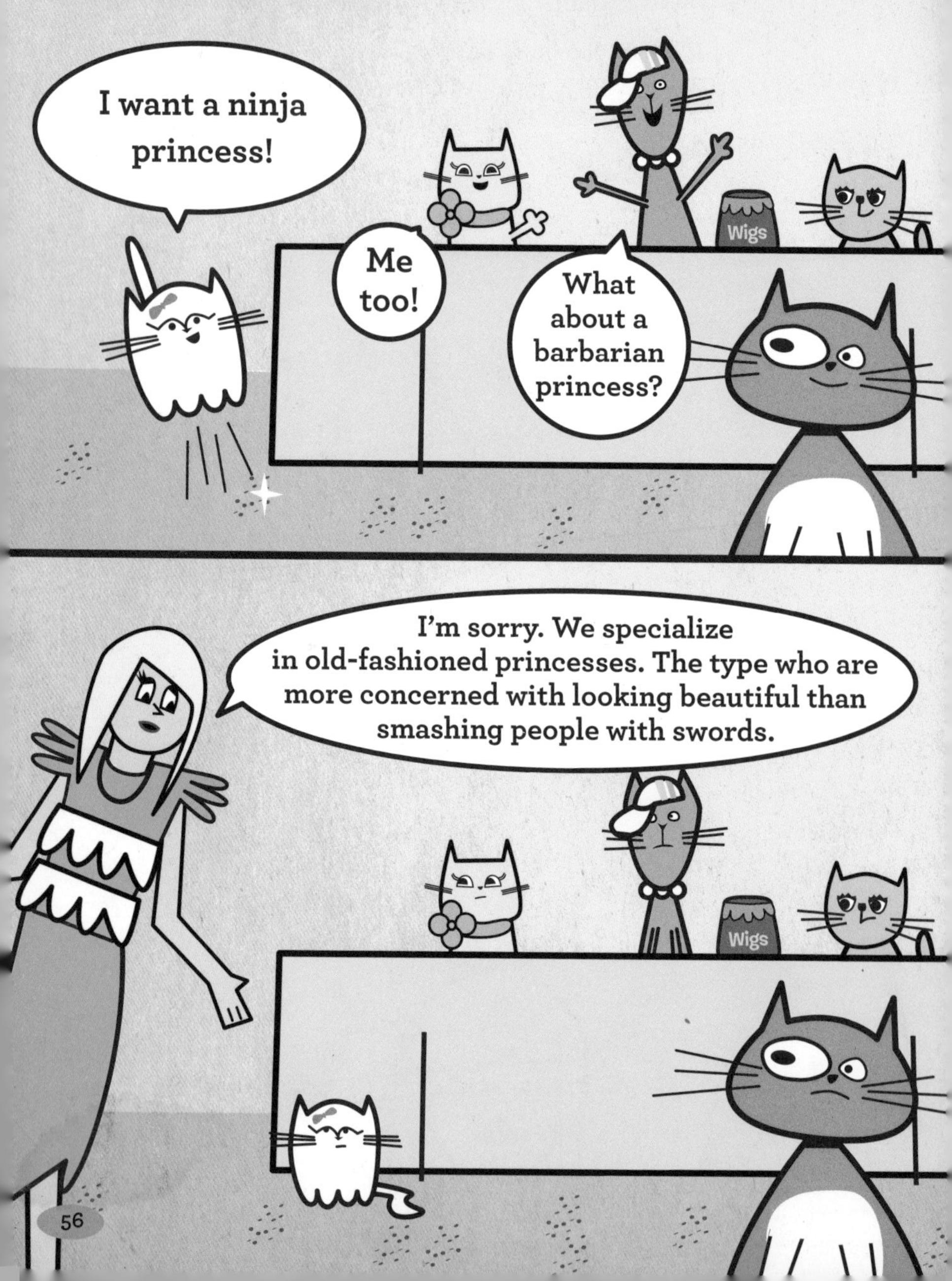
I want a ninja princess!
Me too!
What about a barbarian princess?
Wigs
I'm sorry. We specialize in old-fashioned princesses. The type who are more concerned with looking beautiful than smashing people with swords.
Wigs

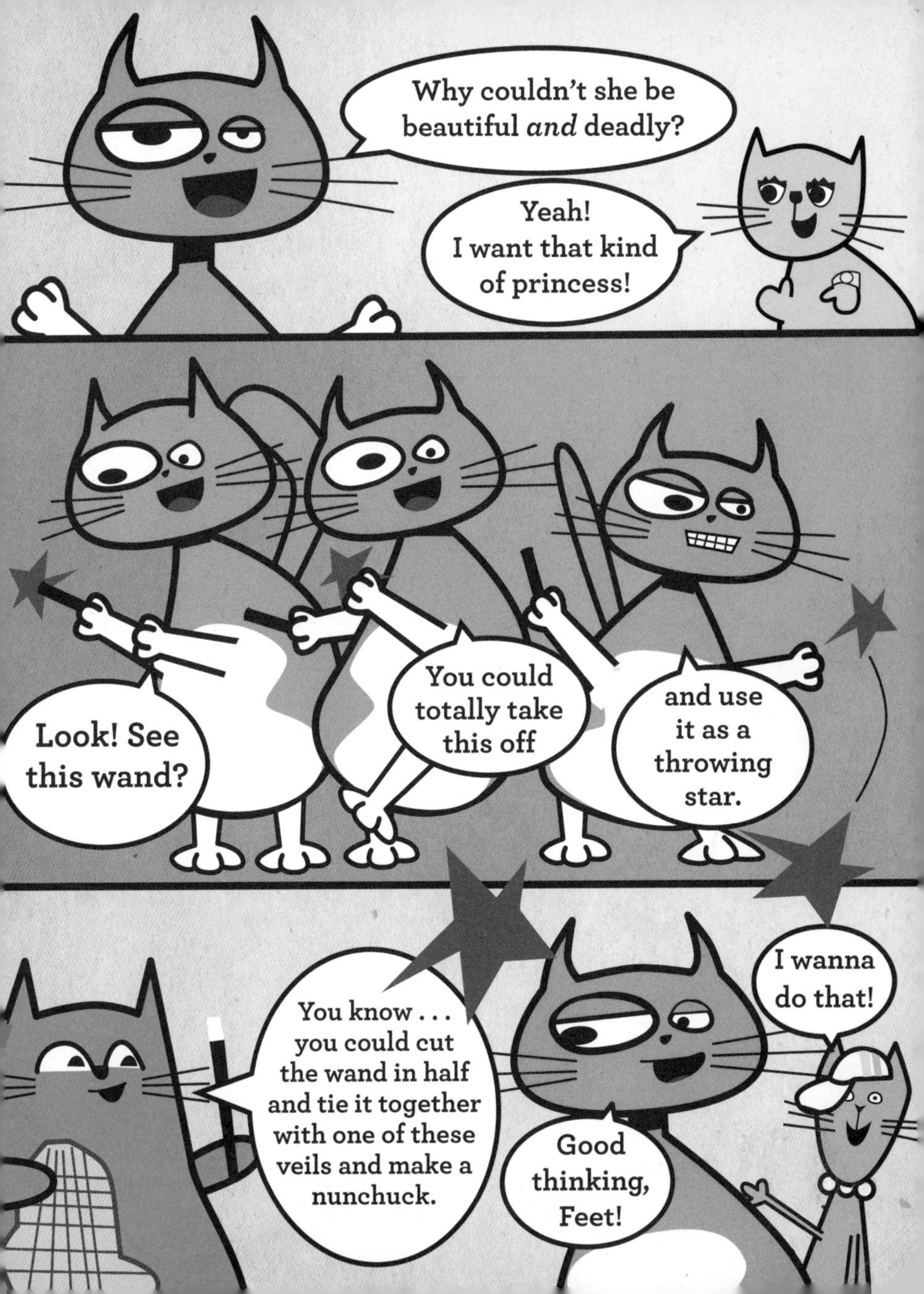
Why couldn't she be beautiful *and* deadly?
Yeah! I want that kind of princess!
Look! See this wand?
You could totally take this off
and use it as a throwing star.
You know . . . you could cut the wand in half and tie it together with one of these veils and make a nunchuck.
I wanna do that!
Good thinking, Feet!

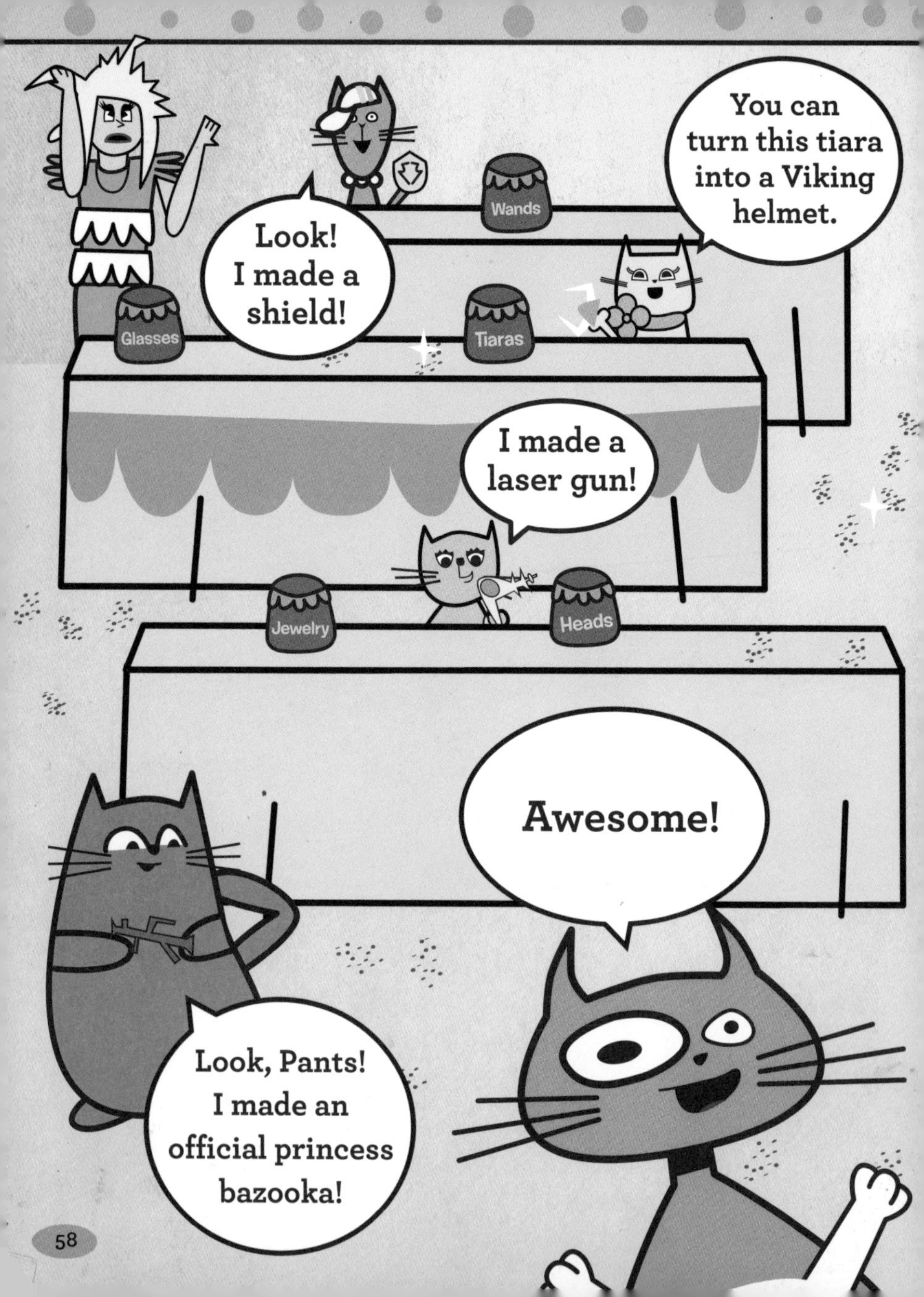
Wands
You can turn this tiara into a Viking helmet.
Look! I made a shield!
Glasses
Tiaras
I made a laser gun!
Jewelry
Heads
Awesome!
Look, Pants! I made an official princess bazooka!

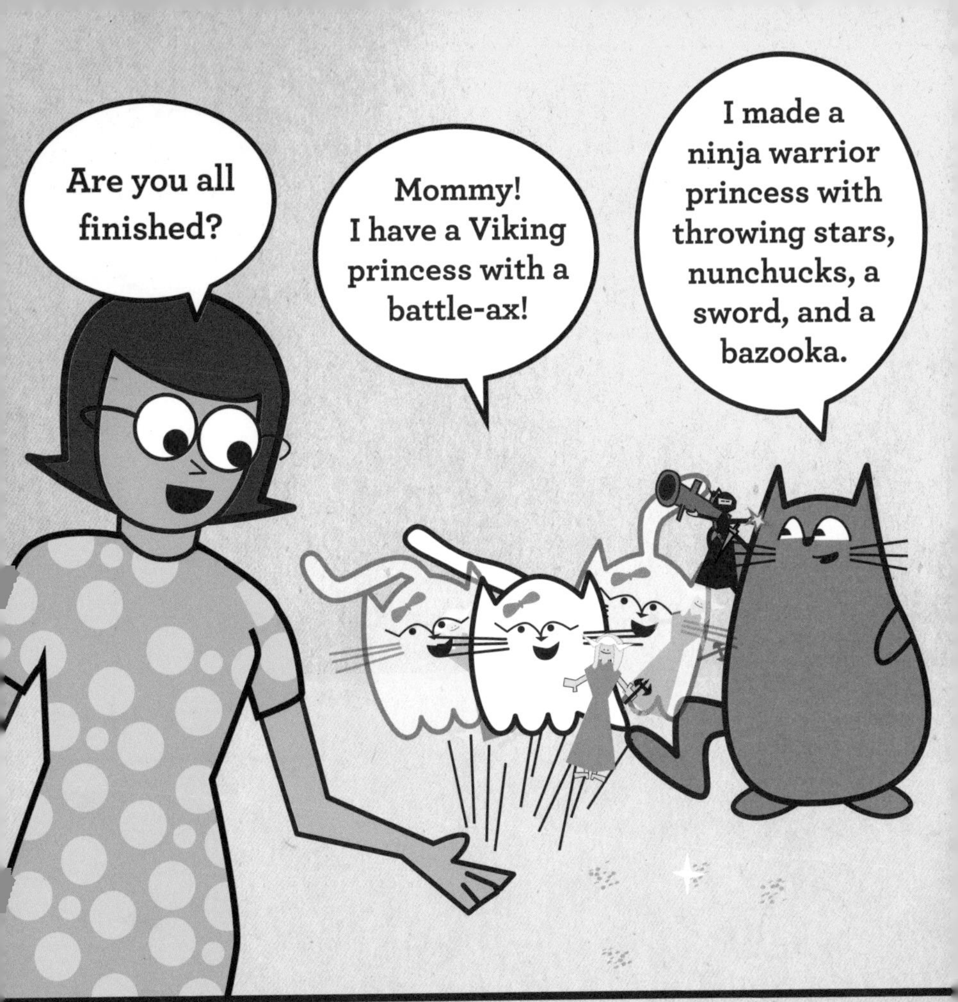
Are you all finished?
Mommy! I have a Viking princess with a battle-ax!
I made a ninja warrior princess with throwing stars, nunchucks, a sword, and a bazooka.

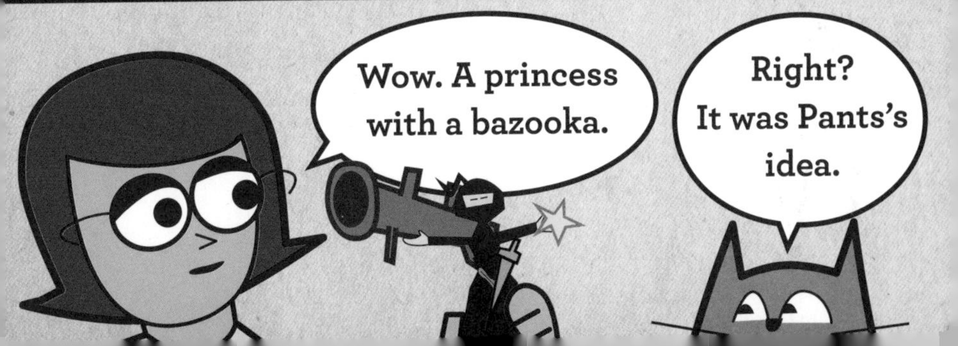
Wow. A princess with a bazooka.
Right? It was Pants's idea.

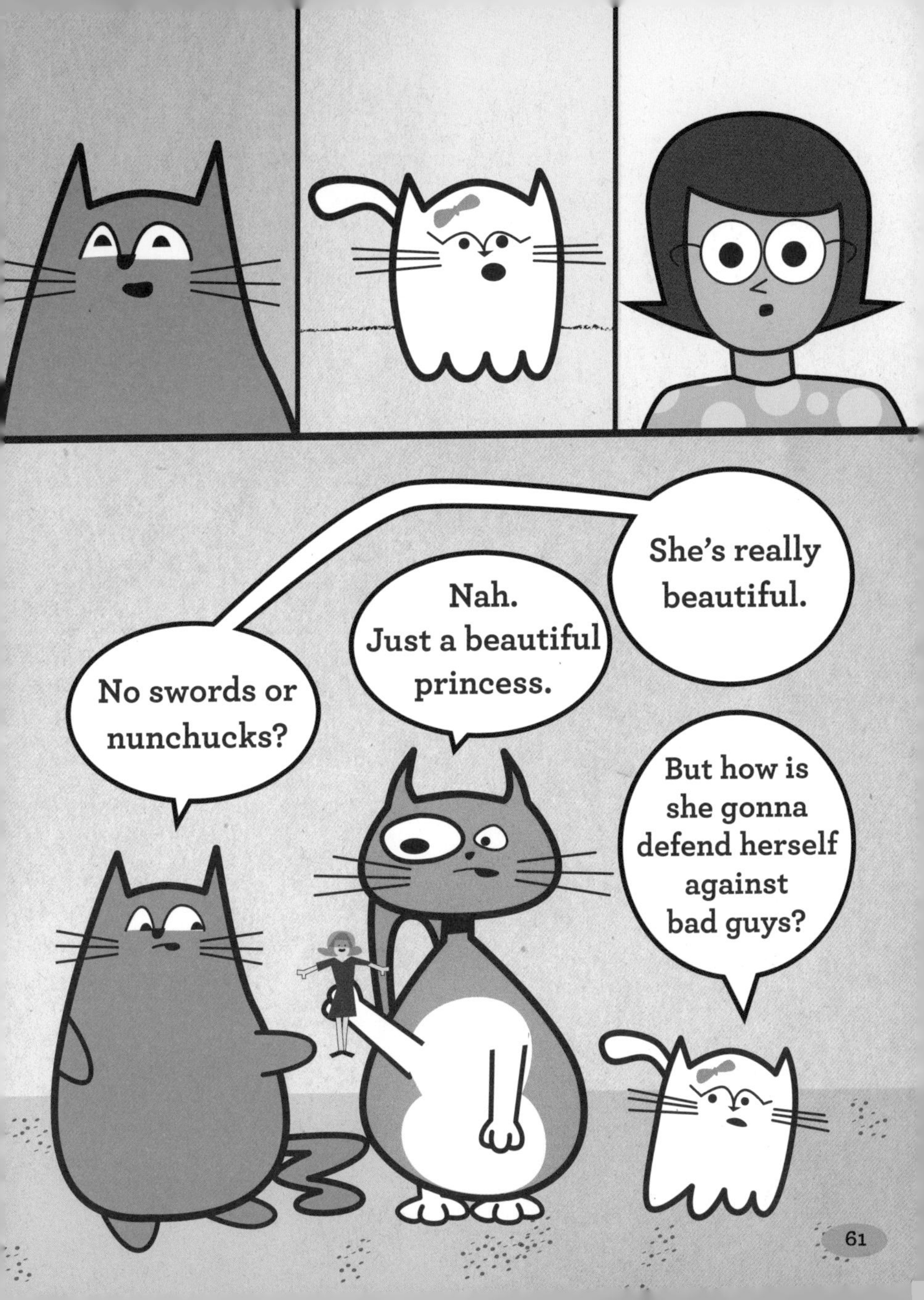
No swords or nunchucks?
Nah. Just a beautiful princess.
She's really beautiful.
But how is she gonna defend herself against bad guys?

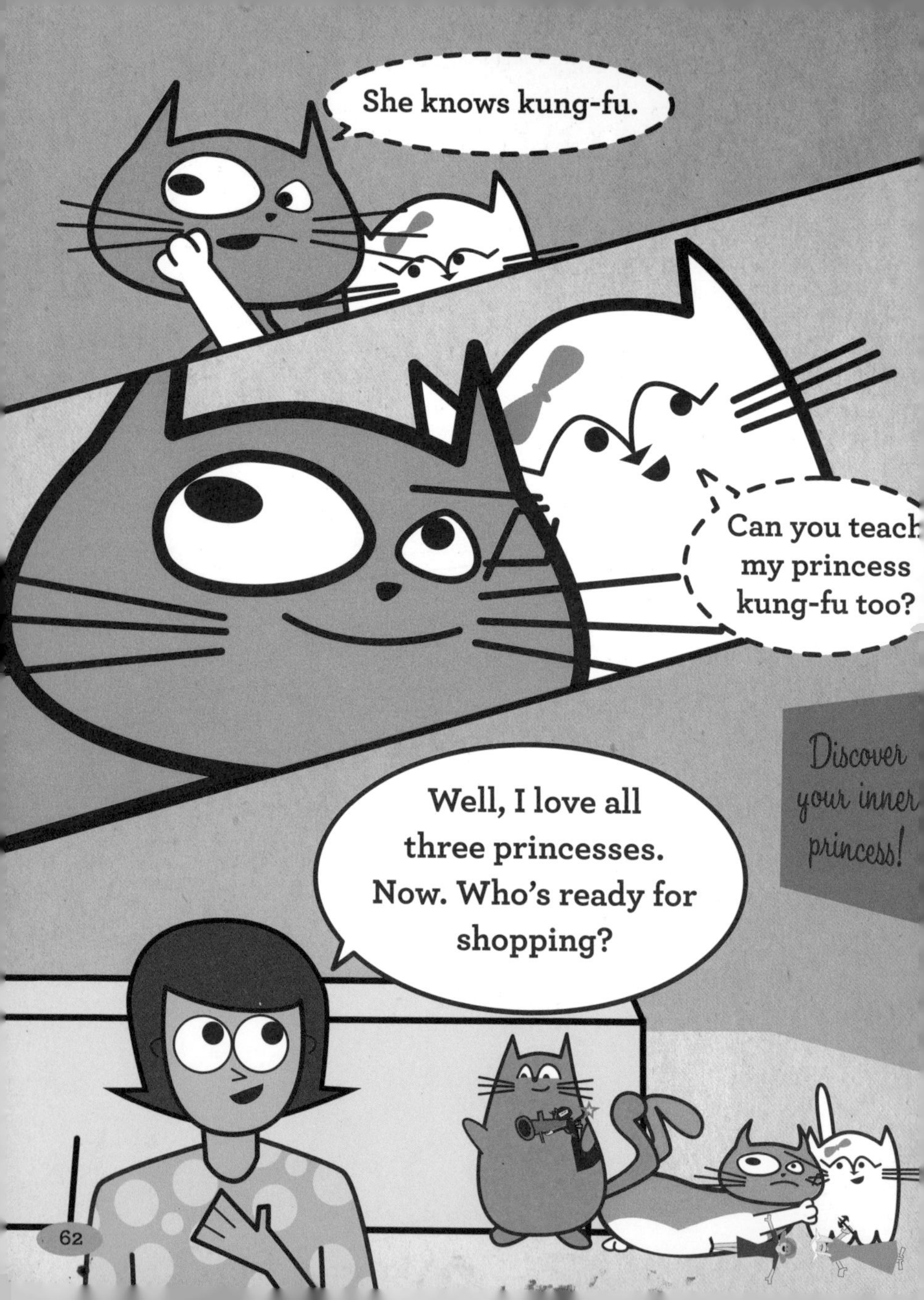
She knows kung-fu.
Can you teach my princess kung-fu too?
Discover your inner princess!
Well, I love all three princesses. Now. Who's ready for shopping?

# Chapter Four:
# IT'S GO TIME

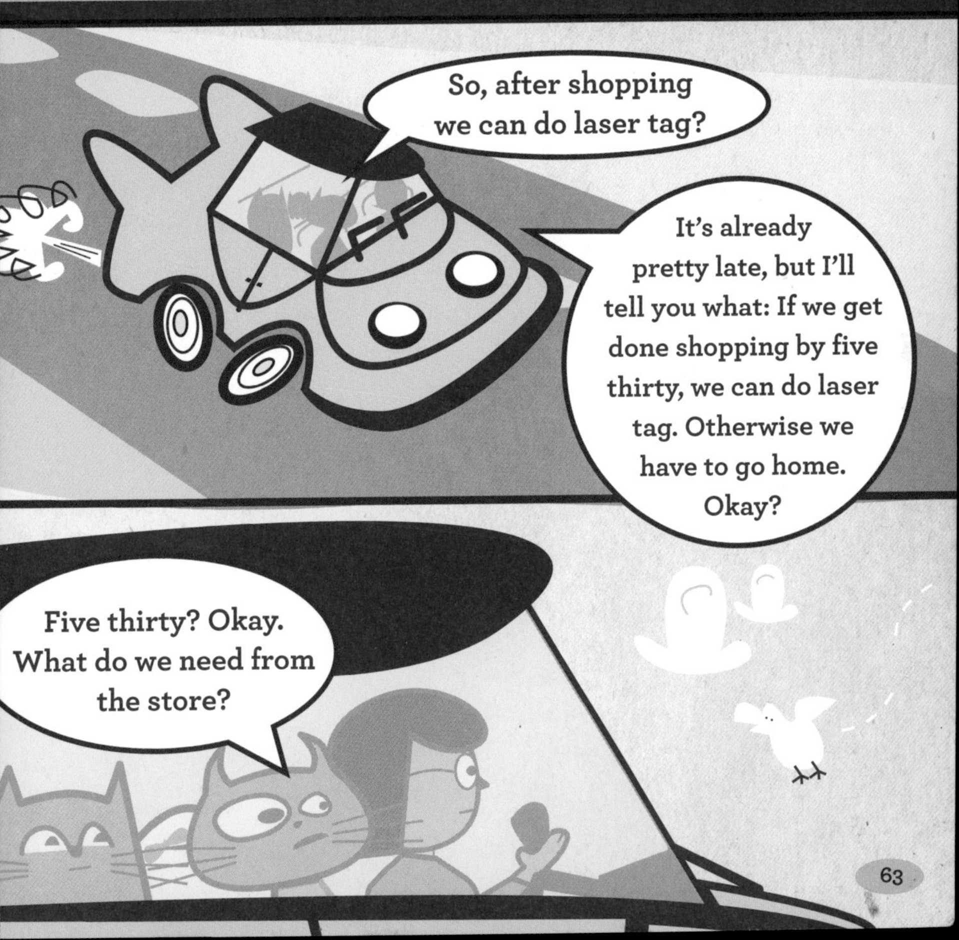
So, after shopping we can do laser tag?
It's already pretty late, but I'll tell you what: If we get done shopping by five thirty, we can do laser tag. Otherwise we have to go home. Okay?
Five thirty? Okay. What do we need from the store?

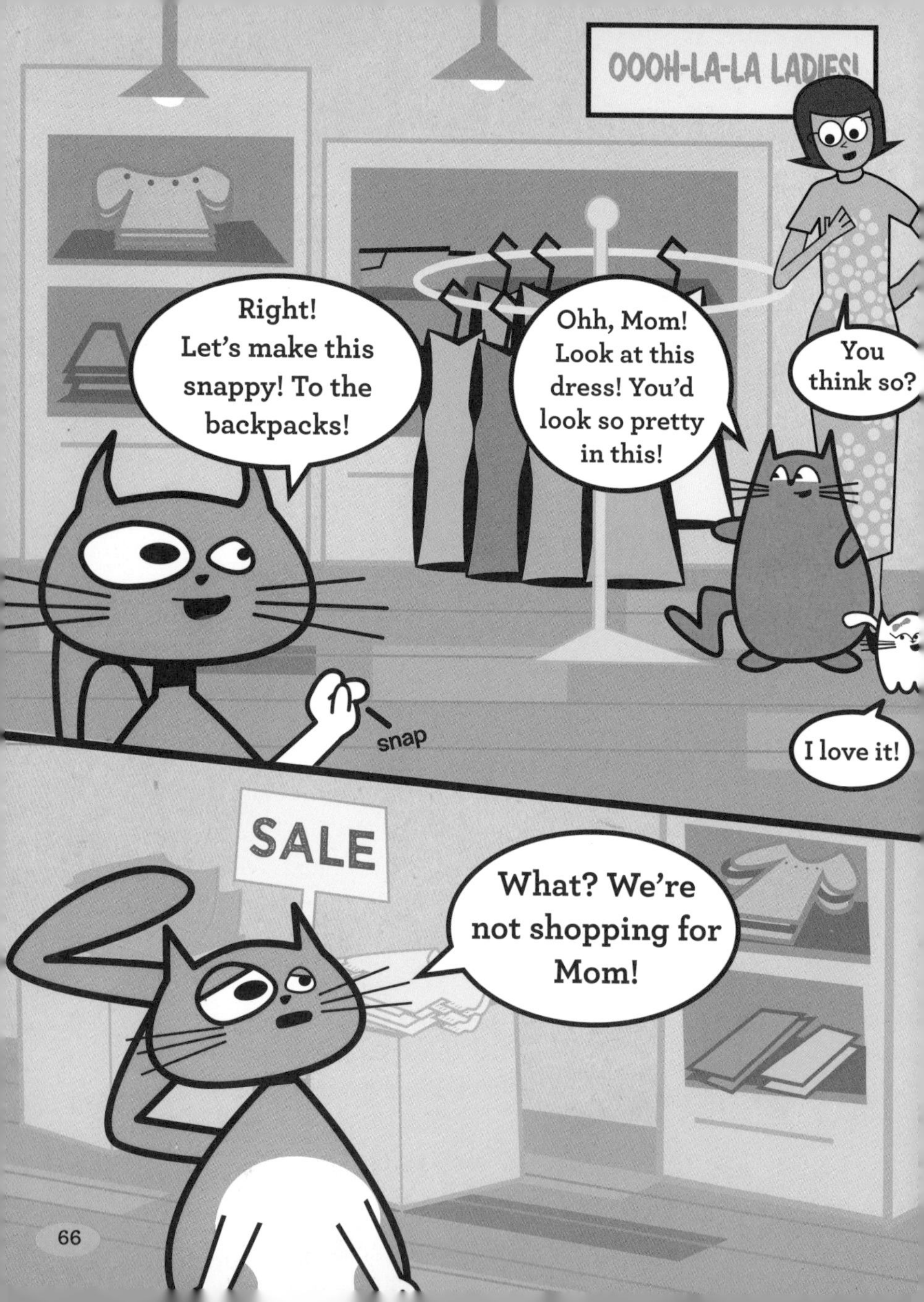
OOOH-LA-LA LADIES!
Right! Let's make this snappy! To the backpacks!
Ohh, Mom! Look at this dress! You'd look so pretty in this!
You think so?
snap
I love it!
SALE
What? We're not shopping for Mom!

67

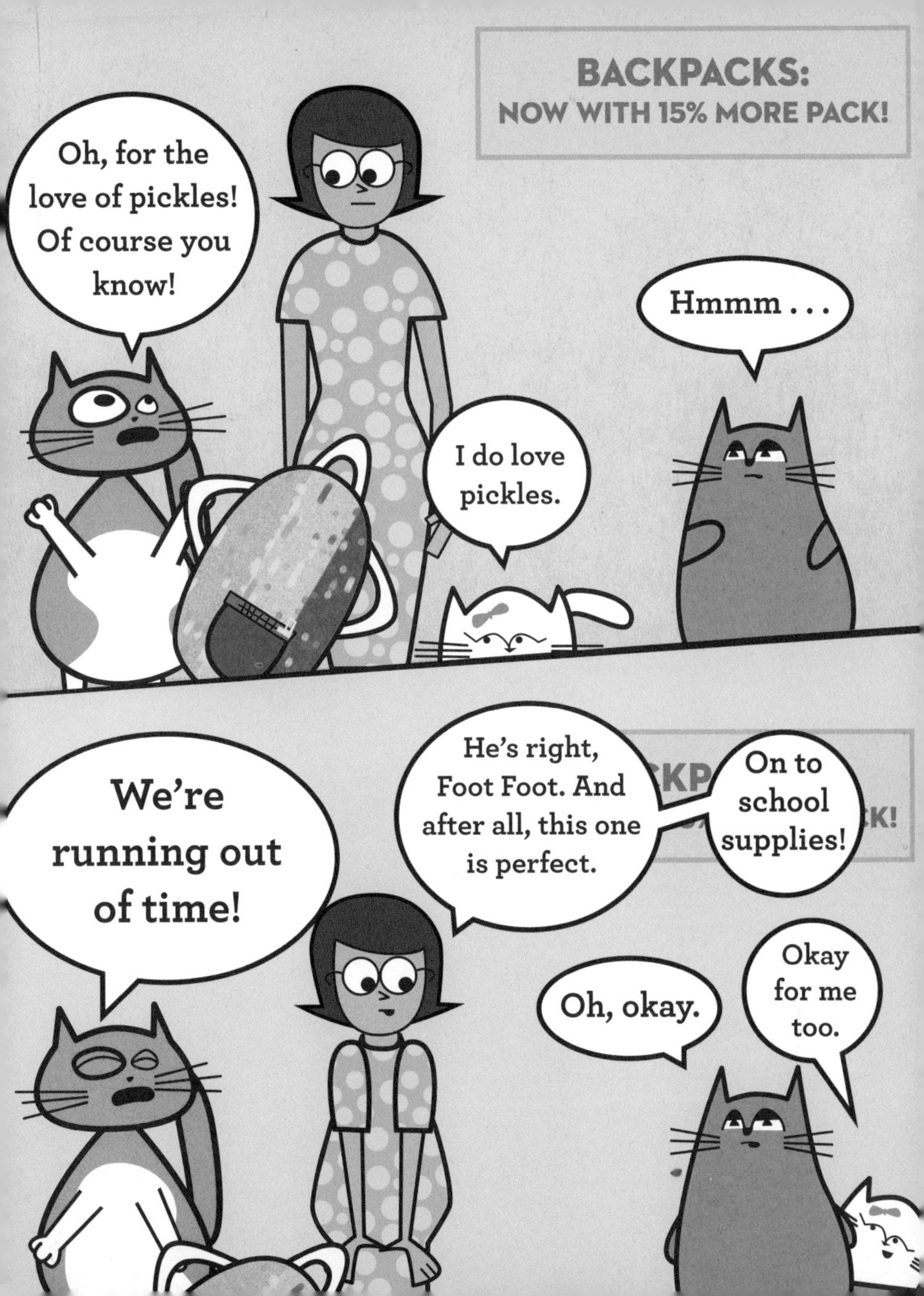
BACKPACKS: NOW WITH 15% MORE PACK!
Oh, for the love of pickles! Of course you know!
I do love pickles.
Hmmm . . .
We're running out of time!
He's right, Foot Foot. And after all, this one is perfect.
On to school supplies!
Oh, okay.
Okay for me too.

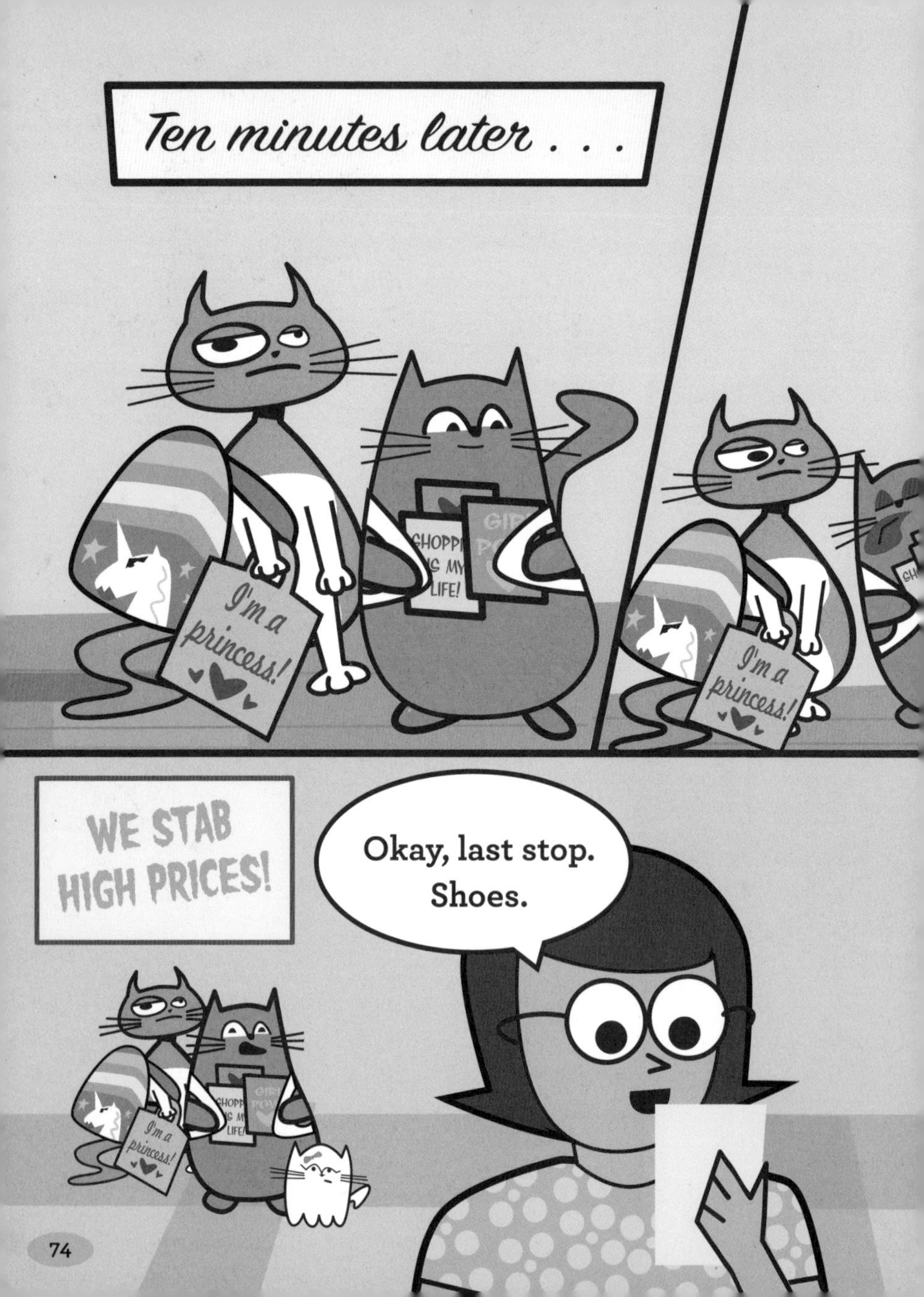
Ten minutes later . . .
I'm a princess!
SHOPPING IS MY LIFE!
I'm a princess!
WE STAB HIGH PRICES!
Okay, last stop. Shoes.
I'm a princess!

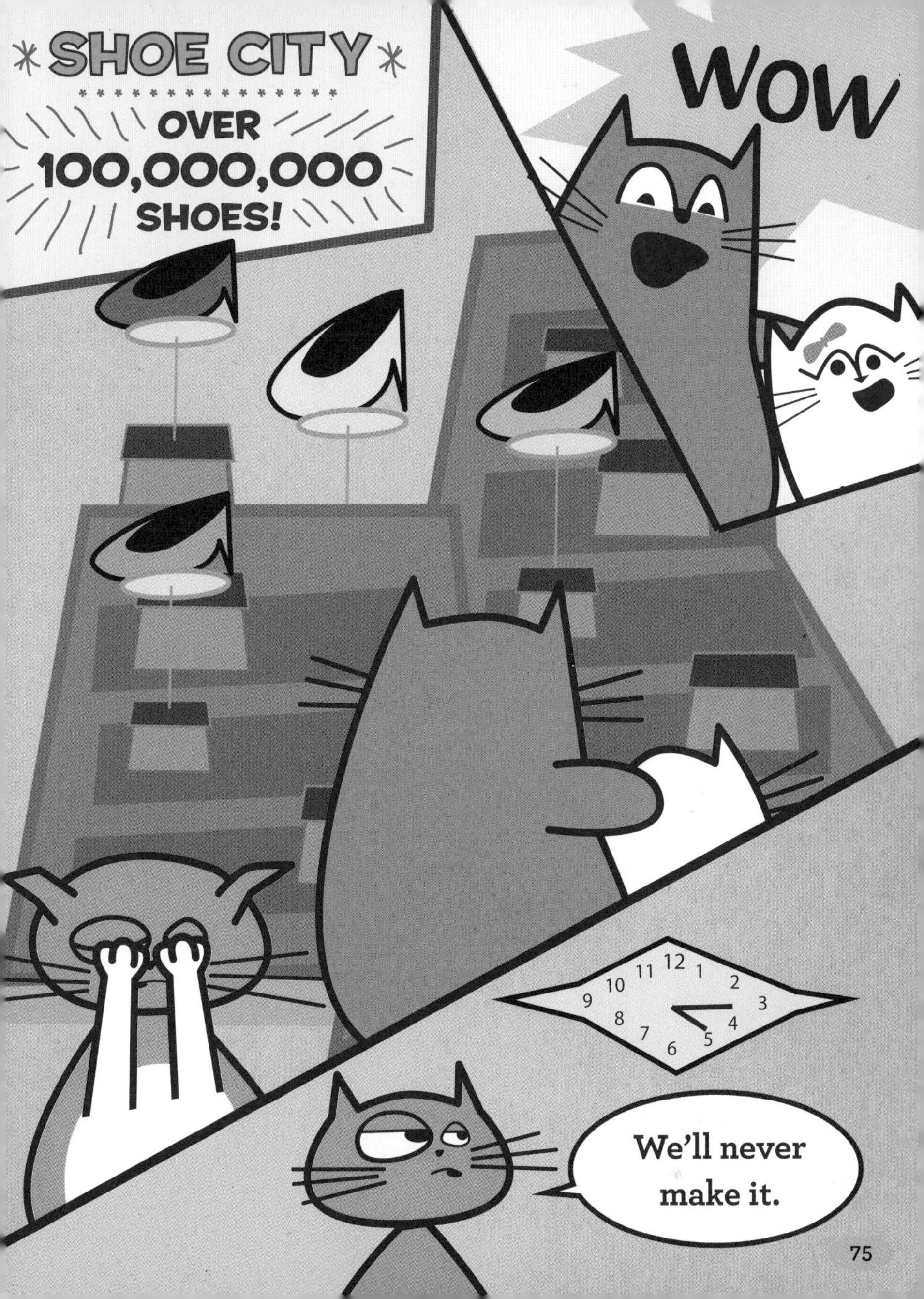
SHOE CITY
OVER 100,000,000 SHOES!
WOW
We'll never make it.

77

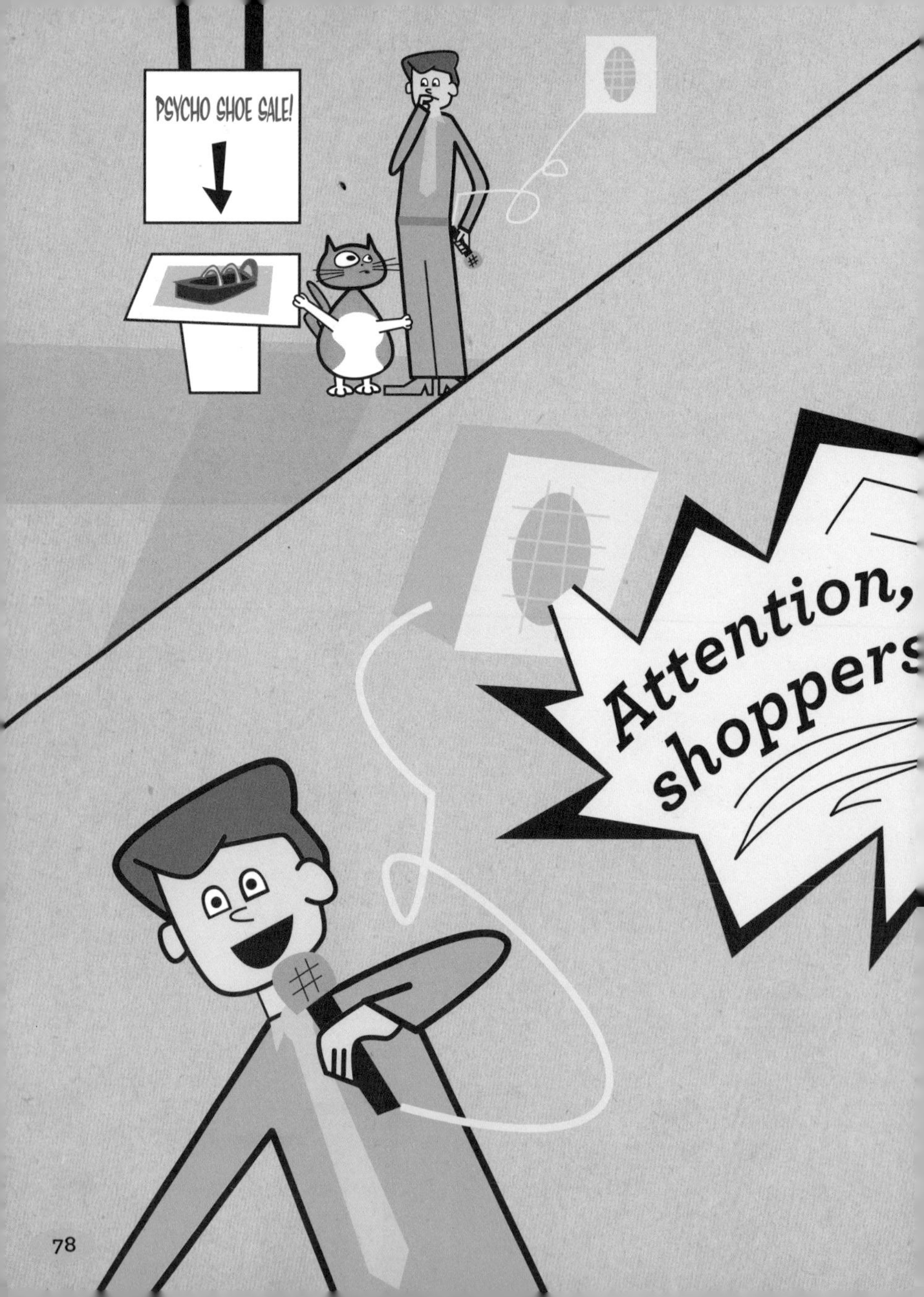
PSYCHO SHOE SALE!
Attention, shopper

# Chapter Five:
# A TREAT FOR FEET

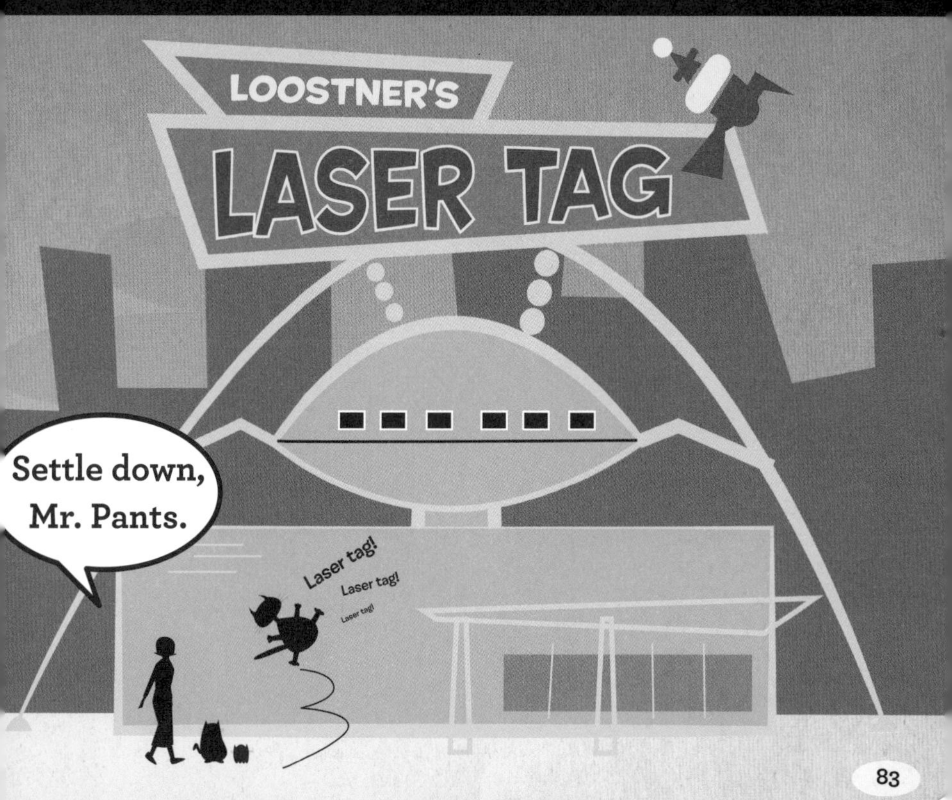
LOOSTNER'S
LASER TAG
Settle down, Mr. Pants.
Laser tag!
Laser tag!
Laser tag!

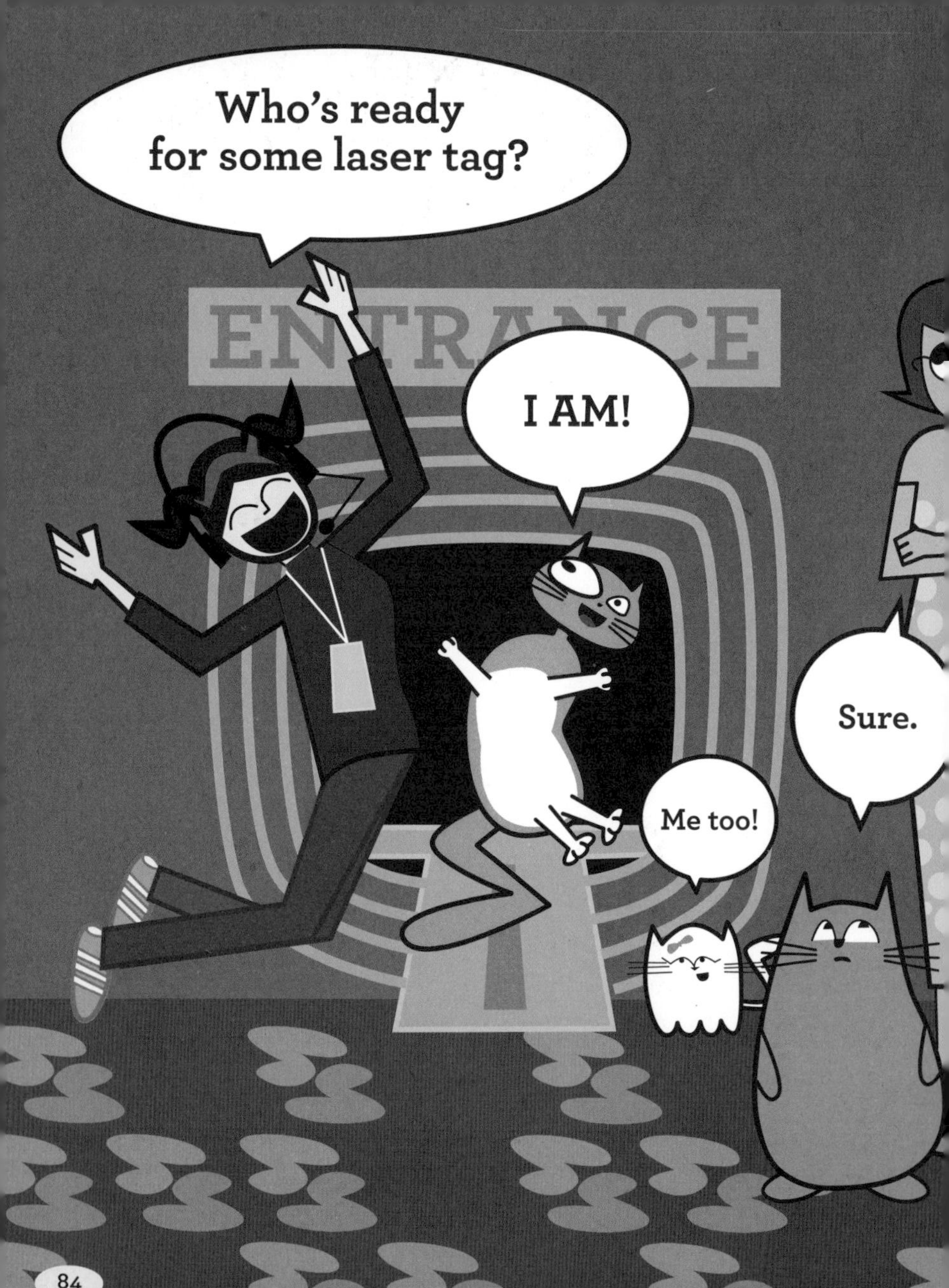
Who's ready for some laser tag?
ENTRANCE
I AM!
Sure.
Me too!

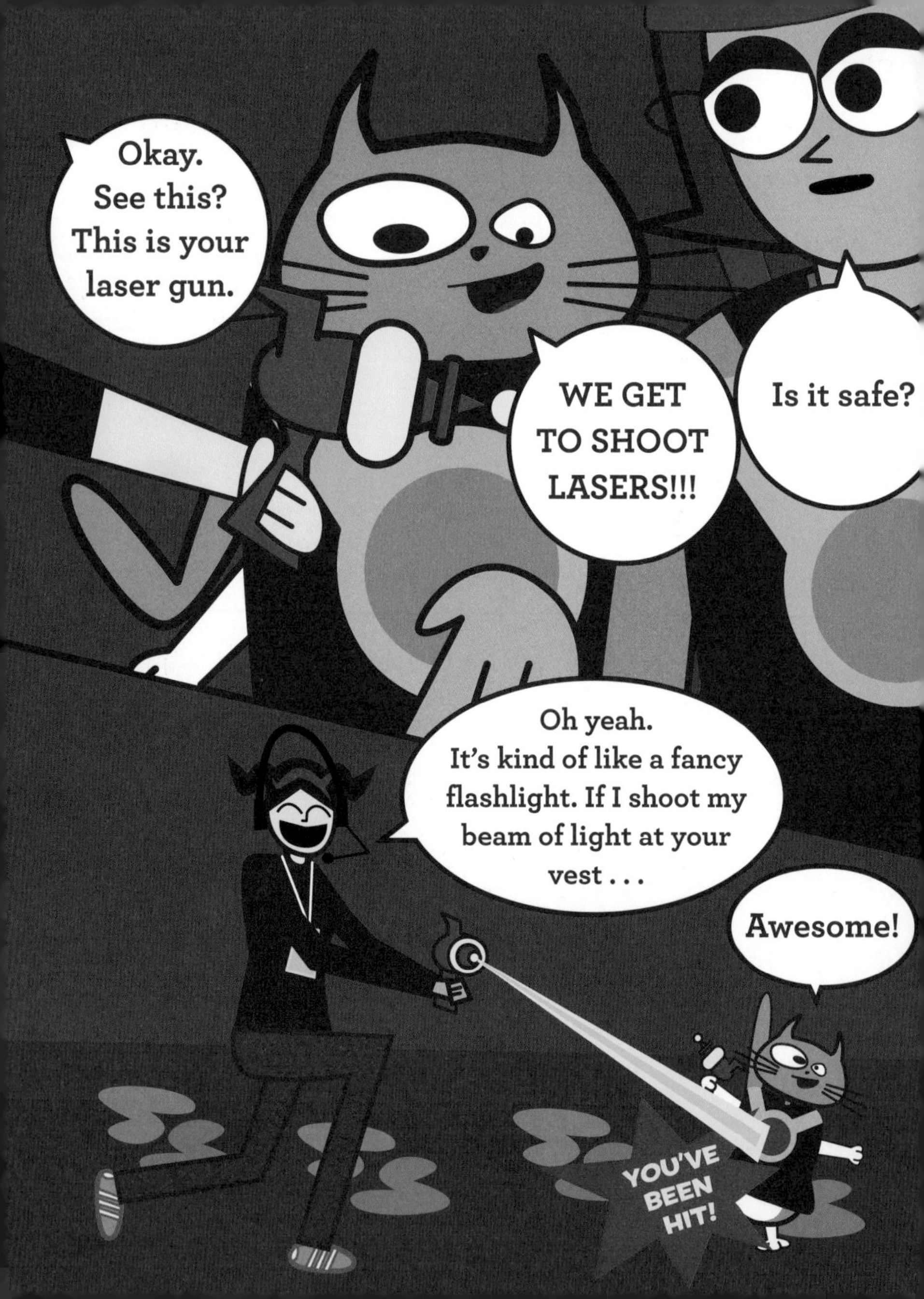

Okay. See this? This is your laser gun.
WE GET TO SHOOT LASERS!!!
Is it safe?
Oh yeah. It's kind of like a fancy flashlight. If I shoot my beam of light at your vest . . .
Awesome!
YOU'VE BEEN HIT!

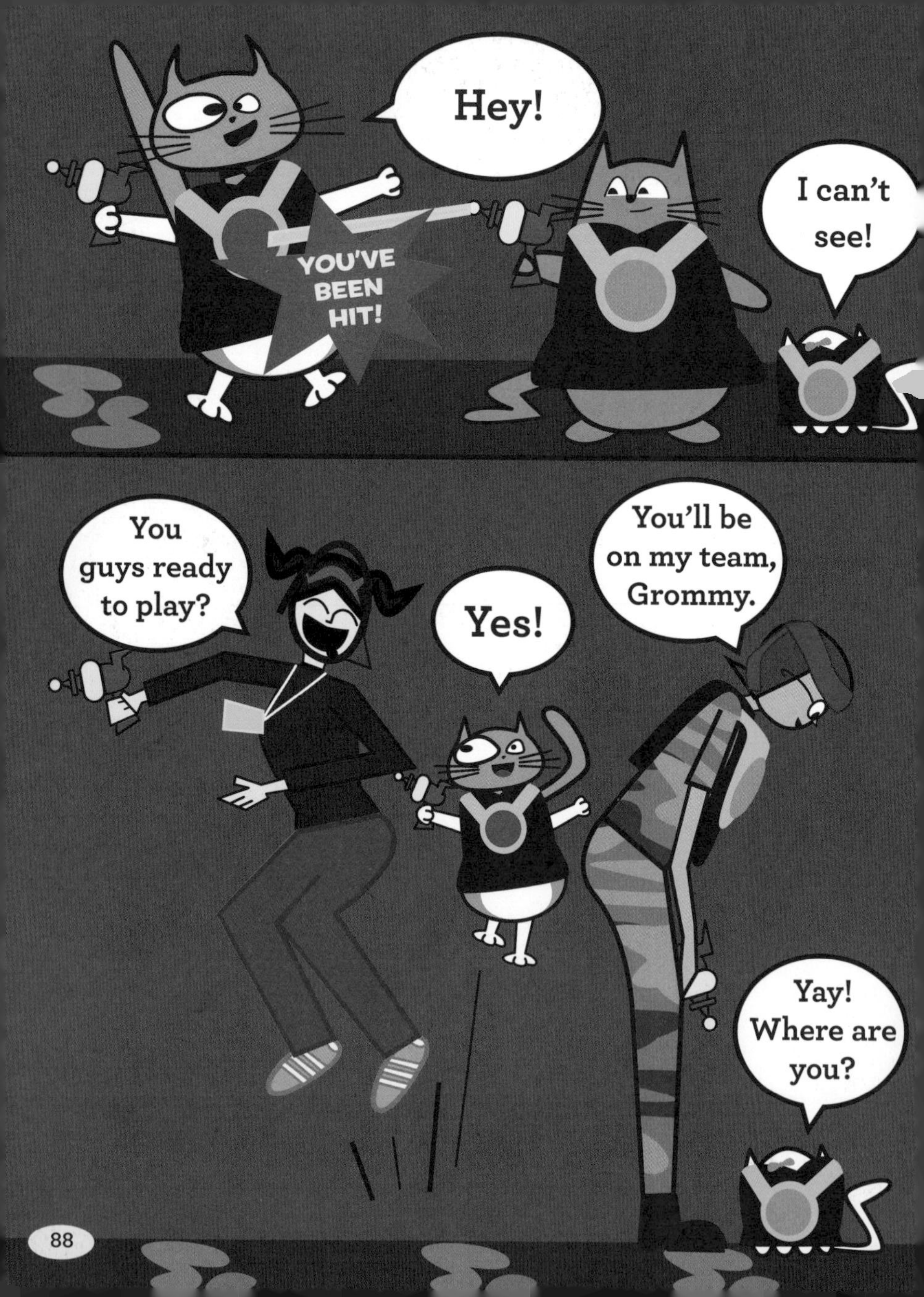
Hey!
YOU'VE BEEN HIT!
I can't see!
You guys ready to play?
Yes!
You'll be on my team, Grommy.
Yay! Where are you?

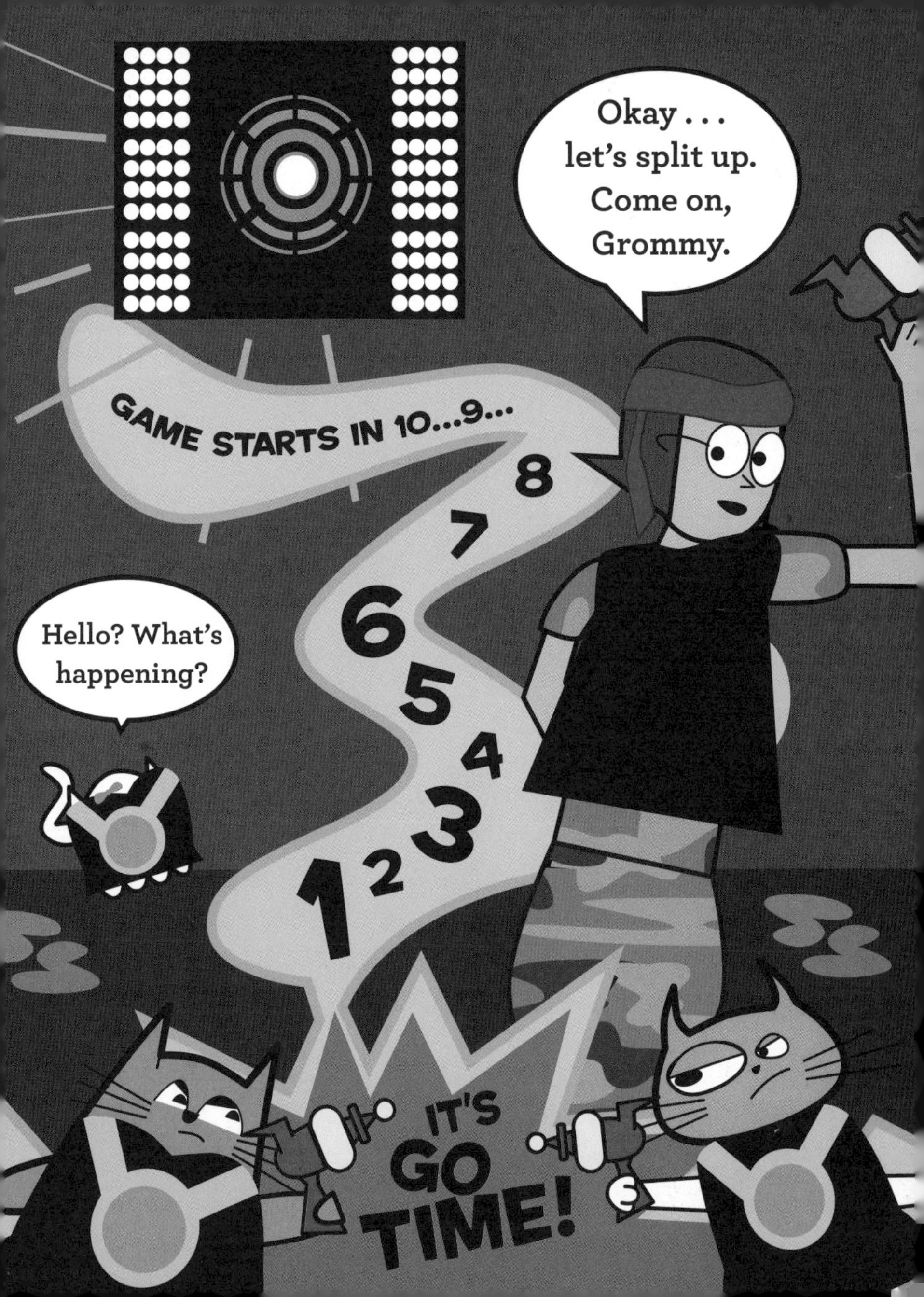
Okay . . . let's split up. Come on, Grommy.
GAME STARTS IN 10...9...
8
7
6
5
4
3
2
1
Hello? What's happening?
IT'S GO TIME!

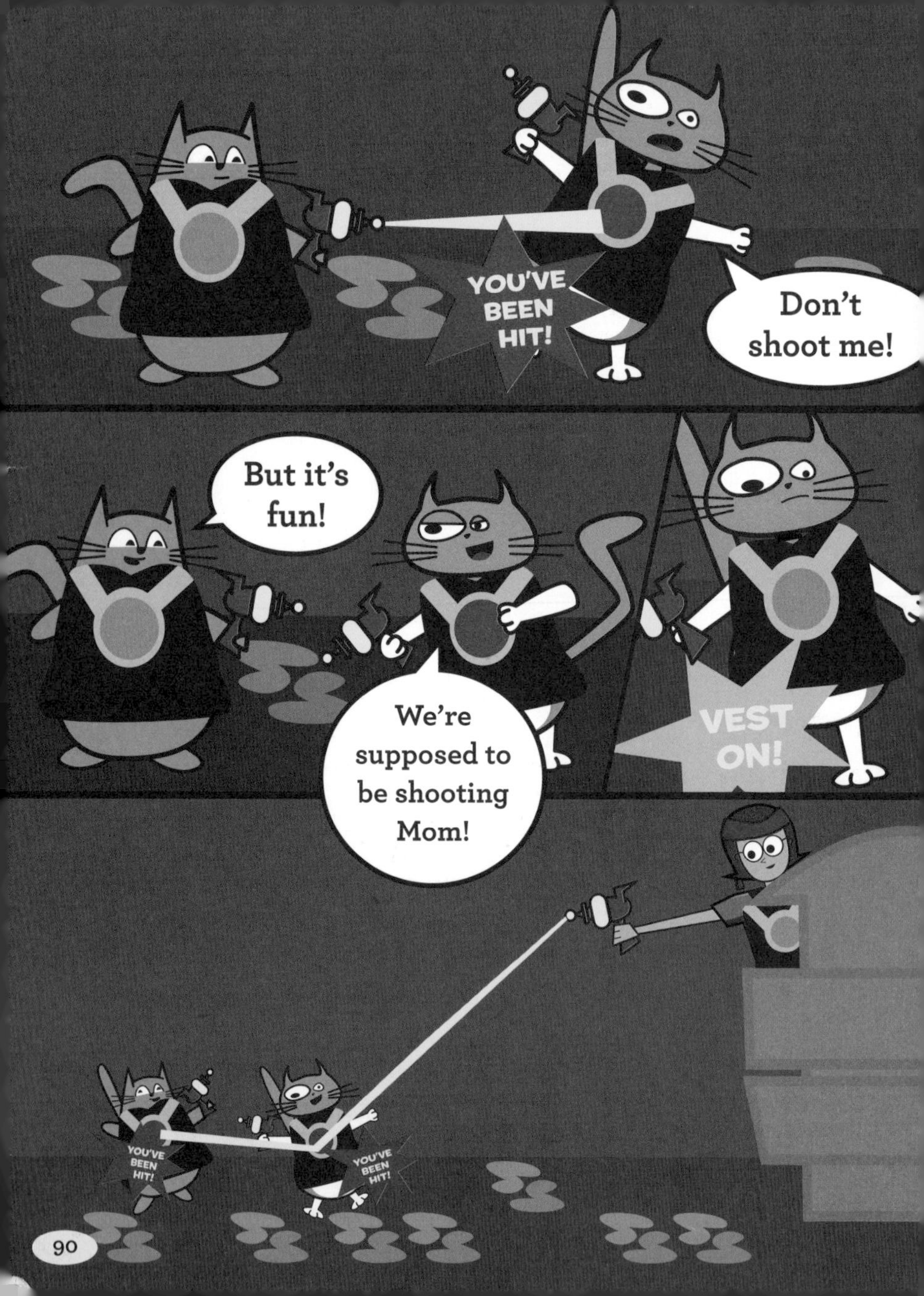
YOU'VE BEEN HIT!
Don't shoot me!
But it's fun!
VEST ON!
We're supposed to be shooting Mom!
YOU'VE BEEN HIT!
YOU'VE BEEN HIT!

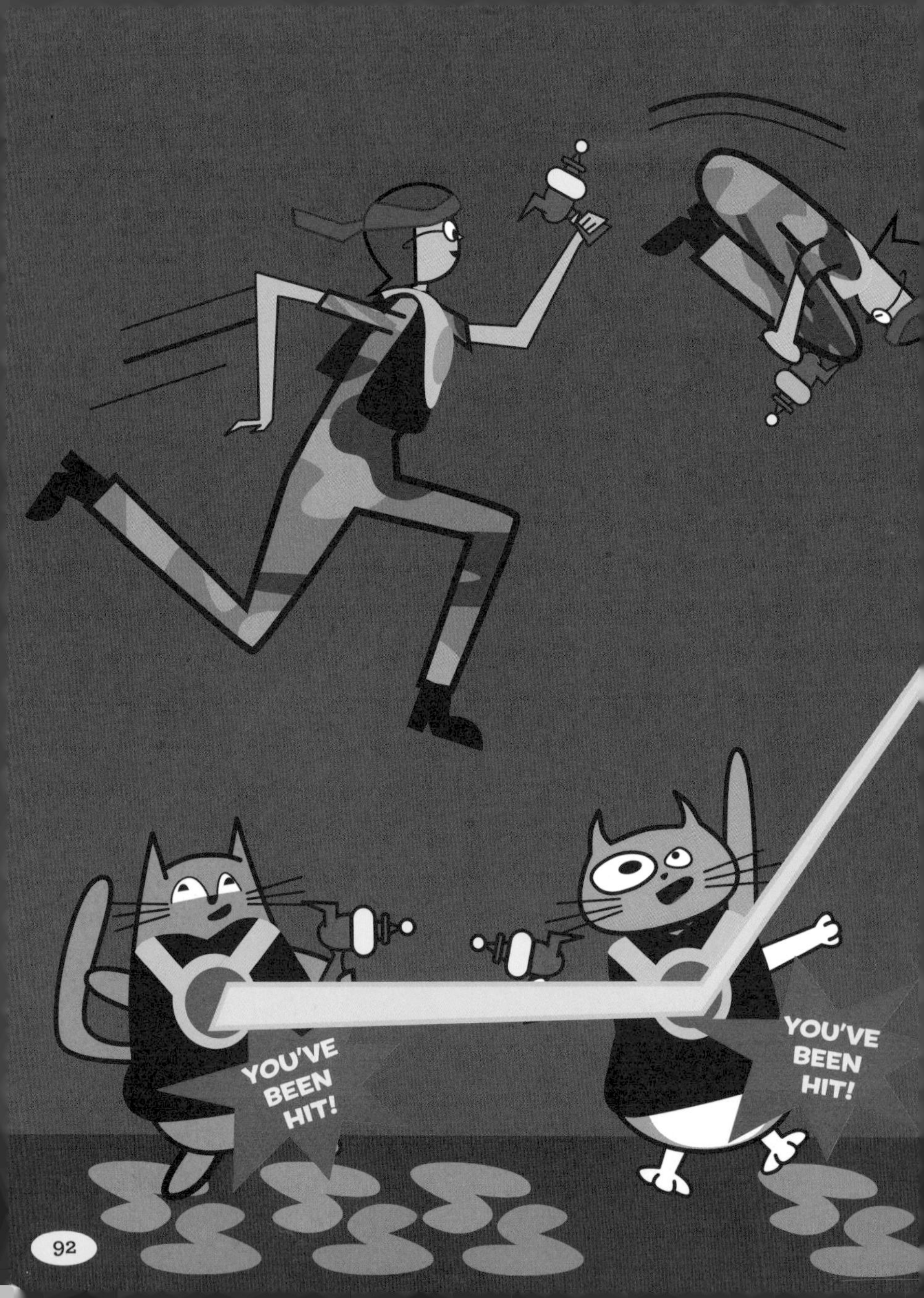
YOU'VE BEEN HIT!
YOU'VE BEEN HIT!

93

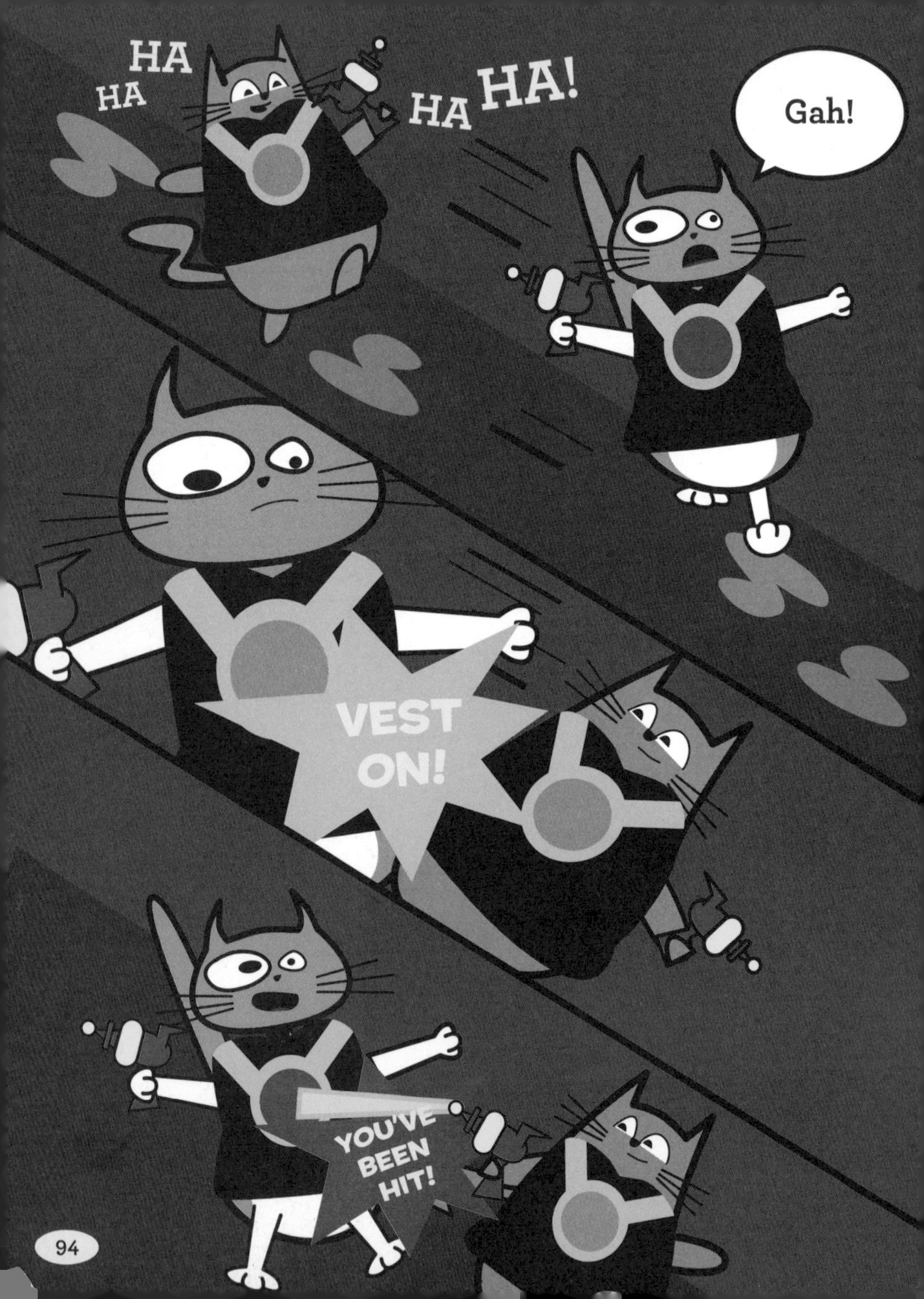
HA
HA
HA
HA!
Gah!
VEST ON!
YOU'VE BEEN HIT!

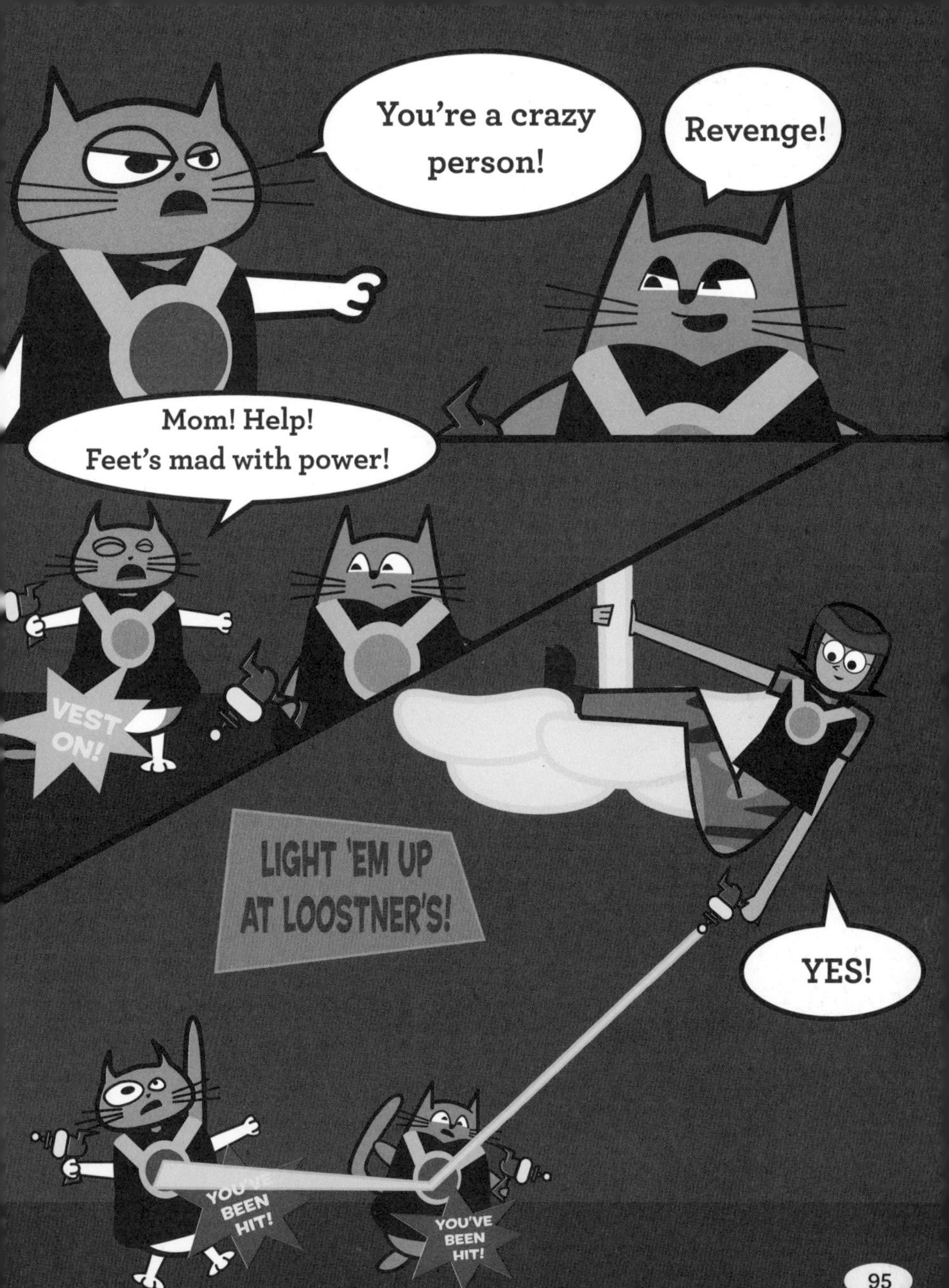
You're a crazy person!
Revenge!
Mom! Help! Feet's mad with power!
VEST ON!
LIGHT 'EM UP AT LOOSTNER'S!
YES!
YOU'VE BEEN HIT!
YOU'VE BEEN HIT!

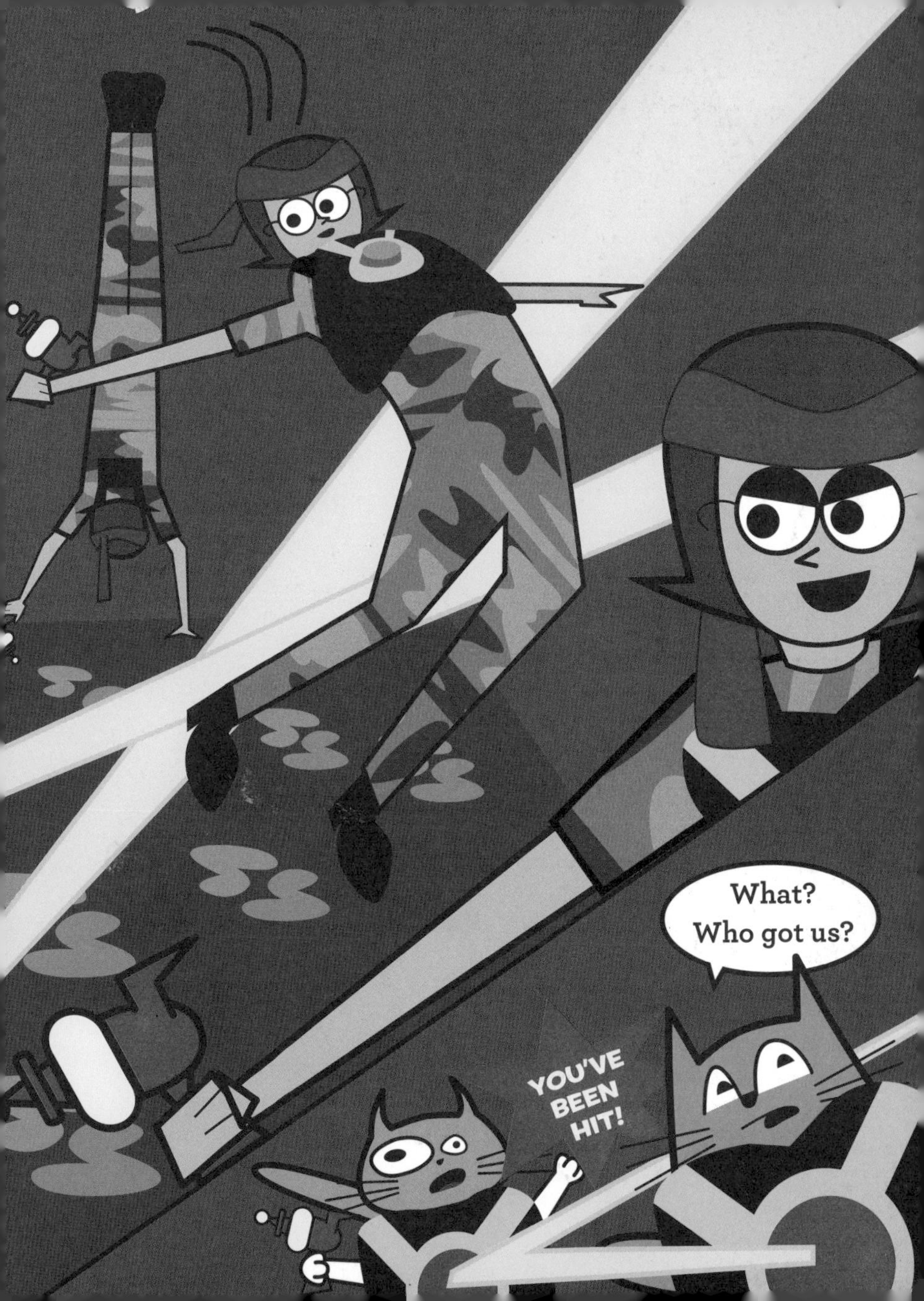
What?
Who got us?
YOU'VE
BEEN
HIT!

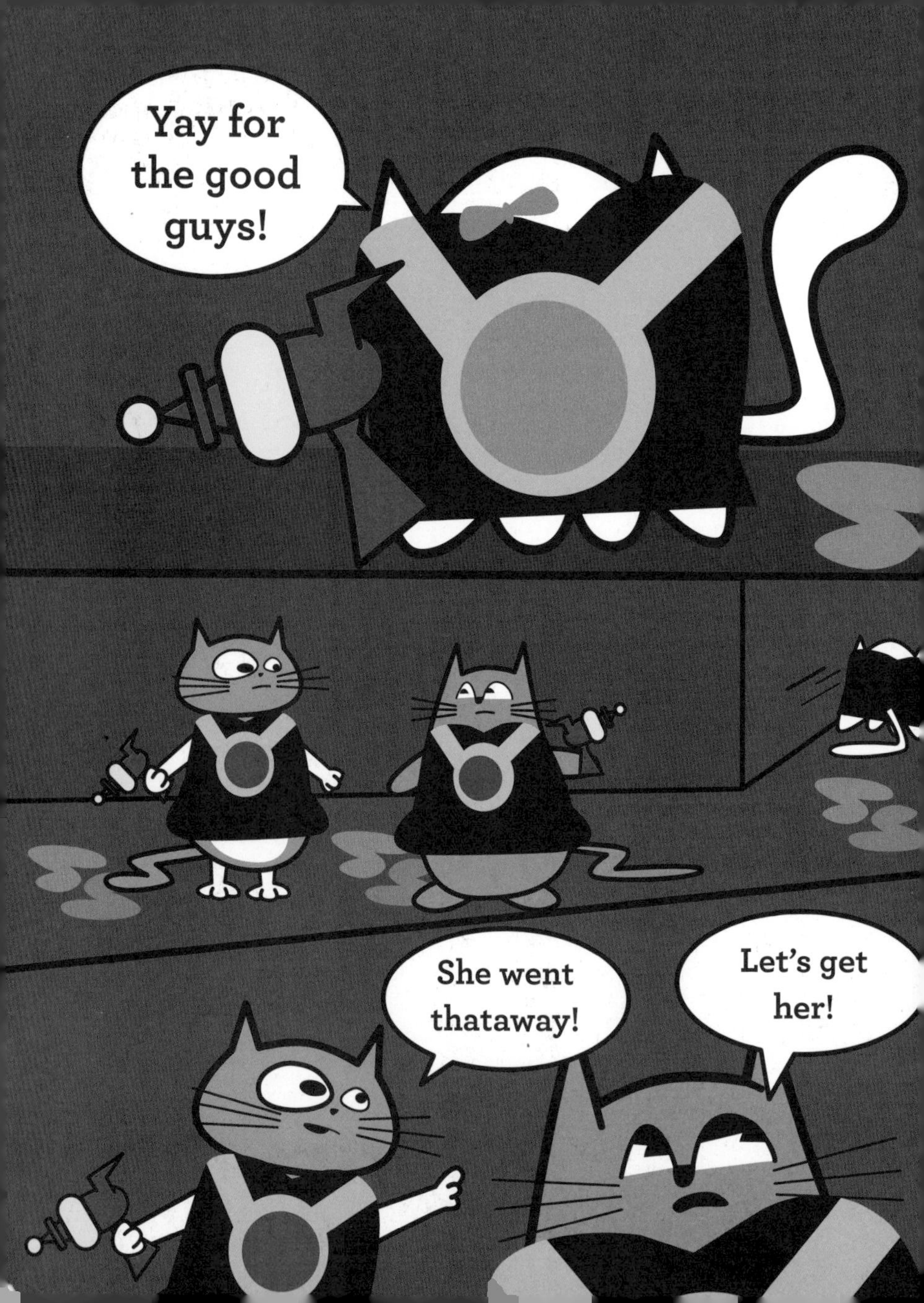
Yay for the good guys!
She went thataway!
Let's get her!

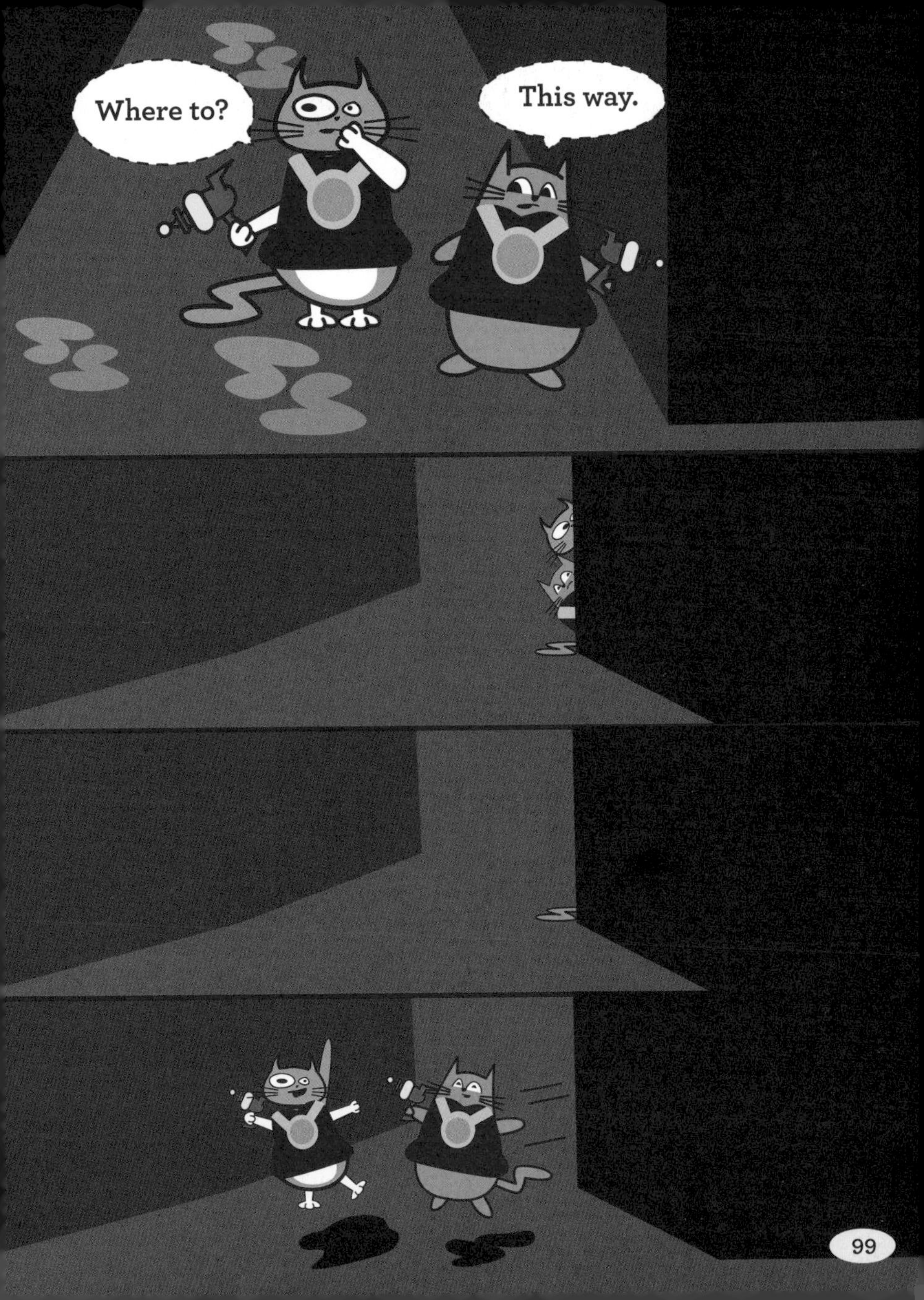
Where to?
This way.

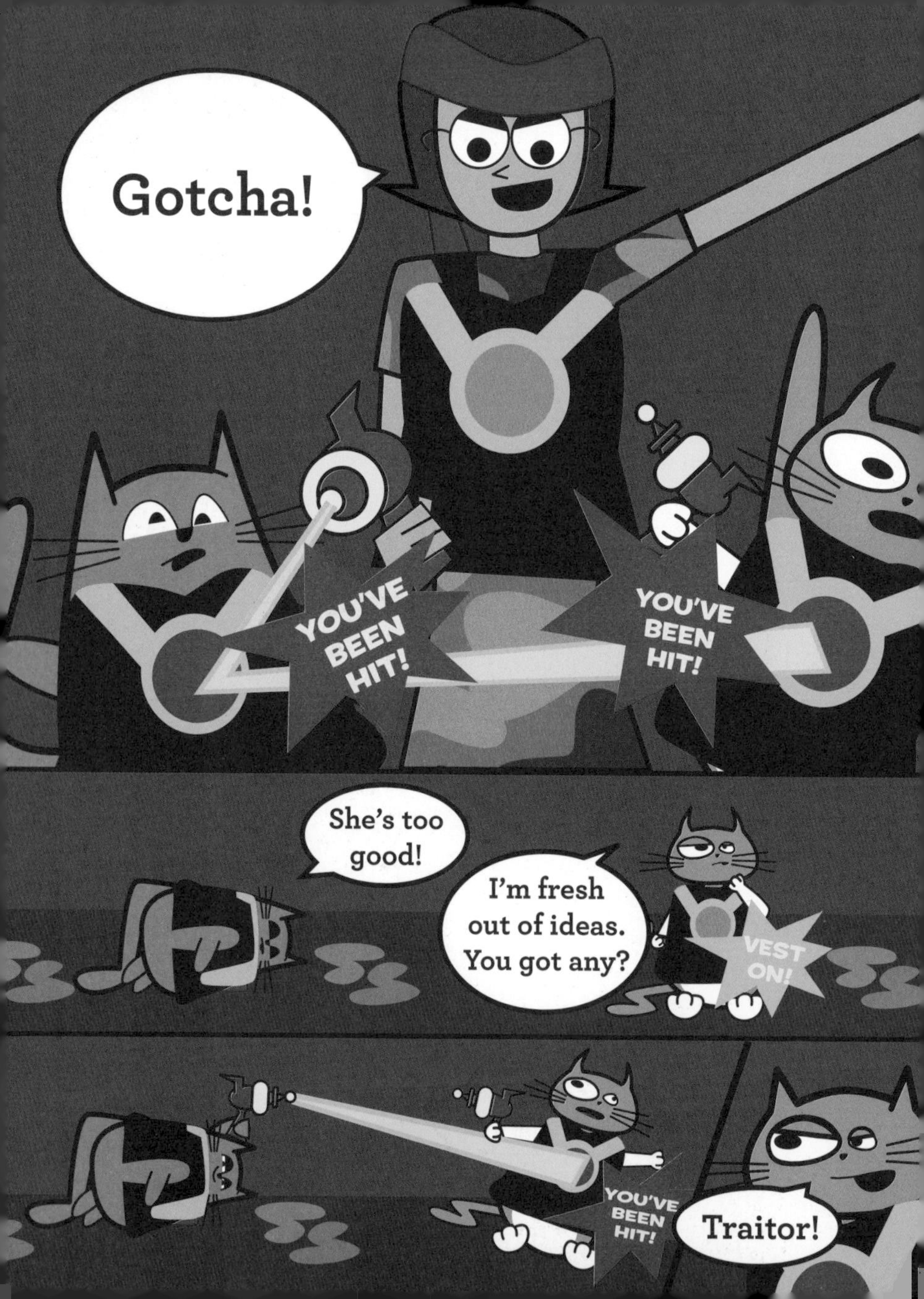
Gotcha!
YOU'VE BEEN HIT!
YOU'VE BEEN HIT!
She's too good!
I'm fresh out of ideas. You got any?
VEST ON!
YOU'VE BEEN HIT!
Traitor!

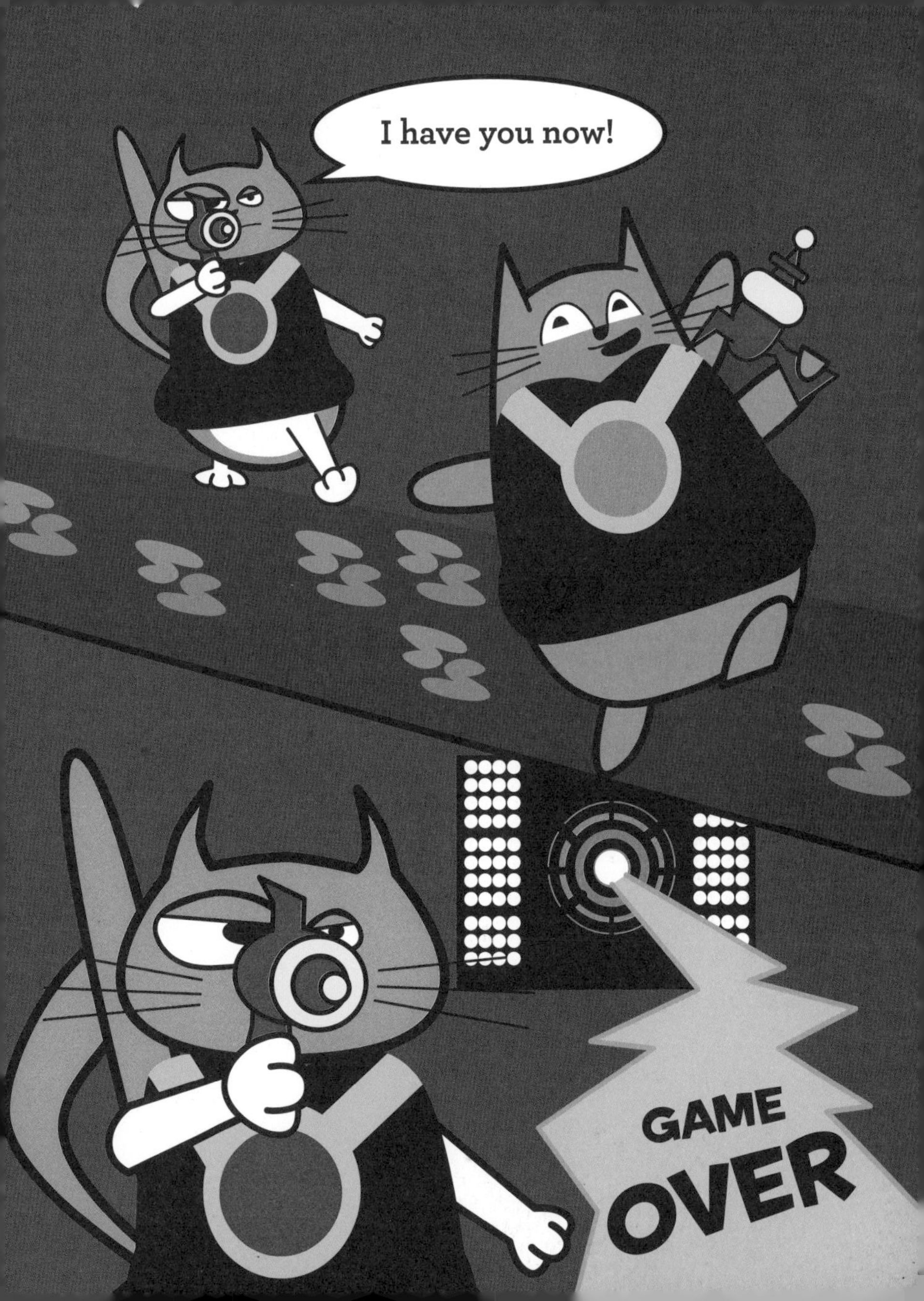
I have you now!
GAME OVER

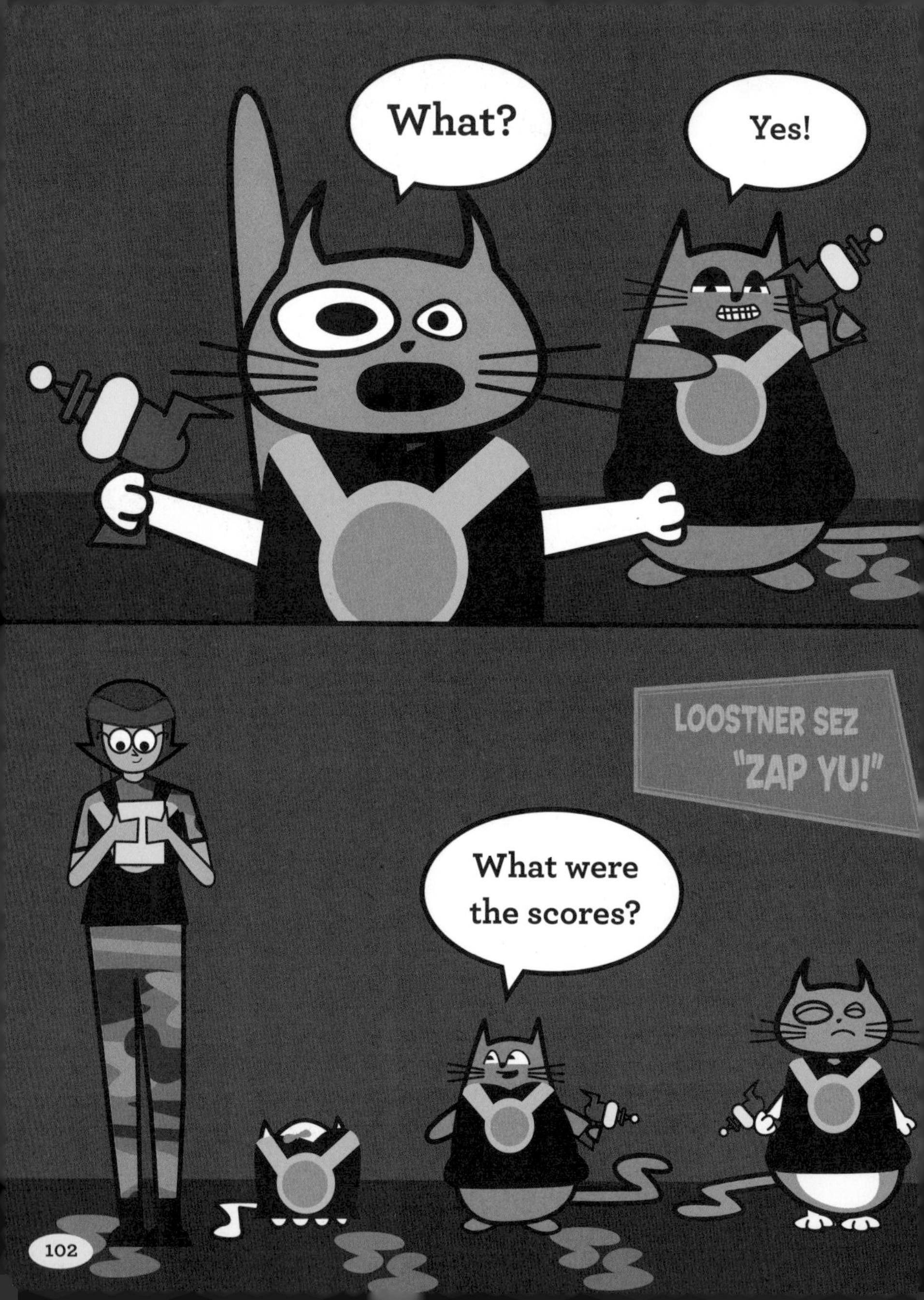
What?
Yes!
LOOSTNER SEZ "ZAP YU!"
What were the scores?

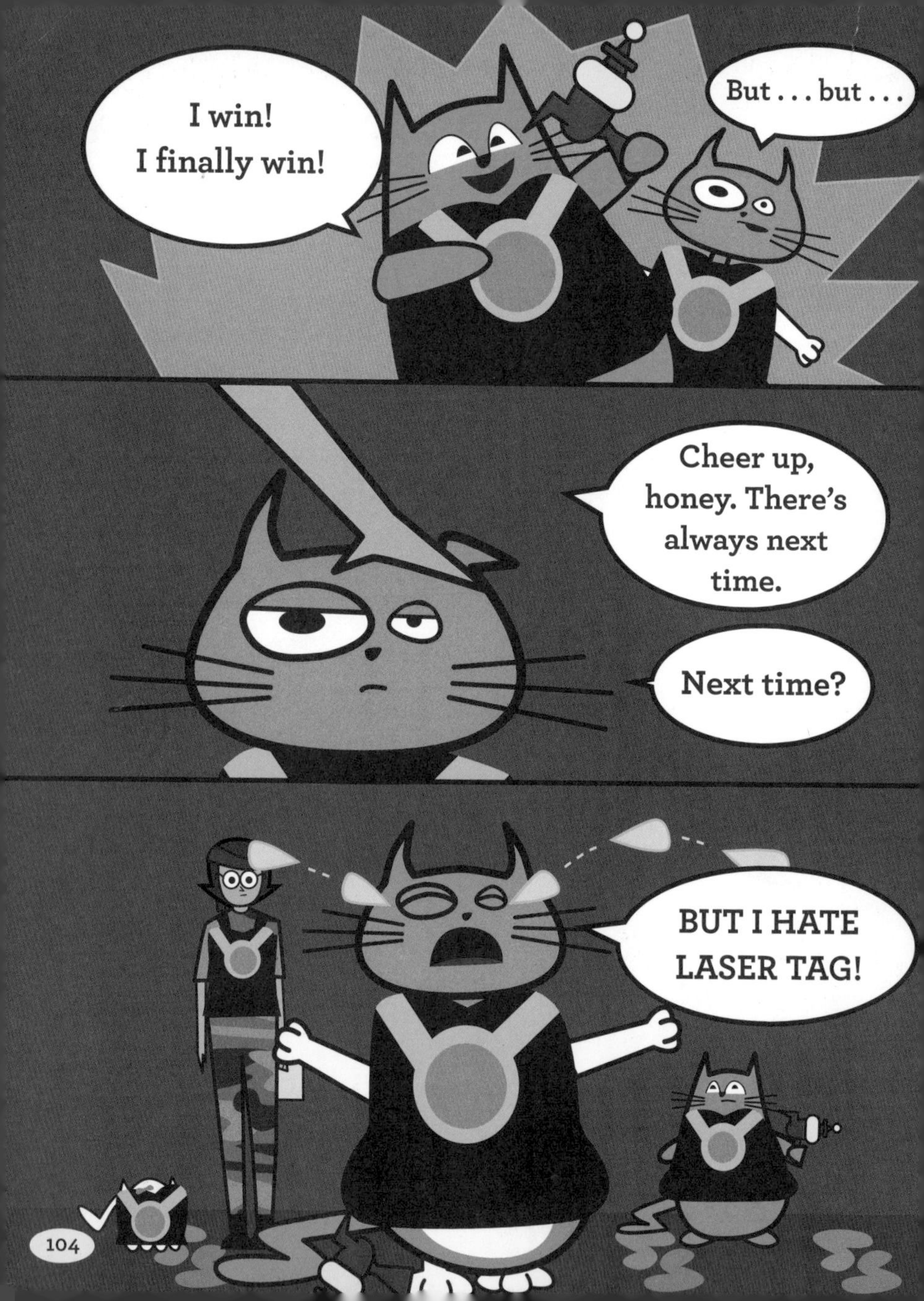
I win!
I finally win!
But . . . but . . .
Cheer up, honey. There's always next time.
Next time?
BUT I HATE LASER TAG!

# Chapter Six: BATTLING BEDTIME STORIES

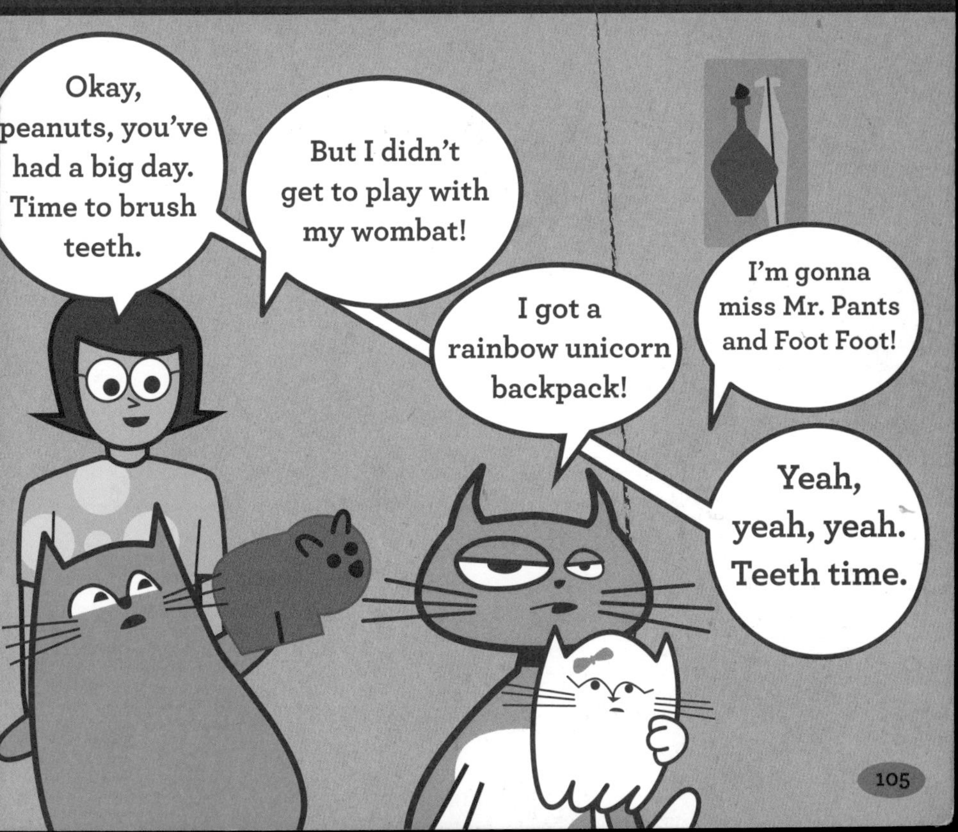
Okay, peanuts, you've had a big day. Time to brush teeth.
But I didn't get to play with my wombat!
I got a rainbow unicorn backpack!
I'm gonna miss Mr. Pants and Foot Foot!
Yeah, yeah, yeah. Teeth time.

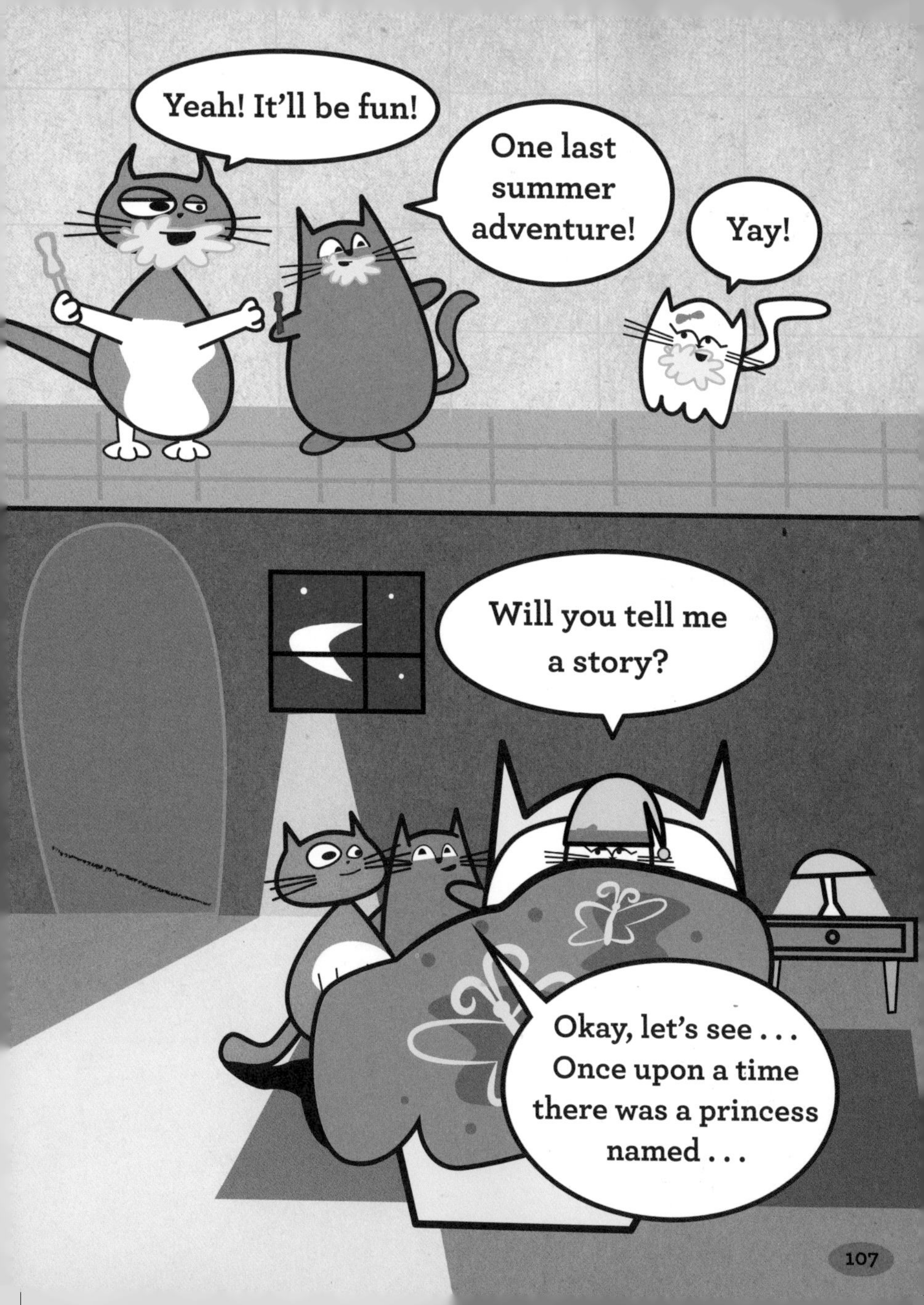
Yeah! It'll be fun!
One last summer adventure!
Yay!
Will you tell me a story?
Okay, let's see . . . Once upon a time there was a princess named . . .

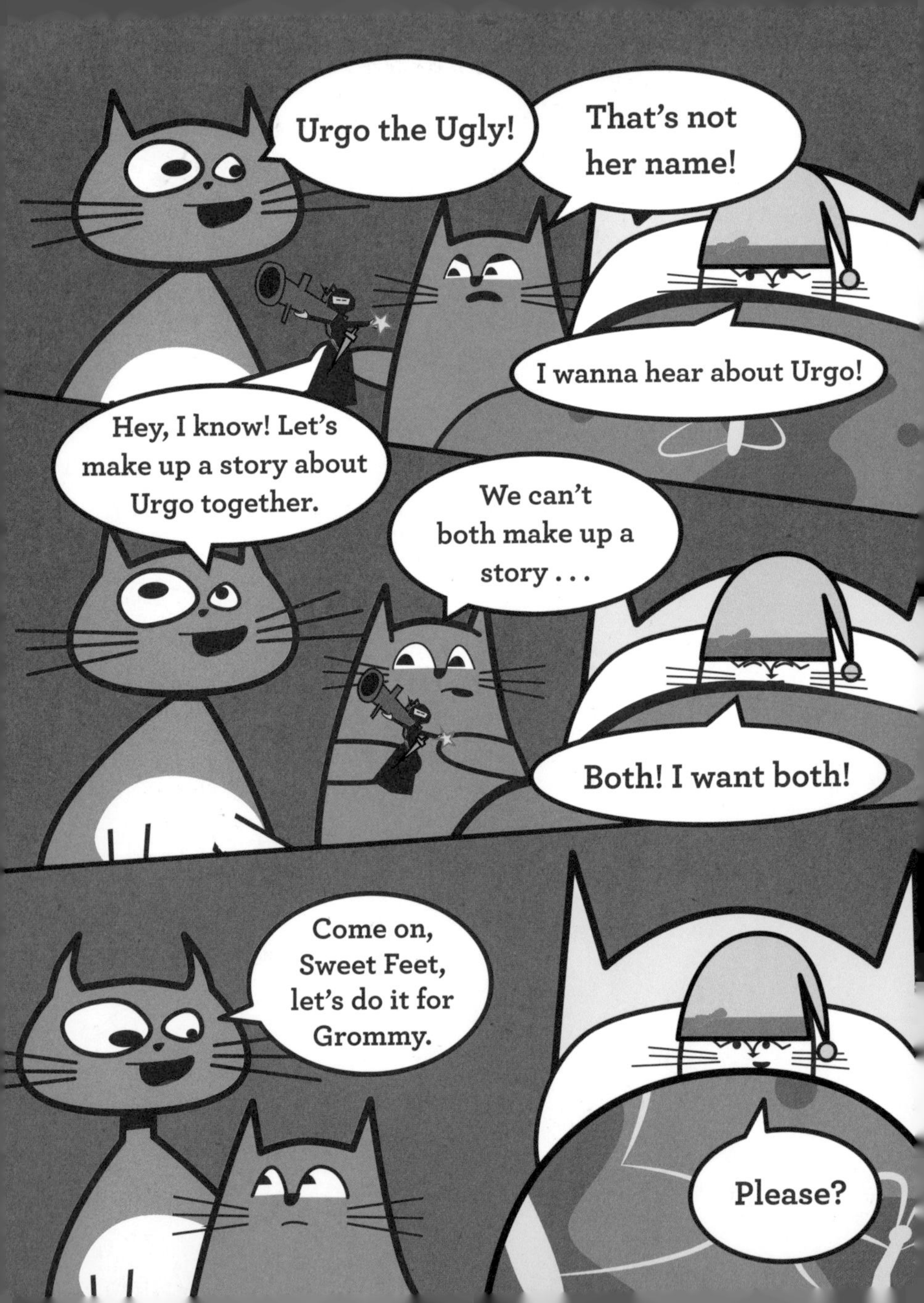
Urgo the Ugly!
That's not her name!
I wanna hear about Urgo!
Hey, I know! Let's make up a story about Urgo together.
We can't both make up a story . . .
Both! I want both!
Come on, Sweet Feet, let's do it for Grommy.
Please?

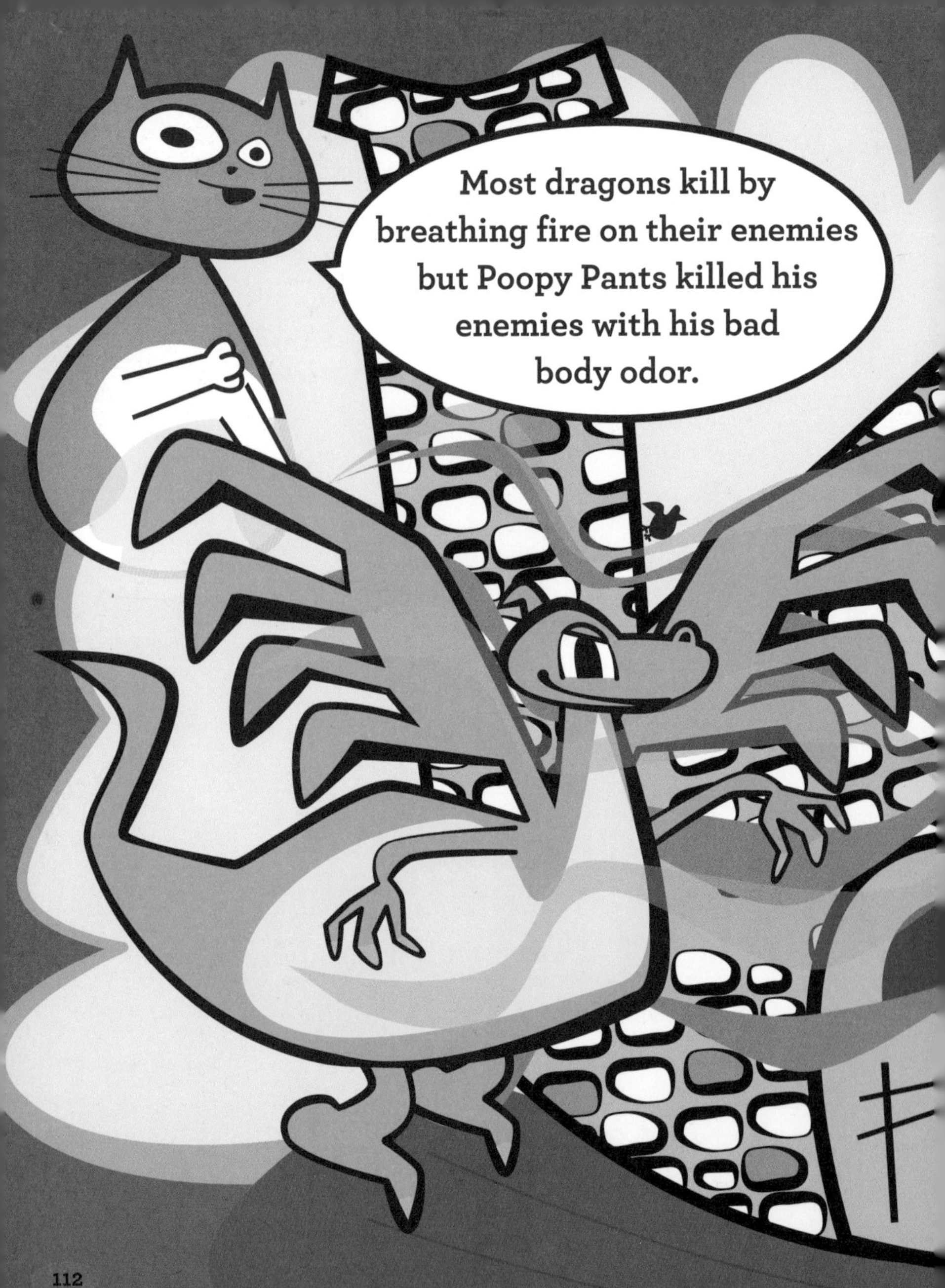
Most dragons kill by breathing fire on their enemies but Poopy Pants killed his enemies with his bad body odor.

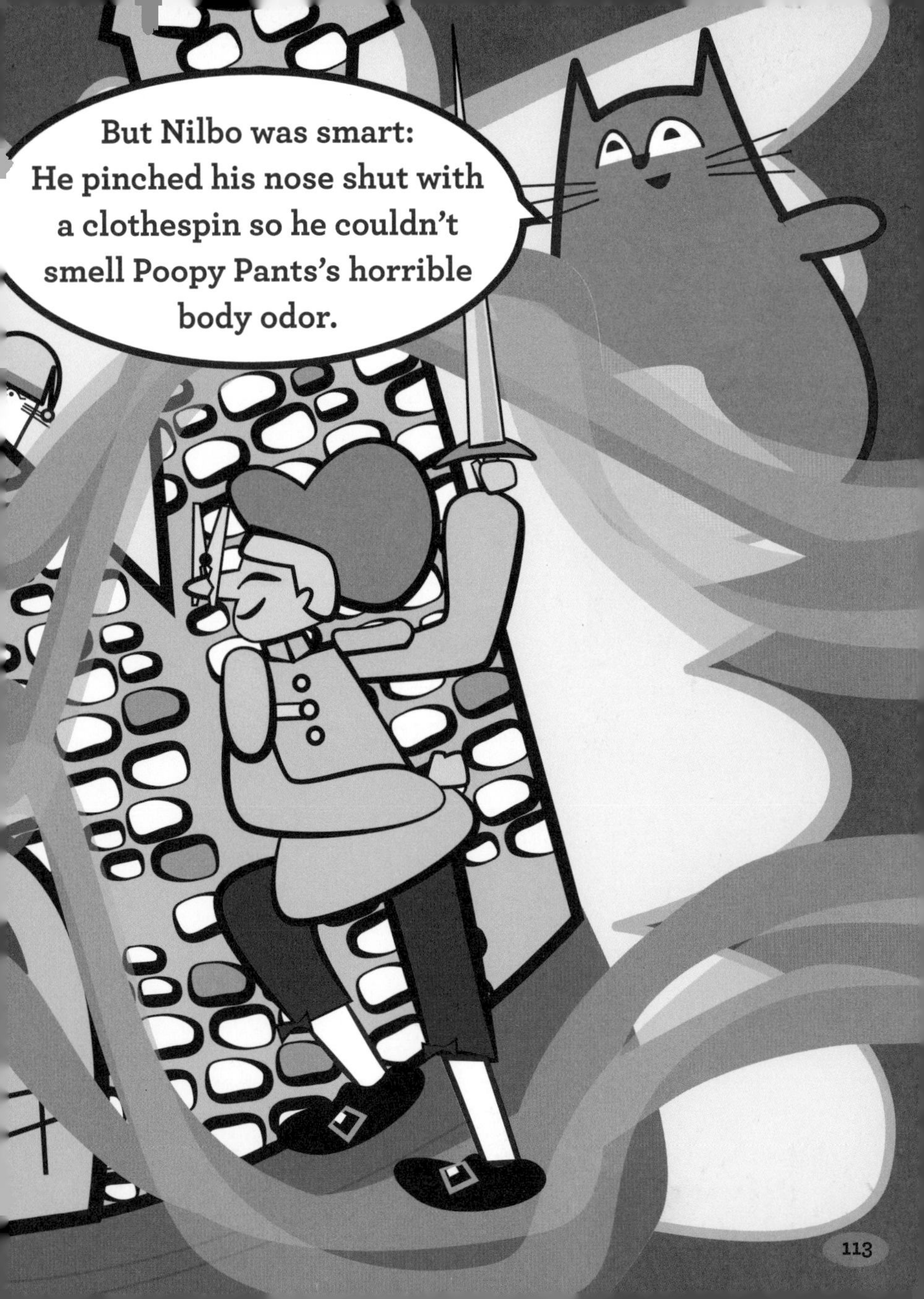
But Nilbo was smart:
He pinched his nose shut with a clothespin so he couldn't smell Poopy Pants's horrible body odor.

114

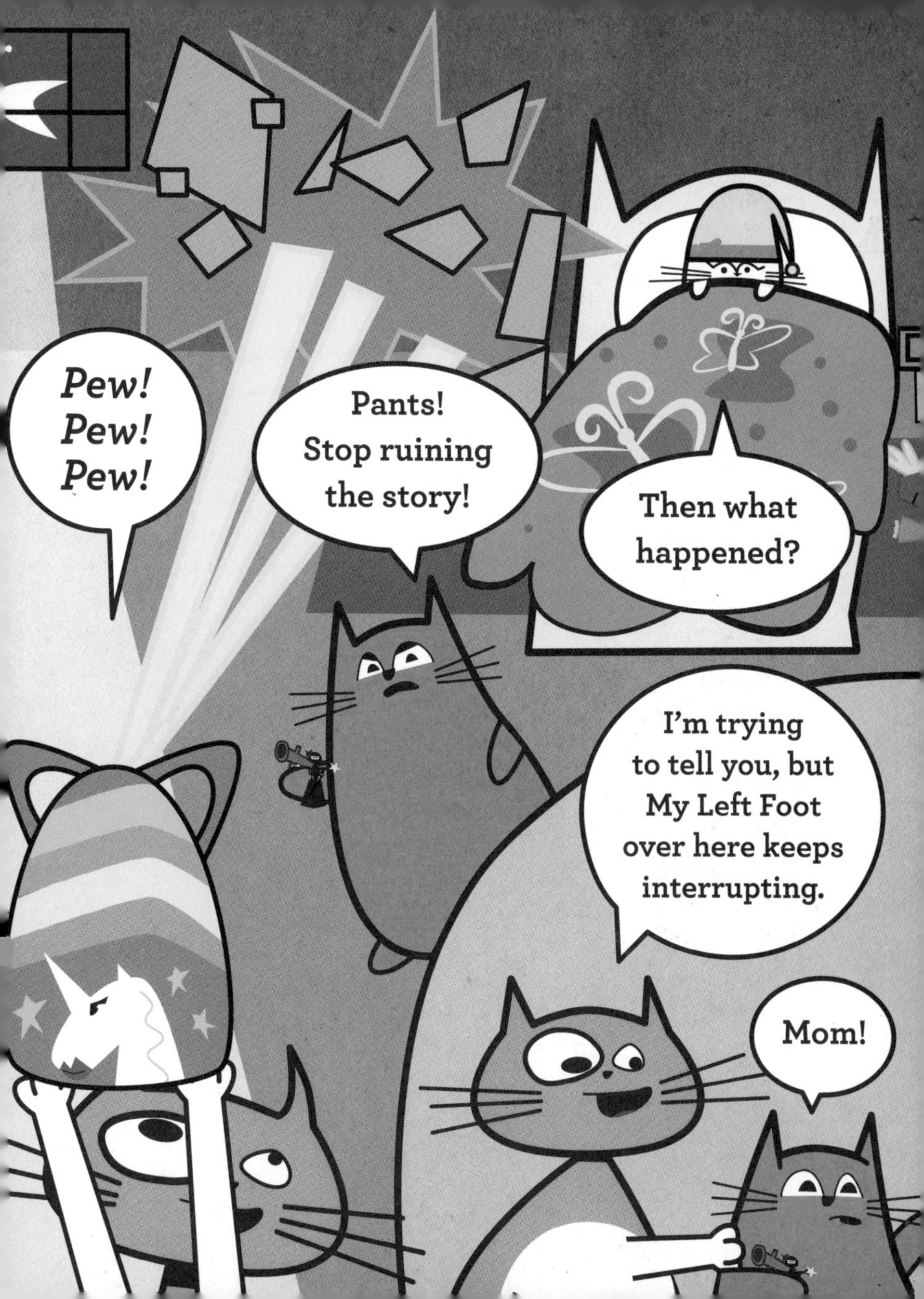

*Pew! Pew! Pew!*
Pants! Stop ruining the story!
Then what happened?
I'm trying to tell you, but My Left Foot over here keeps interrupting.
Mom!

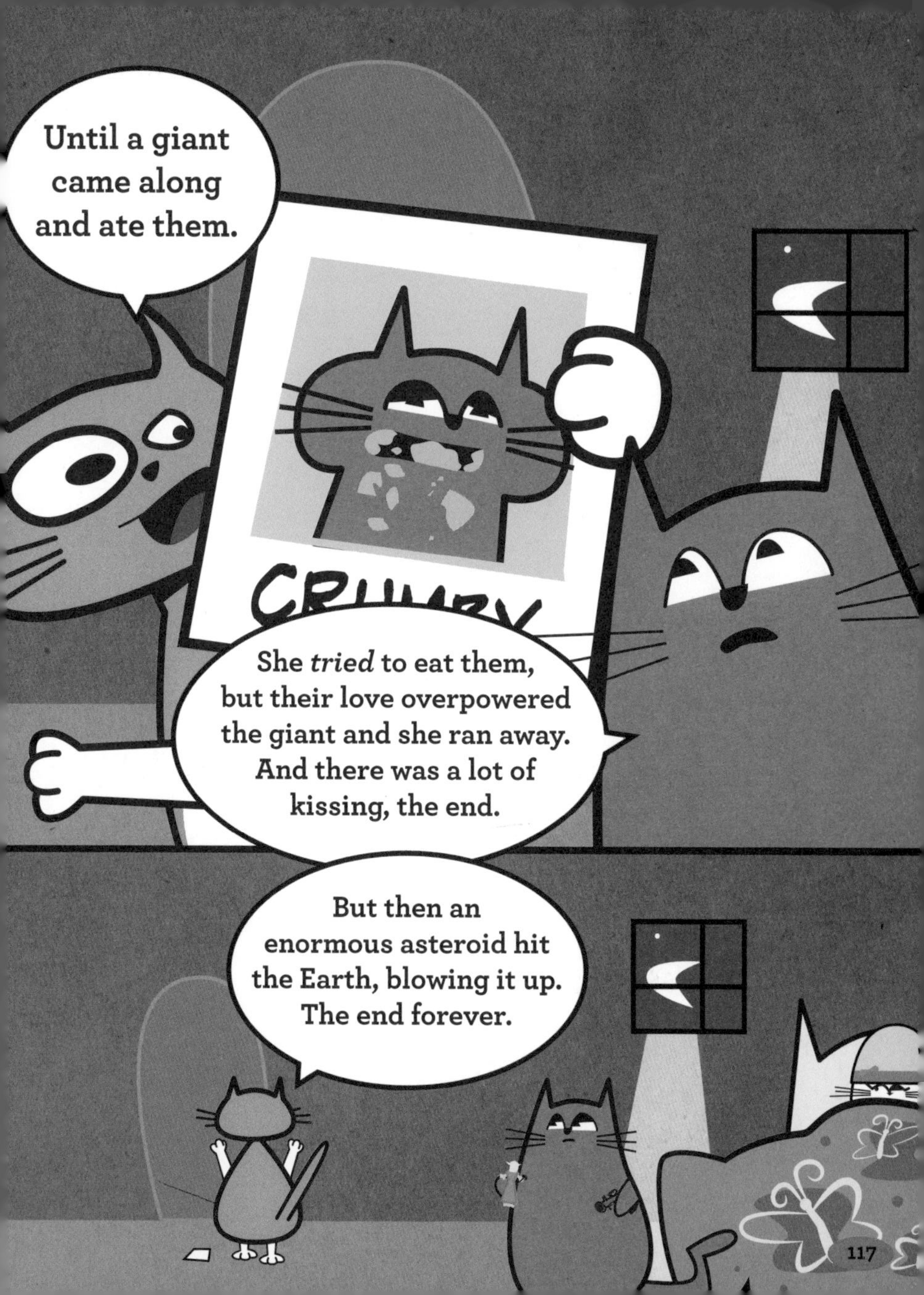
Until a giant came along and ate them.
She *tried* to eat them, but their love overpowered the giant and she ran away. And there was a lot of kissing, the end.
But then an enormous asteroid hit the Earth, blowing it up. The end forever.

# Chapter Seven:
# WUB-BY! WUB-BY! WUB-BY!

SUMMER SCHMUMMER!
WELCOME BACK TO SCHOOL!

Room 237

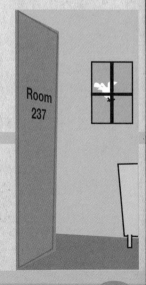

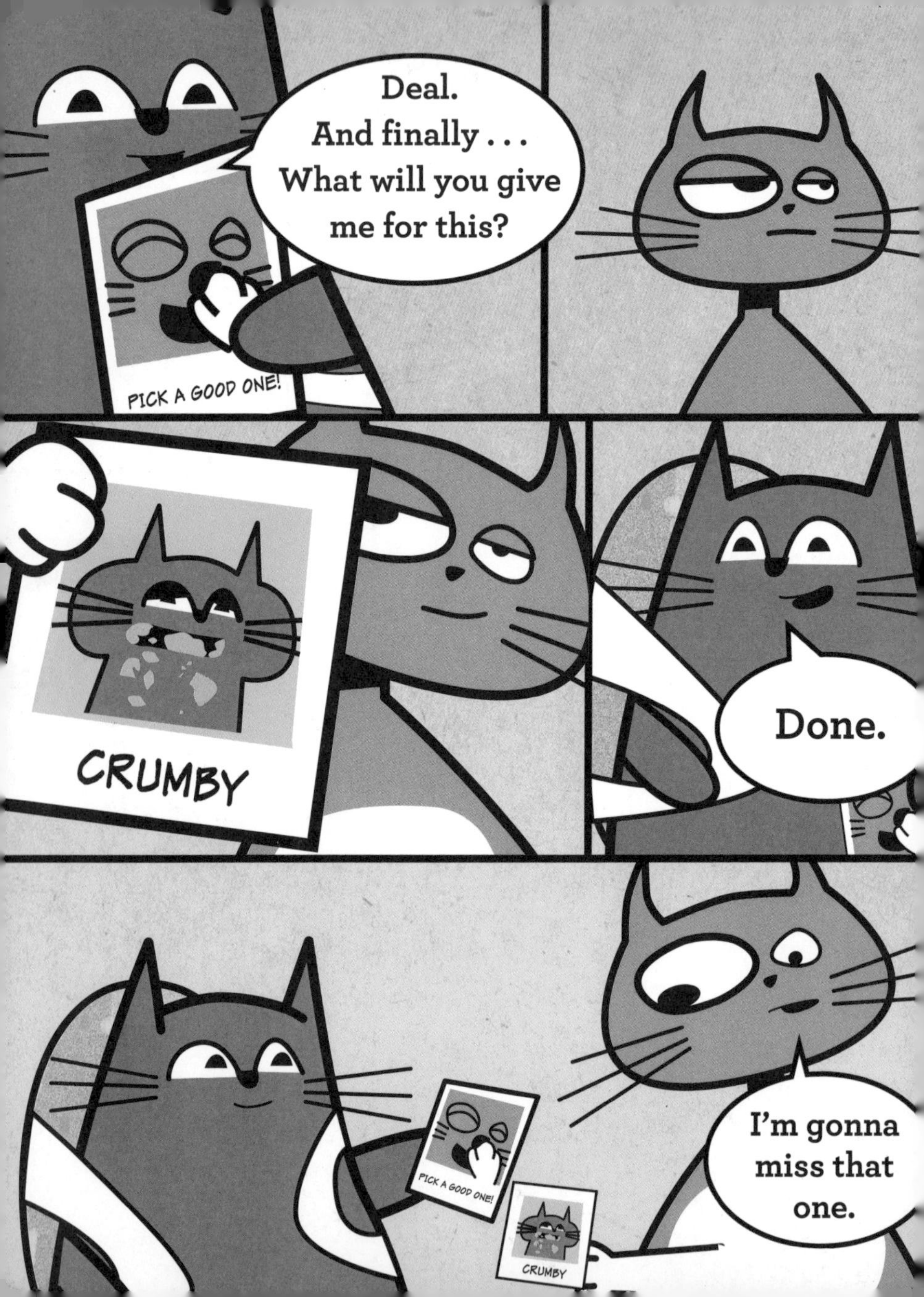
Deal.
And finally . . .
What will you give me for this?
PICK A GOOD ONE!
CRUMBY
Done.
PICK A GOOD ONE!
CRUMBY
I'm gonna miss that one.

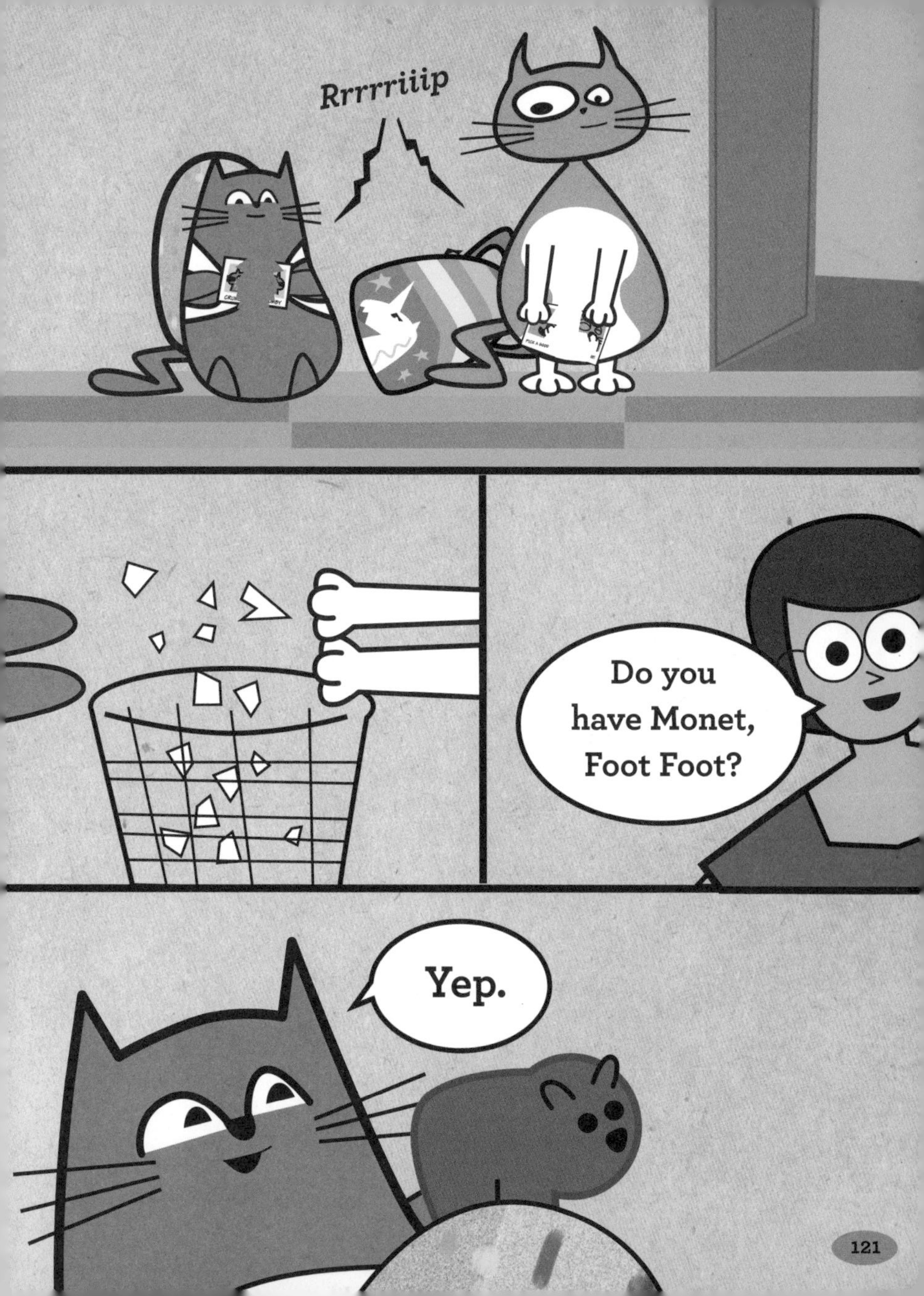
Rrrrriiip
Do you have Monet, Foot Foot?
Yep.

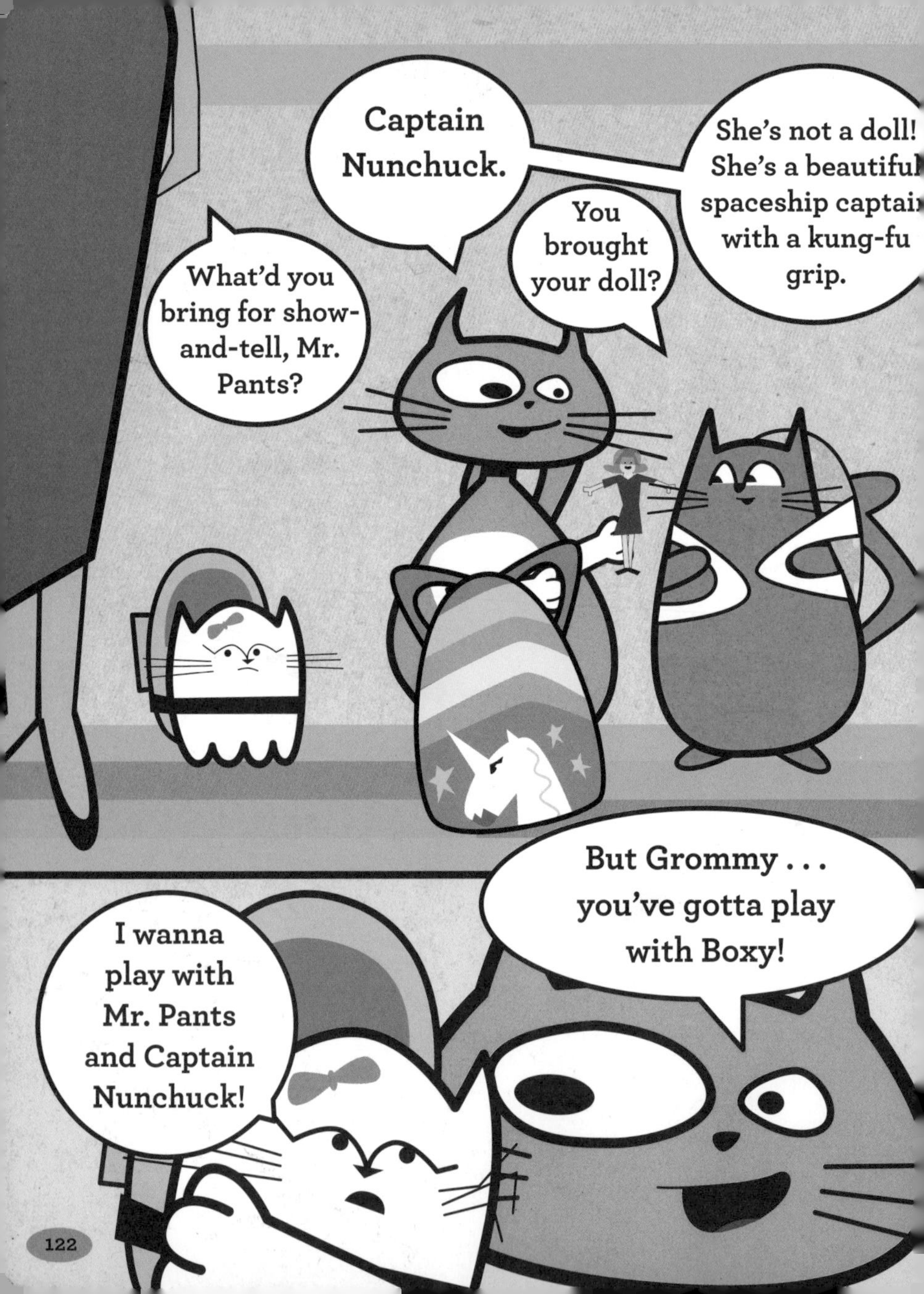

What'd you bring for show-and-tell, Mr. Pants?
Captain Nunchuck.
You brought your doll?
She's not a doll! She's a beautiful spaceship captain with a kung-fu grip.
But Grommy . . . you've gotta play with Boxy!
I wanna play with Mr. Pants and Captain Nunchuck!

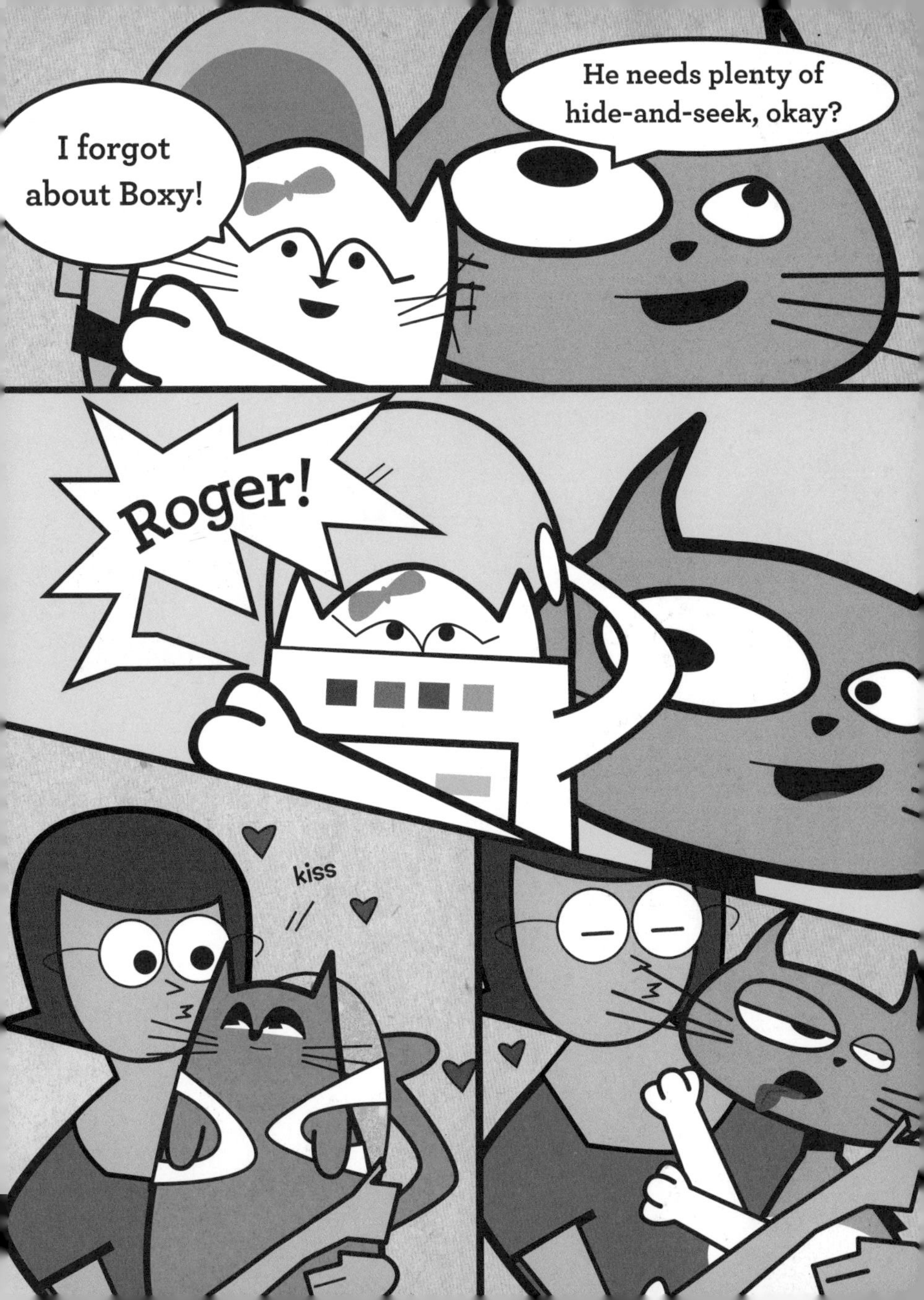
I forgot about Boxy!
He needs plenty of hide-and-seek, okay?
Roger!
kiss

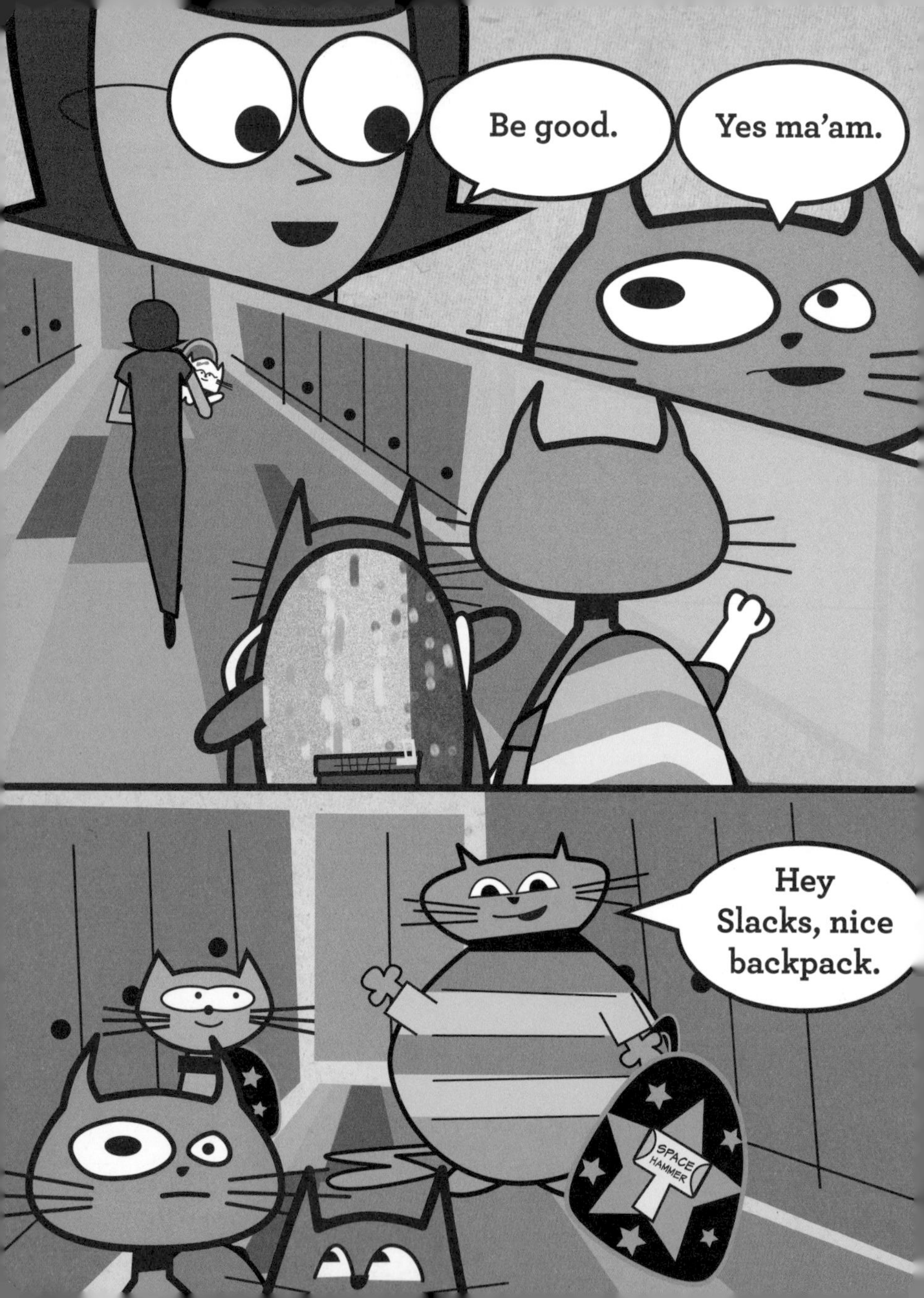
Be good.
Yes ma'am.
Hey Slacks, nice backpack.
SPACE HAMMER

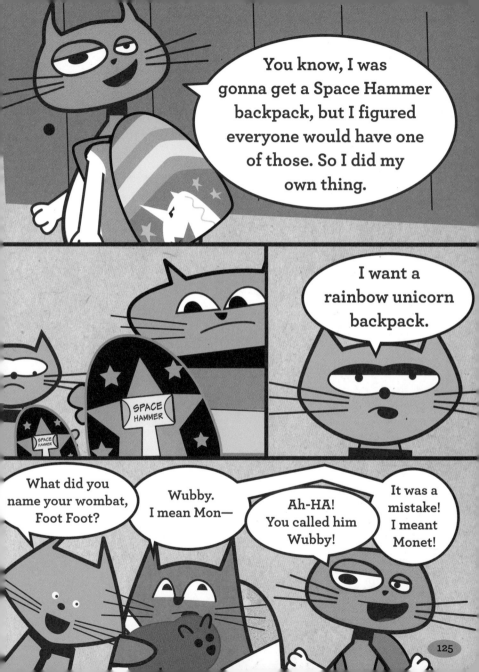

125

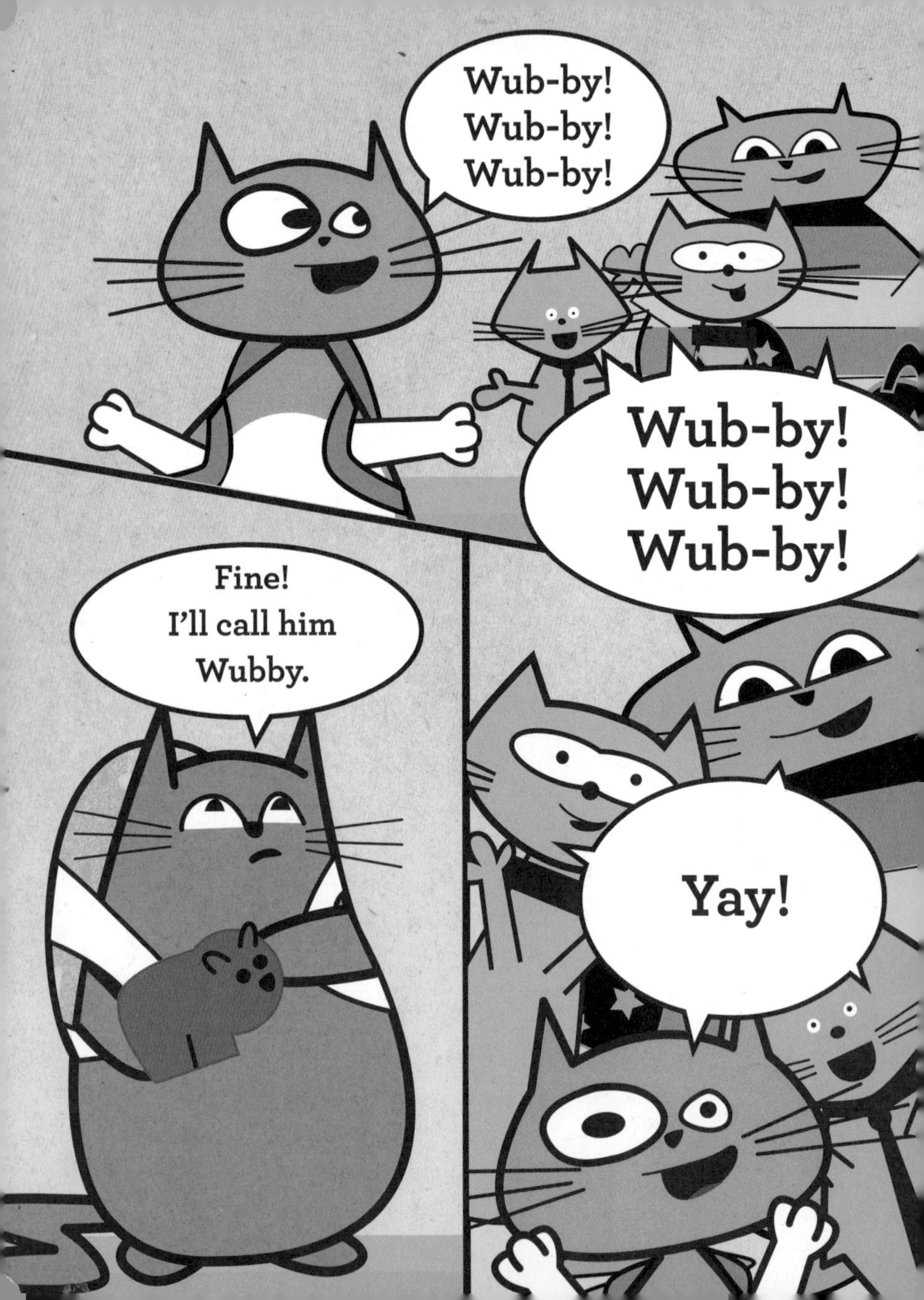
Wub-by! Wub-by! Wub-by!
Wub-by! Wub-by! Wub-by!
Fine! I'll call him Wubby.
Yay!

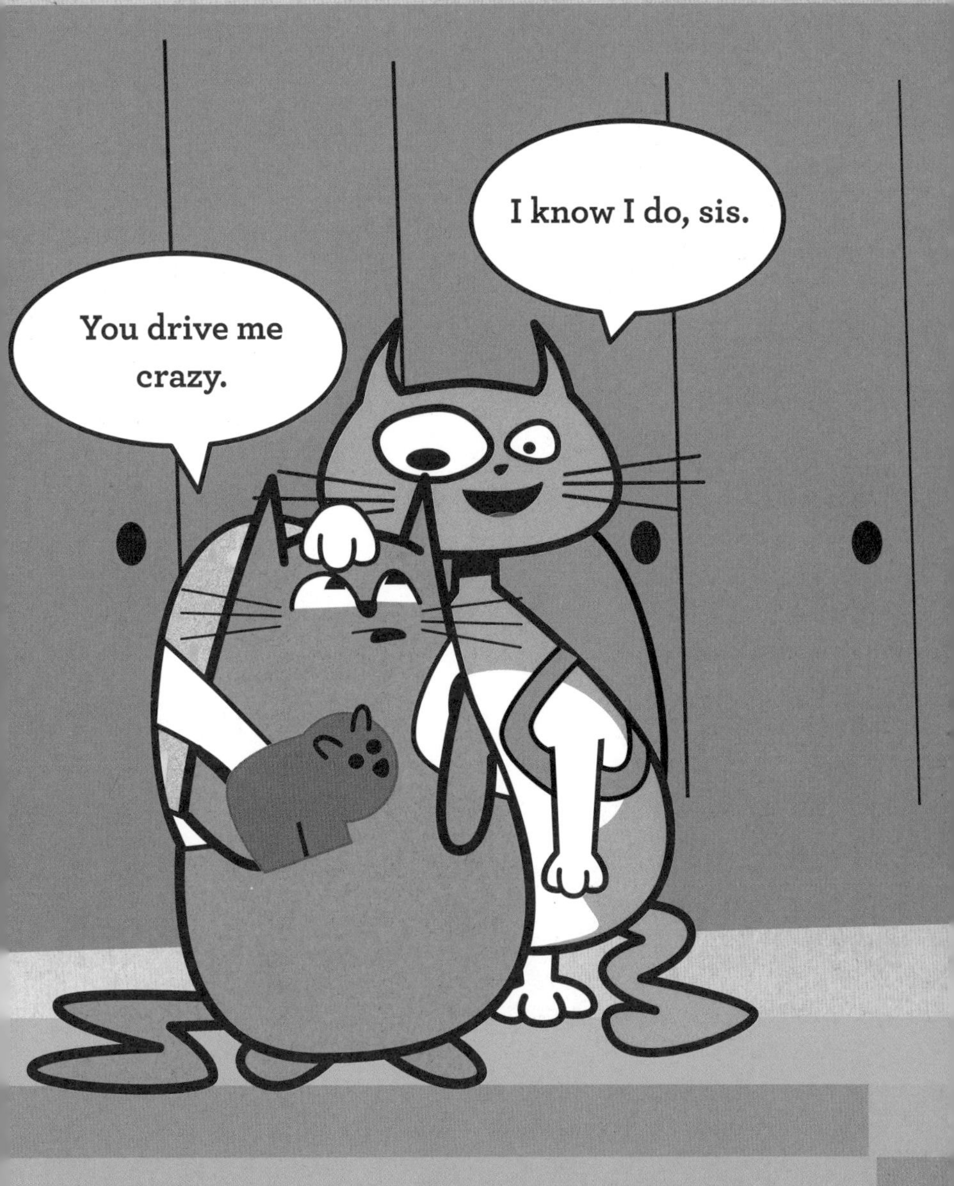
You drive me crazy.
I know I do, sis.

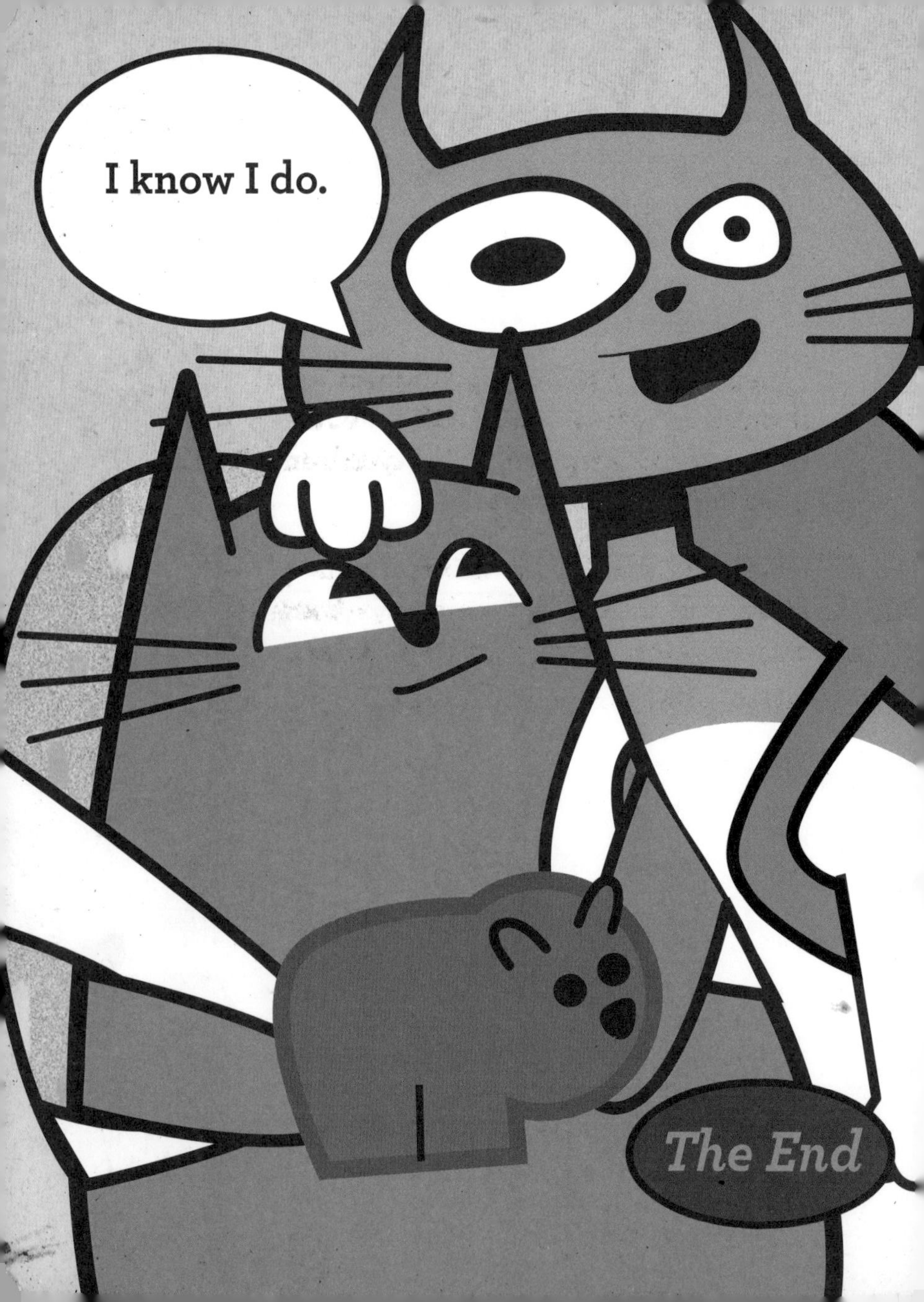
I know I do.
The End